ARK

CWC Collaborative Fiction Novel
Written by 20 International Authors

ISBN: 0-9863159-5-8
ISBN-13: 978-0-9863159-5-4

ABOUT CWC

Collaborative Writing Challenge is aptly named to describe what we do. We bring aspiring writers together from all over the world to collaborate on a full-length fiction novel. We accept writers of all ages with varying degrees of experience, as we believe everyone has something to offer.

Each chapter is written by three or four different writers, and each week, one chapter is selected to form part of the ongoing novel. The experience is challenging and unique, as the writers never meet or discuss their visions for the story.

The book is guided by a story coordinator, who checks names, facts, and integrity, and who works with each chapter writer to get the best results. This story has been kissed by many hands who have yet to read the completed novel.

We also introduced a new element to CWC, a short story competition, to give our writers a chance to submit a stand-alone story to be published in the novel of the same genre. At the end of this book, you will find 'Human Against All Odds' by **Cayce R Berryman**. Her story was selected as the winner. Our close runner-up was written by **Mike Smith**, titled 'In the Blink of an Eye'. You can find Mike's story on the CWC website. Congratulations to both Cayce and Mike.

For more information, please visit:
www.collaborativewritingchallenge.com

IBBY

As this is CWC's third project, 10% of profits from the sales of this book will be donated to the charity IBBY. This is a wonderful organization, dedicated to providing children from all over the world access to books.

We will be donating to the specific project called the **IBBY Fund for Children in Crisis,** which provides support for children whose lives have been disrupted through war, civil disorder, or natural disaster. The two main activities that will be supported by the Fund are the therapeutic use of books and storytelling in the form of Bibliotherapy, and the creation or replacement of selected book collections appropriate to each situation.

Please see further details about this charity by accessing their website: **www.ibby.org**

DEDICATION

This book is dedicated to all the writers who dared to get involved in a CWC collaboration. The interest in each new project is phenomenal, allowing us to start multiple projects of varying genres. This has resulted in better-quality submissions, giving the collaborations the best chance possible at being successful.

I would also like to mention my online writing friends who have brought so much fun and inspiration into my life. This encourages me to continue growing CWC and bringing people from all walks of life together!

Laura Callender - CWC Founder

THE WRITERS

We had over 35 writers involved in this project, twenty of which had chapters selected for ARK. The authors came from 6 different countries: America, Greece, Singapore, UK, Canada, and Buenos Aires.

Rather than fill these pages with details about all twenty authors, all their pictures and bios can be found on the CWC Website. Please do stop by and learn more about our talented contributing writers. Some have very little writing experience, and some have reels of accomplishments under their belts. I think you would be hard-pressed to identify their individual chapters, and it's just possible that your favorite chapter could have been written by a fresh-faced, up-and-coming writer. There are certainly a few names that we will be looking out for in the future.

With this project, it is inevitable that some writers will have their chapters rejected. We had some incredible submissions that we just couldn't use. These chapters were integral to shaping the story, as the variety in chapters gave us the chance to find the best fit. These writers are as much a part of the teamwork that brought this project to completion, so to those who go unnamed: Thank you for your wonderful contributions and effort!

ACKNOWLEDGMENTS

This project has brought together so many talented people. First, I would like to thank **Robert Mackey**, who had his starter chapter ARK selected by his fellow writers from over 10 submissions.

Second, I want to thank Raven Blackburn, who designed the cover art for ARK, which was voted the favorite out of 8 options. She very kindly donated her work for this book. I urge you to check out her premade covers here:
www.selfpubbookcovers.com/Ravenborn

We have had a number of people donate to CWC to help with running costs and to help CWC continue to grow. A huge thanks goes to **Jean Grabow**, **Jason Pere**, and **Sharon Flood**, whose generosity has helped CWC get to where it is today!

Our chief editor **Kathrin Hutson** has done an outstanding job getting ARK ready for publication. I don't know what I would do without her!

As always, my biggest thanks must go to **all of our writers** who agreed to participate in this project. It amazes me every single time, and with every new genre, just how successful collaborating can be. ARK is testament to the dedication we see from our writers time and time again. We are very proud of this book, and it's thanks to you *all*.

Thank You!

A NOTE FROM THE STORY COORDINATOR

Ark is CWC's third project, but the duration of any project lasts over eight months. It was our first Sci-Fi collaboration, and the response for first chapter submissions and writers wanting to be scheduled to participate in the project was pleasantly overwhelming. Our starter chapter, which the writers voted to be Chapter 1, may have been the most blatantly "Sci-Fi" submission we received, but with a mix of quirky characters and odd situations. I honestly didn't know if this was going to be a Comedy of Science Fiction Errors or an overly exaggerated study of nonexistent alien species. But the further along the story progressed, the more I came to realize that we have a huge number of particularly talented writers among our ranks, even those who have never specialized in Sci-Fi.

With only about half of our submitting writers ever having had any experience writing Science Fiction, I was a little worried about just how goofy and/or off-topic this project might become. But I was blown away by the writers' abilities to introduce and then elaborate on complex ideas, incorporate the elements of good, detailed, vivid Sci-Fi writing, and at least sound like they knew what they were talking about. In a genre that is so incredibly detail-oriented, the writers submitted chapter after chapter so brilliantly crafted from nothing but the complete chapter before theirs and the chapter summaries and reference notes of every previous chapter. Some of them even picked up on and used details which I had completely written off as fairly mundane and unimportant, yet it drove the plot forward with such power that I couldn't help but be awed by the skill on this project.

There are always obstacles with these projects, the most frequent being weeks where none of the scheduled writers were able to submit chapters, leaving me with empty hands and biting my nails. But a number of incredibly talented writers (and apparently immune to time-crunches) were gracious enough to step up to the plate when asked to write an "emergency" chapter with just twenty-four hours' notice. And even those chapters flowed with the narrative voice and plot to read as though this entire novel was written by just one author.

8

I definitely had a hard time some weeks choosing only one chapter out of three or four submissions. So I accepted two instead, most of the time because it seemed as though the authors had gotten together and planned out their chapters to fit perfectly side-by-side with each other (of course, they hadn't). Some chapters I'd even accepted to "use later", but didn't insert them consecutively into the book during the week they were written. This might have been the most difficult part of my job as Story Coordinator—finding the appropriate "slot" for a winning chapter that *wasn't* in consecutive order with the week it was submitted, simply because I couldn't let such imaginative writing and brilliant character development go to waste. As it turns out, I think I've done a pretty decent job fitting all the puzzle pieces together. Every chapter received a minor touchup. Changes were always received well by the writers, and the chapters went on to get a full consistency edit once the story was completed.

It was incredibly difficult to choose the final ending chapter, as each submitting author tied up the loose ends of the story in such a variety of ways that I wanted to incorporate them all. But of course, I had to choose just one. Writing the ending chapter must have been particularly difficult for this project, as the motivations for half the characters' actions were explained in the last chapter or two, almost like a mystery but on a grand galactic scale. Some of the final chapter submissions literally gave me chills with the ideas they presented, which was an incredible feat all on its own.

Our ranks of authors continue to grow as we get set to publish *Wytch Born*, our fourth collaboration, and we're almost halfway through our fifth collaboration, *The Map*, and will soon be starting our sixth.

I've had more fun than I can say coordinating *Ark*, and I can't wait to share with you all the great things CWC has in store for the future.

Kathrin Hutson
CWC Chief Editor & Story Coordinator of ARK

CONTENTS

Short Story Winner:

CWC's Fourth Collaboration:

Chapter 1

T he two suns of Santelli Minor peeked over the horizon in perfect harmony to the east. Mearon, Santelli's only moon, faded from view in the west as the light of the suns effortlessly erased it from the mauve sky. Dirk Forrett walked across the coarse red sand, taking in the spectacle—wondering if there would ever come a point during this expedition he would tire of the view.

It was another new planet, and while the *Ark* was his home, he took solace in sampling the breathable, untouched air for himself. He reached down and patted his Chihuahua's head, who was named after Dirk's favorite zoologist, Alfred Kuhn. "Well, Kuhn, time to get back. Another day, another specimen. Or fifty."

Unlike his idols Achille Valenciennes, Adison Verill, Alexandre Brongniart, and of course Alfred Kuhn—Earth's first zoologists in the eighteenth and nineteenth centuries—Dirk traveled the cosmos for his research. As a planetary zoologist, he spent his existence identifying, categorizing, and studying the behaviors of creatures from dozens of planets.

The man looked more like a high school kid, much too thin to betray his thirty-seven years. His pocket-laden pants sagged with the weight of their cargo, and he belted them just above his navel to compensate. He readjusted the trifocal horn-rimmed glasses, more than occasionally the butt of fashion jokes, under-neath his jet black crewcut.

He strode casually back to the parked ship, stark against the background of one of Santelli's mountain ranges, and reassured himself with a quick pat to the breast of his long-sleeved shirt. It was his favorite shirt, completed by two pocket protectors holding pens, tweezers, and an array of carefully wrapped instruments de-signed for probing, separating, and clipping for specimen analy-sis.

Kuhn scratched at Dirk's leg, hoping to be picked up and held tightly as was the routine whenever they boarded. Holding his only true friend, Dirk marveled at the sight of his creation. He couldn't believe that he'd actually designed and overseen the building of that ship. He had dreamed of such a craft back in his early college days, when traveling to distant planets had barely be-come a reality. His single goal back then had been to create a ship which could be piloted to newly discovered planets—a home-base, traveling laboratory to temporarily store the new lifeforms they discovered and document them. He'd been blown away by the speed of those technological advancements and how quickly his dream had been realized.

Kuhn clamored up Dirk's chest and buried his head in his owner's armpit. The huge door on the side of the ship lowered to the ground and out danced a monster of a man. Dirk struggled to get the dog back on the ground.

"You stay right there, Kuhn. Here comes foul-mouthed Franklin."

Franklin was nearly seven feet tall under a head of dirty blonde hair which curled down to the middle of his back. There wasn't an ounce of fat on his herculean body, and Dirk was certain he felt the ground tremble under the man's feet as he sprinted the forty yards toward them.

Breathing as if he had just awakened from a nap, Franklin said, "Hey, Dork Ferret, have I got some cool shit for you!"

"Why do you insist on calling me that?"

"What the hell do you want me to call you?"

"You could call me Doctor Forrett, or Dirk, or anything else fitting your superior. Not Dork Ferret." Dirk expected the exploration pod to have already returned by the time he and Kuhn finished their walk, but he could have done without Franklin's greeting.

"Well now, you're touchy today," Franklin mocked. "Hey, check this little fucker out. This'll blow your shit back a couple hundred feet."

Franklin tilted his head back and looked to the sky as he dug around in his shirt pocket. He fished out a four-inch-long, zebra-striped worm with an enormous head and presented it to Dirk. "Ain't he the cutest thing? And check this shit out." He grabbed a pebble from the ground and laid it before the worm in his hand.

The worm swallowed the pebble, and the lump it created in the middle of the worm's body disappeared rapidly. The creature then excreted a small amount of a black, soil-like substance.

"We threw him in a terrarium filled with pea gravel. This little fucker ate every last pebble and pooped out this dirt shit. Your hot little assistant Jenny, she says the stuff is just like peat moss. I bet this guy could shit a cubic yard of this stuff in the course of a day. Just think about it. You turn a couple hundred thousand of these guys loose in the Sahara, and the next thing you know, you got fucking farmland."

Yes, Dirk's dreams for an exploratory ship had come true, but that ship had unfortunately not been fully equipped with the most brilliant minds.

"Franklin, you have to stop carrying specimens around in your pockets. You have no idea what it's capable of."

"Quit being such a pussy. There ain't no harm to him. He's cute. Eats rocks and shits soil." Franklin stroked the top of the worm's segmented body.

"Cuteness is not an excuse to keep specimens in your pocket." Dirk swallowed and adjusted his glasses once more.

Franklin's eyes lit up. "Hey, speaking of cute, I've got another surprise for you." He grabbed Dirk by the wrist and half dragged him with surprising speed back toward the *Ark*. Kuhn stood where he had been left and shook feverishly.

Dirk tried to pull free to turn back for a check on Kuhn. Franklin kept an iron grip on his wrist, but the zoologist managed to catch a last, fleeting glimpse of his four-legged friend, curled up now in the sand. He called quickly to the dog, but Kuhn made no move to follow.

The *Ark*'s cargo hold housed cages and specimen carriers, serving as a place for the pod to unload its findings after each excursion. They stopped in front of the first occupied cage, and Dirk blinked at the reptilian specimen inside. Franklin eyed him for any sign of shared excitement, but Dirk only stared.

"C'mon, Dork. It's a fucking lizard! They apparently feed on the pebble-eatin' zebra worms. Hot stuff cut one open and found a bunch of them in his gut."

Again, Dirk had nothing to say. How many times did he have to tell the man he would not respond to any information not properly documented in an initial report?

Franklin sneered and raised a thick eyebrow. "I got an even better thing to show you, Dork." He spun off down the walkway, lined with cages that increased in size the further they walked. They kept the larger specimens in the back of the cargo hold before transferring them to the *Ark*'s research facilities closer to the bridge. Franklin skidded to a halt in front of a large wire enclosure and grinned. "Huh? Do these things qualify as cuter than shit or what?"

Dirk looked into the enclosure in horror. 'Cuter than shit' was not a phrase he would have chosen, but his mind was now too muddled with potential consequences to correct the description. "Franklin! You've disregarded the first protocol directive. We don't take humanoid specimens, don't engage them at all unless the safety of the *Ark* or her crew is threatened. That is a 'no exceptions' mandate. What were you thinking bringing them aboard?"

With his standard amount of over-exuberance, Franklin defended his actions. "They didn't utter a sound. They didn't even move. We found them sitting cross-legged and silent just as they are now. They're so beautiful." He opened the door to the enclosure and stepped inside. "Come on, touch one. They're so soft, like…I don't know. Does exquisite describe them? Hell, if you gave them a pole to dance around, you could probably hire them out at strip clubs. Fucking gorgeous!"

Despite his colleague's obtusely crude comment, Dirk couldn't argue with that observation—found something strangely alluring about the serenity of the sleeping humanoids. They may have been female under the wavering layer of what seemed to be scales *and* fur, looking so strangely soft. But he couldn't ignore the protocols, nor the gut instinct that something was wrong here.

"Get out of there," he yelled at Franklin, feeling his face flush hot. "Close the door. Lock it. And set the quarantine field!"

"Really? They don't even move. Haven't moved once since we found them. They're perfectly harmless." Franklin reached out a hand in an effort to stroke one of the creatures.

"Do it."

Franklin froze, staring at the new specimens, and gave them a weak wave. "Sorry about this," he whispered, then left the large wire cage and did as Dirk had ordered.

Dirk reached up and grabbed Franklin's shoulders, trying to exude more authority than panic as he stared up into the wide eyes of the security officer who was definitely not a scientist. "Where is everyone, Franklin? There are usually a lot of people here when the pod returns with specimens. Is there something you aren't telling me?"

Franklin looked up and down the corridor. "Maybe they're in the cafeteria. We had a helluva morning."

"Get up to the bridge and tell Johnson to sequence a pod for an unplanned excursion so we can return these creatures. What quadrant of Santelli did you find them in?"

"P13-04."

"Oh, you can remember *that* piece of information, you overzealous…" Dirk took a deep breath and briefly closed his eyes. "Just do it."

"Yes, sir," Franklin said and ran off.

Dirk watched him round the corner of the hold, then slid the thick glasses back up his nose. He'd go to the lab and speak to Jenny, see what she could explain of the situation. As much as he wanted to entirely blame Franklin, he had a feeling the man wasn't alone in this dangerously careless blunder.

The *Ark*'s hallways were unusually silent, unusually empty. He couldn't justify passing the lab to get to the cafeteria just to check Franklin's hypothesis. But he soon became quite aware of the fact that he hadn't passed a single person in the normally bustling corridor, had not been greeted by his usual team of scientists on the way out of the *Ark*'s cargo hold. He felt his heart racing, and it was not from exertion from the walk he took every day.

At his arrival, the lab's hydraulic door hissed open, and Dirk stepped very slowly inside. The room's walls were lined with shelves and a few specimen carriers, and two stainless steel counters ran the length of the lab, leaving an open isle down the middle. There in that isle sat almost half the ship's personnel, positioned in a perfectly straight line one after the other. They sat cross-legged, their hands folded in their laps, unmoving. Their eyes focused on something ahead of them he could not see, glazed over and absent. They did not blink, did not look at him, and he thought of the humanoid specimens in the cargo hold.

Stepping around his closest associate, Dirk whispered a few names in wary greeting. There was no response, not even when he raised his voice in what was supposed to be a command. It sounded only like terror. He ran down the line, saw Jenny's brunette ponytail, and hovered over her. "Jenny? Jenny! Wake up!" He grabbed her by the shoulders and gave her a violent shake. She didn't move a muscle.

Dirk weaved through the line of sitting personnel, throwing his arms in the air and shaking clenched fists. He felt like he was going to explode and finally roared the first expletive of his life.

"Shit!"

Chapter 2

F ranklin rushed through the *Ark*'s endless hallways. The Ferret had chewed his ass real good this time. He'd never seen the zoologist so ruffled before.

It was true, they had ignored a few security measures. Hell, he should know, he was the frigging security chief. But at this point in an investigation just about everyone knew that. As soon as a planet earned T-rating confirmation, with carbon-based lifeforms and all the atmosphcric and geological features neces-sary to sustain them, they were no more dangerous than any of Earth's species. Anatomy differed with every species, but there wasn't a real risk of harmful contamination anymore. The only one who worried about following all the protocols *ad nauseam* for fear something might happen was the Ferret, and then again, the man worried about everything. Besides, it wasn't like it had been Franklin's idea to bring the scaly-furry people onboard.

A pair of sliding doors opened before him after a quick iris check, and he stepped onto the bridge. "Hey, Johnson," he called, only to be rewarded with the usual grunt of acknowledgement. Franklin always felt creeped out around Johnson, but sucked it up when forced to deal with him. "Forret says we gotta—"

The intercom system buzzed to life. It ran in every room of the ship but was supposed to be reserved for emergencies. It was designed to work even if everything else failed, but they used it all the time. It was ridiculously useful to locate staff members when they were needed somewhere in particular. The voice behind the speaker was Forret's now, though, and for the first time it looked like the device would serve its intended purpose.

"A-anybody who's still there... Meeting at the bridge. Right now. We have an A-Type emergency. I repeat. We have an A-Type emergency. All personnel to the bridge. Now."

The communication ended without ceremony. After a few seconds, Franklin realized he was shaking his head and stopped. "A-Type..." he whispered. That was like fucking Defcon 5 in the ship. That usually meant an alien attack or...

"An epidemic?" Johnson muttered.

Fucking probably, Franklin thought without amusement. Nobody seemed to be shooting them, after all.

"But…" Johnson continued. Geez, he was on a roll. "How did it get inside?"

A knot drew tight in Franklin's chest, compressing his heart. Well, he kinda had an idea about that.

***

Dirk felt he couldn't run fast enough to the bridge. His entire scientific team had fallen into a trance, if that's at all what it was, and there was no way of telling if they'd come back. They were his people, the ones he was supposed to lead. And Jenny...Jenny, above all. Jenny, whom he... But no. He couldn't let himself think like this. He'd figure it out. They would come back, he'd bring them, and Jenny would be fine.

He was almost at the bridge when he remembered and stopped in his tracks "Kuhn." He turned around in agitation and went in the opposite direction. He had to get his dog. He was ashamed that he'd forgotten him, if only for a moment, and realized that his little buddy had obviously noticed something neither he nor Franklin had detected. Kuhn's reluctance to follow him into the *Ark* hadn't made much sense twenty minutes ago, but now it did. It made way too much sense.

He found the dog as he'd left him by the cargo hold's entrance, barking and jumping in useless warning. His agitation spiraled into obnoxious canine insanity when he saw his master approaching, and even as he was held tightly against the zoologist's chest, the Chihuahua let out a string of doggy wails when they stepped back inside. "Easy, Kuhn. It'll be all right."

Four minutes later, he stepped onto the bridge. He sighed with relief at the sight of the crowd gathered there. If he guessed right, the remaining half of the staff was alive and well, and here. He counted uniforms: security, cooks, medics, mechanics, maintenance... Just what he'd feared. As happy as he was to see them, this meant that he had no scientists aboard. Conscious ones, at least.

Franklin's voice screeched through his inventory like nails on a chalkboard. "What the fuck's going on, Dirk?" His deep voice came out airy and weak, and he really looked rather sick.

The scientist swept his gaze over the rest of the crowd, found the same expression on every single face—anticipation, fear. "Just listen to me," he said. "And please don't panic."

There was a nervous silence as the remaining crew tried to process Dirk's words, interrupted only by Kuhn's chattering little steps. The dog had calmed down as soon as they had left the cargo hold, and now Dirk had let him down to walk freely about the bridge as he told his crew what he'd witnessed.

This was the *Ark*'s first real crisis, and nobody had been prepared. They needed to take measures, and it had to be now. "Well, I know we're all unnerved by the situation," he started, "but since this thing doesn't appear to be contagious, I suggest that everyone who hasn't been involved in this morning's mission goes back to their respective stations. Work will carry on as close to normal as we can manage. The rest of you, please stay here. I have a few questions to ask regarding…this thing."

Most of the crew went out in relative order. A few snide and thinly-masked comments were made, but Dirk tried to pay no attention to them. As expected, the only ones remaining after the little exodus were Franklin and his boys from Security.

"So," Franklin said, "what do you want us to tell you?"

The fact that the man had managed a complete sentence without including some kind of profanity both pleased and worried Dirk. "Well, it would be nice if you told me exactly what happened today. Start from the moment you found the humanoids. Oh, and I need to know who was in charge of—"

"Korsakov."

"What?"

"Korsakov was in charge." Franklin stood and paced the room. His hands were closed into fists at his sides. "He was the one who insisted we brought these fucking things aboard. Shit, I never imagined they could be so dangerous. I...I..."

"We loaded them," said a boy in a security uniform. He was red-headed, that natural carrot shade of red that indefectibly

24

comes with a spray of freckles. He couldn't have been more than twenty and looked like he was fighting tears. "He told us to load the cages onto the pod, and we did."

Dirk cursed himself. He should have known. Dr. Korsakov was his second in command, the man who always headed missions Dirk wasn't available to make. He was the only person who could give that kind of order without being questioned. But why?

"Look, guys," he said, trying to comfort them. He really didn't want to see Carrot-top cry. "I really don't think that bringing them here made any difference. If we look at the facts, only the scientists were affected. The rest of the crew is all right. So are all of you, and so am I. Franklin even touched them, and he's...still Franklin. So whatever this is, I think it started before you returned to the ship. I need you to think about this. Did my team have contact with something you didn't? Is there something special you remember that..." They were already shaking their heads. He was tempted to curse for the second time that day, but there were people this time to hear him. Instead, he kept it to a good rub on his temples. "Okay, let me think. I—"

"Maybe it was somethin' in that big-ass altar?" Franklin blurted. Then his face shrunk into itself, like he wasn't quite sure.

"Come again?"

"Well, this is going to sound nuts, but we found this altar. It was all white, with the creatures sitting all around it. Doc Robinson said it might be an altar, because it was all carved and stuff—"

"Franklin." Dirk couldn't help but chide the man. If he would just get to the point...

"Okay, okay," Franklin said, a bit annoyed. But the red-headed boy was already looking at him, nodding as he too remembered. "Jenny and a couple of your science people came in the pod with us. Just about everybody touched it. Well, everyone but us. We were surveying the perimeter, or loading cages, or..."

Dirk held out a hand. "Fine," he said.

Dr. Robinson was an anthropologist, a middle-aged woman who had been part of the *Ark* Project from the start. She had been excited about finding new cultures, and look where that had gotten her. No, stop it. Focus. "Are you sure none of you got close to it?"

"Yes, sir," answered a chorus of guards.

"Okay, let me think..."

"But how can contact with a piece of rock induce a trance from a long distance?" Asked Johnson, who had remained silent during the whole meeting.

Dirk scoffed whilst everyone turned to look at him with expectation.

"I don't know," he said. "But it's all we've got. Maybe we need to go see for ourselves, check the place out and see if we find something else." He looked at Franklin. "Which sector did you say it was?"

"P13-04."

"That's about sixty miles from here, Sir," Johnson added.

"Very well. So in a pod we could be there in about twenty minutes." He pondered this idea for a moment, then turned to the security team. "You're all coming along. I'm going to need each pair of hands I can use."

"Yes, Sir."

"And you," he told Franklin, "go fetch Dr. Rowens. Tell her to get her people ready." Dr. Rowens was the leader of the medical team, and now the docs were the closest thing he had to a squad of scientists.

He smiled, thinking of the expression on her face when she

26

found out she would now be required to sink her pristine black shoes into the mud. But hey, there were lives at stake here.

Johnson's grumbling escalated into a roar as his hands crashed down on the controls and he collapsed back into his chair. Dirk and security stared at him. "Something's interfering with the pod com," he said. He didn't turn around to look at them, but only brooded in his pilot's chair.

"What the hell does that mean?" Franklin snapped.

Johnson finally did turn to glare at him. "It means that some *thing,* or some *person,* messed with the connection from *my* bridge controls," he stabbed a finger at the keys in front of him, "to the pod controls. They're not responding. I can't even turn them on."

"Ah, fuck it!" Franklin shouted. Kuhn barked.

There was no emergency protocol for that kind of failure. Dirk knew it could take ages to repair, even after finding the cause, and they didn't have ages.

"Well..." Dirk sighed. "It looks like we're going to have to walk."

Chapter 3

A pale, blue-white funnel in the bright purple sky glowed over Dirk's team as they marched through the thick crimson sand. Within a few hours, and for the second time since they'd left the *Ark*, the two suns would be slowly setting in the mountains behind them. Then, once Mearon appeared, the singing and shuffling of the night creatures would accompany them until the morning.

Back on Earth, the average distance soldiers could cover on foot was twelve miles in three hours. Dirk had calculated that, with a team of doctors, untrained as they were to marching long distances and on sandy terrain, it would take them approximately fifty hours. This included breaks to eat and sleep before they reached sector PI3-04. Almost everyone in the group had studied maps of their path, but none of them had actually walked it. Pods were convenient, fast, and able to transport a decent amount of specimens at any given time. Even Dirk, who took frequent strolls with Kuhn by his side as a means to clear his head and ponder upcoming projects, never strayed too far from the *Ark* without an accessible pod nearby. As a matter of fact, Dirk had never spent a full day away from the *Ark* since the day he started building it.

With his favorite shirt sticking to his torso like second skin, his heavy glasses having glided half an inch down the bridge of his nose, and raw, red sand dripping out of his shoes, Dirk recalled the sight of the *Ark* the day before. They had reached the peak of a tall, smoothly scaled mountain when Dirk had turned around for a final look. Like the zoologist he was, he had given his home an organic look—curvy, with no corners. Standing on six solid, flask-shaped legs, the fuselage was designed after the *Shovelnose Guitarfish*— a triangular ray fish with smooth edges—its twin engines located where the tail of the fish would have been. The numerous windows placed along the length of the aircraft made life onboard more pleasant to the crew than most other crafts of its time, while undoubtedly the best view was enjoyed from the cockpit's large elliptical windows.

As was the case with several batoid fish, the *Ark* was painted uniformly in a shade of white-gray with a matte black belly and two neutral-gray platforms—one in the middle and one in the rear. Seeing the *Ark* covered in clouds of red dust in the distance had made Dirk smile at his masterpiece, and he had turned back toward his team only after Zoe called out to him.

"Care to share?" Dr. Zoe Rowens asked. Her London accent seemed to intensify her disdain as she dragged her feet next to Dirk. A transparent pink scarf, which she occasionally pressed against her mouth as if to breathe in through her gloved fingertips, was wrapped around her face. Only the eyes of the thirty-three-year-old doctor and established professional were directly exposed to air.

Dirk took a look at his extra-large multi-function watch. "Not just yet, I'm afraid." Rowens dismissed him with a wave of her hand. "Why are you wearing that thing over your head? They're harmless, you know." He pointed to the suns behind them without turning to look.

"It's the sand…" Rowens stopped in her tracks to dust off her initially white but now reddish-gold trousers. Dirk waited for her. "I hate sand, especially when it gets in my hair. I also hate dust. And mud. And tiny nests the little zebra worms crawl into. I want to go back to my sickbay." She reluctantly started walking again, and Dirk followed.

"Kuhn over there struggles to keep up with us, but you don't hear him complain." Dirk nodded at Kuhn a few feet ahead, sliding in the sand every now and then yet never giving up. Dirk had been carrying his friend through most of the journey, but from time to time Kuhn needed to stretch his legs. Rowens waved a hand in front of her. "What do you think's happened to our scientists, Zoe?" Dirk asked after a while.

Rowens shook her shoulders. "I've no idea. Their vital signs appear to be fine, but there's no response to either pain or retinal stimuli. Their bones are locked in place, and I'm sure they wouldn't move even if I set them on fire. Perhaps I could tell you more after a few biochemical tests, but for some reason, you wanted to rush the whole medical team out to that altar."

"I need you guys there. We don't know what we're up against. None of you got this…thing."

"Why? Do you think we're immune?"

"I don't know."

"Hey, Ferret!" Franklin waved Dirk over.

"How many times have I told you—"

"Check out this other crazy fucker, here." Franklin held the familiar stripped worm in one palm and another two-headed worm in the other. Apart from the extra head, they were identical. "This one's Jim, and the big one's Frankie".

"You didn't…"

"Come on now, Ferret, there's nothing wrong with naming them. They have their own cages, and we—well, *you*—can examine them on the road. Something to do on the way back, right?"

"We can't just carry them around, Franklin. I told you before. It's bad enough that we have to carry this cage of sleeping humanoids with us—"

"Those were Korsakov's orders, to take those things. These two are harmless." Franklin placed the worms into small cages he had strapped over his shoulders.

Dirk still could not fathom why Dr. Rodney Korsakov would give an order against the first protocol. Security personnel were trained to follow orders, not question them, so he couldn't blame Franklin and his team for not having any further information on the issue. Dirk hadn't mentioned it to anyone yet, but the thing that unnerved him most was Korsakov's disappearance. He hadn't seen the man once since they'd discovered the humanoids and couldn't possibly imagine what had happened to him.

Dirk had known immediately that the only way to get answers was to go on this journey himself. Even if Dr. Rowens nagged about it. He hadn't been to sector PI3-04 before and didn't remember anyone ever mentioning an altar. What security staff seemed to remember the most was its bright white pillars and how the humanoids had gathered around its entrance. Sure, they had noticed some strange patterns on those pillars, a number of which had even been broken or cut in half, but their job wasn't about taking out a magnifying glass and studying abstract paintings.

"Dork Ferret?"

"Hm?"

"Why didn't we take the *Ark* to the altar? It's a ship. It can fly."

Dirk smiled at Franklin's naivety and readjusted his glasses on his nose. "As you well know, the *Ark* is a very sophisticated piece of machinery which includes a very advanced, state-of-the-art laboratory. Despite our current, and hopefully temporary, crisis, very delicate specimens, plants, animals, and samples are still in the *Ark*'s lab waiting to be analyzed by exemplary scientists. Right now, lifting the *Ark* into the air and risking potential damage to our research is unnecessary. Besides, we can always call our highly decorated pilot if we need to evacuate as soon as possible. Isn't that right, Johnson?" Dirk spoke into the radio placed over his shoulder.

"That's right, Sir," Johnson responded from the other end.

After a short break for food and some rest, the group resumed their course. Dirk looked at his watch. It would take them a few more hours, but they would be there before sunrise, he thought. Dirk lifted his head to the mountains ahead. Apart from worms and lizards, they hadn't come across any other species larger than a fly. It was quite possible that the humanoids actually lived in and around that altar, while the lizards preferred to be under rocks in the mountains and the worms in the sand.

The sand…something was happening in the sand.

At first, Dirk heard the grains of sand, as loud as receding water over pebbles. Then he saw small, intermingled clouds of dust dancing in place on the ground before him. A part of him wanted to approach the spot, but the part of him that prevailed advised him to stay still and watch.

The grains whirled to form the shape of an animal Dirk

33

recognized as the *Maltese tiger*—once a mythical creature but not so long previously identified and documented in China as a mammal of the *Panthera tigris* family. Dirk had read about it while he was on another planetary expedition. Before he could admire the shape of the proud, blue-gray, striped cat, the grains of sand began a new dance, this time shorter and subtler. In place of the tiger appeared the Peruvian endemic *white-bellied cinclodes*—a rare black, white, and brown bird, much like a large sparrow, which had become extinct.

As much as Dirk enjoyed the presentation, in the back of his mind, he couldn't help but wonder what was actually happening. Before he could move, another cloud of sand rolled over the shape of the bird, which gave its place to that of a blue dragon sea slug. Normally, the slug was no more than an inch long, fitting in the palm of one's hand, but Dirk saw it drawn by the invisible wind as large as a cat. Named after the mythic Glaucus, the fisherman who became immortal after consuming a magical herb, Dirk found that *Glaucus atlanticus*' shape was the most impressive of the three, with its blue-black camouflage depicted in red and yellow tones, its thin, long tail, and three pairs of symmetrical, tentacle-like appendages.

Without warning, Dirk heard the sound of thunder behind him. With a quick turn of his head, eyes wide open, he saw another funnel had appeared in the sky behind them. Only this second funnel grew larger by the second, doing what it was not meant to do; it was approaching. Giant white roots flashed in the sky as the funnel turned clockwise with abnormal speed. The galactic spiral had turned into a gigantic whip, preparing to lash at Santelli Minor's surface.

Dirk yelled at his crew to take cover in any way they could, but his voice seemed nonexistent when a sudden, powerful wind lifted massive clouds of gravel and dust toward the group. The freckled, red-haired kid appeared by Dirk's side, grabbing his arm and crying in his ear for help. Dirk regretted never having gotten around to asking the young man's name. While they were immobilized in the eye of a sandstorm, the funnel had almost reached the planet's surface. Dirk felt his strength failing him, gradually losing his hold on the man being sucked into the spiral. It wasn't long before the funnel blocked Dirk's entire field of vision, and Carrot-top became invisible.

In the midst of the chaos, Dirk tried to spot Kuhn but couldn't see clearly since his glasses were no longer on his face. All he could hear were distant cries in the storm. He felt a numbness in both his arms, starting at his fingertips and spreading up to his elbows. He couldn't determine if it was from his effort to keep Carrot-top on the ground or something else entirely.

And then Dirk saw home. Not his superficial home—the one made of materials which allowed faster-than-light air travel and carried people he called family. He saw the home in which he was born. He thought he had forgotten everything that had happened until it all reappeared in the center of the spiral. Dirk stretched out his hands with tears in his eyes, yelling at the storm to take him too, but the numbness had travelled through his shoulders and into his throat. Unable to stand any longer, Dirk crashed hard against the alien ground.

"You all right, buddy?" Franklin shook Dirk's shoulder. "Lost you here for a second." Franklin let go of him, casually clearing his throat. "We don't want you getting all fucked up on us, now."

Disoriented, Dirk checked his watch once again. They had been walking for hours, and it was only a matter of time before the suns set. Everyone around him, including Carrot-top, still marched east in almost the same formation as before he'd lost track of time. Everyone except one. "Where's Kuhn?"

"Why are you asking *me*? You're the one holding him all the fucking time." Franklin seemed to have regained his composure after the momentary lapse in apathy.

"No. No, he was… He was right there. I could see him. He's gone!" Dirk yelled.

"Fine, whatever. I'll go look for him, already. Just stop screaming in my ear. The hell were you thinking, bringing a puppy along, anyway?"

"He's not a puppy, he's a full-grown… Look, just help me find him, okay?"

As the two men searched among moving boots and sandals for the missing Chihuahua, a shot rang out over the valley. They ducked and spun, searching for the source. A small circle had already formed over a collapsed body on the ground, making it impossible for them to see who it was. As they ran towards the incident, a security officer pushed another, the second waving his arms and screaming.

Once finally there, Dirk approached the officer who had pushed the other. "What happened?"

"That son of a bitch shot Alby!" The man nodded at his colleague in security uniform who was being handcuffed on the ground by his fellow officers. He was so agitated, he had to be held down.

"Why?" Dirk asked, even though he didn't know who Alby was.

"Why don't you ask *him*?"

"Hell, that's Ron," Franklin said, once the man was dragged and lifted by his armpits. It wasn't a gentle lift, and his colleagues were now shouting back at his protests. "Hey, break it up!" Franklin shoved the men aside. "What the hell did you do, man?" he asked Ron.

"I didn't do anything! We were just standing there talking, nothing wrong. Hey, I'm not fucking crazy!" Ron wasn't making much sense, and Franklin examined him from head to toe.

"Sir, we were right behind them. We saw what happened." Another officer, fresh out of the academy like most of security, looked with pleading eyes toward Franklin. "Ron just lifted his weapon and shot Alby in the head without warning. He didn't say anything."

Franklin had made up his mind. "Fine. Stick to protocol. Arrest him," Franklin ordered loudly, then whispered to his closest officer. "Just put something in his mouth too. He's too loud. We'll lock him up for an investigation when we get back to the *Ark*." The officers did as they were ordered, sealing Ron's mouth with the latest invention of synthetic tape.

"Wait," Franklin spoke up again. "We don't know what actually happened, and I don't want him close enough to hurt anyone else. Put him in the cage with the humanoids."

Dirk had never seen his Head of Security quite like this in action. Franklin had been highly recommended when the *Ark*'s team was being assembled, but Dirk honestly didn't know the man actually had it in him. Having observed the incident silently, he told the group to prepare for a stop. They were going to camp there for the night, even if it meant arriving at their destination much later than originally planned. Accidental or not, a death by one of their own was not good for morale.

He went to Dr. Rowens, who knelt next to the fallen soldier as the others solemnly prepared a makeshift camp. Standing over them, Dirk could finally see that Alby was, in fact, Carrot-top.

"He had no chance. Poor kid," Rowens said and stood.

37

Dirk brought a hand to his head, trying to make sense of everything. Of anything.

"Hey, leave it up to me." Franklin pushed Dirk gently aside. "You go look for your dog. I'll take care of this."

Dirk shook his head in disappointment. With the intention of pinpointing their exact location on the map, he took his tablet out of the case strapped to his trousers. As he raised his finger in the air, about to place a black flag on the electronic map, he heard barking from the top of the hill to his left. Dirk immediately dropped his tablet and ran as fast as he could to the hill, earning several looks from his group. It could only be Kuhn, and he was right; he found the dog at the peak of the hill, who only barked louder upon seeing his master.

Overjoyed, Dirk grabbed and held Kuhn in his arms like a baby, unable to believe he had found him again. But the Chihuahua bit him lightly, just like he did when he wanted Dirk to follow him or let him go.

"Okay. What is it, boy?" Dirk hesitantly let him back down to run around freely again.

As soon as Kuhn touched ground, he sprang toward what looked like a piece of white fragment and dug rapidly at it with his front paws. Kuhn never acted like that for no good reason. Dirk ran and slid down the hill to examine the object. Digging with his hands, he uncovered more of the fragment's surface, which by then resembled the top of a pillar. When Dirk reached a surface he could no longer dig by himself, he stopped to inspect the object more carefully. Carved on the pillar were two black circles, one larger than the other, from which white lines spread outward.

"The two suns? Sunrays? An eclipse?" He tried to make sense of the image. "Well, I'm no archaeologist," he told himself, getting up. "I don't even know where our archaeologist is…"

Kuhn barked at Dirk, this time wagging his tail. Smiling, he lifted the dog again. "It's okay. We'll figure it out." He rubbed a playfully barking Kuhn between the ears, then looked up to the sky. Mearon had made its appearance, as brilliant and radiant as always, lighting the way for all explorers. It was there, right under Santelli Minor's stunning moon, that Dirk saw what Franklin had described as an altar.

Chapter 4

"There it is." Franklin had walked up the hill to step behind him and share in the sight.

Presented before them was a large oasis, outlined and shaped by wildlife of all sorts. Rocks lined the edge of a ring in the center while vines draped themselves over the branches of trees, creating a secluded atmosphere. The foliage was thick and would have been impossible to see through had they not found it from the hilltop. Placed within the ring of stones was a large white slab, neatly polished and carefully positioned. The other rocks were dusted in dirt and debris, yet even from Dirk's perspective above, the altar seemed pristine.

"Didn't I tell you it was creepy as fuck?"

"Don't tell anyone about this yet," Dirk said softly, staring down. "We need to rest tonight, and I'll show the others in the

41

morning."

Franklin folded his arms and grunted.

***

"No one touch the white stone, are we clear?" Dirk commanded. He had led them over the crest of the hill once they'd packed up camp and had been met with eager expressions and comments of both relief and hesitation. Now that they were actually here, the team seemed to be a bit more at ease. He stared each person in the eye, making sure they understood, and after nodding in agreement, the group spread out.

"The air reads normal for Santelli Minor," Dr. Rowens said, staring down at the air analysis device in her hand. She was qualified enough to have helped Dirk establish a baseline of air standards each time they landed on a new planet. As a medical doctor, it helped her to alter the methods of administering drugs and medical care to best fit the environment in which they existed.

"No shit, the air reads normal, Zoe," Franklin jeered. "It's not the air that turns people into fucking stone."

"Oh, you're right. That would be the result of you and your poisonous face, Frank." The pink scarf had been abandoned to hang loosely around her neck, but she pulled it up to her face again, almost out of habit, and rolled her eyes.

Dirk could only sigh at their bickering. In reality, he should have expected this. Franklin and Dr. Rowens couldn't stand to be in the same room. From the moment he sent Franklin from the bridge to get the doctor, they had been at each other's throats, throwing insults whenever they could. Alby's death the night before had sobered their hostility, but only for a night.

The two had been acquaintances long before the *Ark*'s completion, much to Dirk's ignorance at the time. When the crew for the first expedition was being assembled, he had taken it upon himself to evaluate each potential candidate. Not once did it occur to him to ask if they had issues with any other candidates—besides the fact that they were all vying for limited spots on the first vessel of its kind to explore extraterrestrial land. A question like that seemed horribly stupid at the time. Franklin and Dr. Rowens, it turned out, had gone to high school together, and consequently, their innate distaste for each other ran deeper than Dirk's own for Franklin. Though he never asked why they couldn't be civil, sometimes he was convinced it was the result of a relationship gone wrong.

"Dr. Rowens, let's examine the altar," he said, redirecting the conversation.

Snapping a pair of gloves on, Dirk walked around the altar, studying it from all angles. Yes, it had looked pristine from the hilltop under the moonlight, but there were far more details up close. There were scratches on the sides, but nothing coherent. Squinting as he leaned forward, he couldn't tell if they were words, hieroglyphs, or accidental marks. He carefully took a slew of photos to reexamine later.

"An altar describes it perfectly," he muttered. "Where's Dr. Robinson when you need her?"

His rhetorical question voiced aloud must have made Zoe uncomfortable, because she ignored it completely and cleared her throat. "Dr. Forret, may I run something by you?" Nodding, Dirk moved to stand beside her, their backs to the rest of the exploring group. "Whatever it is about that white stone affected not only the human crew but the humanoid specimens on board as well, correct?"

"Yes."

"I am a reasonable doctor, am I not?" Dirk's eyes shot up to meet hers. "I have done a lot of good for the *Ark* with my work, for humankind, have I not?"

"You are and have indeed," Dirk said, suddenly feeling anxious. It wasn't like Dr. Rowens to bring her accolades and intelligence into an argument—even an argument with Franklin.

"Whatever it is that causes the dormant state has found the same anatomical target in both species. I have studied the human body since I was a child—I know it inside and out. The humanoid on the inside, however, I have not." She swallowed, and Dirk hoped he misunderstood her.

"Zoe…"

"I would only ever suggest something like this for a good reason, and I think we can agree that our current situation is a good reason." She took a deep breath and lowered her voice even more. "For the sake of the lives of your crew, I would like your permission to perform an autopsy on a humanoid specimen."

The lingering silence drowned out the shuffling of the crew around them.

He had no idea what to say, what the right answer was. A man of science, he wanted to tell her to go ahead and solve this mystery. Yet he was also a man with a heart and a conscience. Even though the humanoids were not Homo sapiens, and even though they slept without response, there was something so *wrong* with cutting them open while they were alive. Even cutting them open while they were dead, because they didn't seem to be dying at all. No one knew to what extent their stasis ran; the possibility of them feeling pain was enough for Dirk to shy away from Dr. Rowens' suggestion.

But these were not normal circumstances. Half the crew, whether they would admit it or not, who trusted Dirk with their lives sat with their legs crossed and their eyes blank aboard the

Ark. Something had taken away the freedom of their minds, leaving them nothing more than empty dolls.

And then, of course, there was Jenny.

Even though he was a man ruled by his brain, he could not stop his heart from aching as he remembered her sitting there, staring at nothing. Doing nothing.

She was always full of energy, anticipating the next adventure. With a passion for discovery and a love for puzzles, there was no one else he would have wanted by his side as he traveled into the unknown. When he had screened her, he was surprised she had made it as far along in the interview process as he had. Lacking formal education in anthropology and biological sciences, her only claim to success was her photographic memory and her pure belief that the *Ark* was the means of finding ways to better society.

She was, in a sense, his biggest fan—a fact of which she had often reminded him, though always worded more discreetly. Would she think he had let her down if he denied Dr. Rowens' request, if he dragged out their comatose state with such an unclear future? Or would she be disgusted if he agreed to an autopsy, repulsed by the abandonment of his scientific morals?

There was so much to consider and so little time to do so.

"I know that this is a difficult choice, but you see our reality, right?"

"I don't know…I just—"

"Dirk, please." She moved herself into his line of vision so he was forced to look at her without causing a scene.

"There must be another way to test it before we cut open an intelligent life form," he reasoned, running a hand through his hair in frustration. He understood her pleas, he truly did, but her knowledge of the body was not enough for him to agree wholeheartedly. It was not that he doubted her intelligence; there was no

45

other doctor he would have wanted as the medical head. But he needed more evidence before he consented to something which might haunt him forever.

What they needed to do was test the effects on some other species, one neither human nor humanoid. If the rock did the same thing to any creature, there would be nothing to gain by an autopsy.

He glanced over at Franklin, who stood a few yards from the altar with his hands on his hips, gazing about. The two cages hung over his shoulders looked like a ridiculous pair of worm-powered spaulders.

Franklin caught Dirk looking at him. "Dork?" he asked, hesitating.

"Give me one of those worms," Dirk said, and offered his palm up for the creature.

Franklin frowned. "Jim or Frankie?"

"Whichever." He hoped he wouldn't have to attack the cages himself, and the man. But Franklin gave up the worm easily enough. Ignoring the raised eyebrow sent his way, Dirk held the worm with his gloved hand out toward Dr. Rowens.

"Jim will serve as our first test." She nodded, and he moved to the altar. The rest of the team had caught interest in actually interacting with the altar, and all eyes were on him. He gently placed the worm on the white stone, not sure what he hoped it would do.

The worm slowly inched around, and time seemed to drag forever as it made its way from one side of the altar to the other before suddenly, in a fit-less instant, it froze. The air hung heavy around them, and Dirk picked up the worm to gently drop it into a separate, closed container. Crouching down, he also picked up a few small chips of white stone he'd noticed scattered around the slab. Turning to meet the curious eyes of his crew, he took a breath.

46

"Dr. Rowens, you may examine *this* for now," he said, passing the tray to her. He focused on Franklin. "Show me where you found the worm. I want to see what happens if we try to feed it samples of the rock."

Franklin eyed the worm named Jim, now passed to Dr. Rowens. "I liked Jim." Then he seemed to realize what Dirk was asking. "You're going to feed the worms pieces of that fucking altar? The thing that left the others like zombies? Are you fucking mad?"

Franklin seemed to have much more empathy for creatures which ate sediment and rolled around, and Dirk had had enough of the comments. "It's either the worms or you," he said.

"It would help to have a larger organism to cut open," Dr. Rowens mumbled as she glared pointedly at Franklin.

"Bitch."

The sound of a cracking twig within the oasis foliage caused them to freeze. A few others of the team had heard it too, and they peered into the trees with visible anxiety. Dragging footsteps slowly filled the air and Dirk felt his breath catch. This was not how he envisioned this trip ending. No one dared move closer to look for what was back there. Yes, it may just be better to die ignorant, Dirk decided.

The leaves rustled at the edge of the stone clearing, and before Dirk could hide behind Franklin's giant frame—an action he would never have admitted to, even if he had the chance to do so—a familiar, exhausted figure emerged from the foliage.

Chapter 5

D irk took a few steps back, adjusting his glasses in hopes of a better view. "Is that…"

"Dr. Robinson!" Zoe ran toward her as the woman appeared from the cover of the foliage. "Where have you been?" Robinson's feet dragged as she slowly walked toward the group, kicking up the red sand. "Dr. Robinson?" Zoe placed a hand on the woman's shoulder, frowning into her colleague's face, which was covered with dirt and scratches. Dr. Robinson just kept walking, her gaze hypnotic and focused on nothing

"Dr. Robinson, can you hear us?" Dirk asked. He stepped in her path and caught the look in her eyes. It was distant, filled with worry and fear, and they opened wide to share her internal battle despite no outward evidence. She continued on without reacting to Dirk's voice. He was suddenly reminded of the visions he'd had—the swirling sand, forming Earth's creatures, and the tornado hurling red sand all around, paralyzing him beyond help.

"That's the same look Ron had," one of the security guards chimed in.

"Where is she going?" Dirk asked, and Robinson never stopped in her path.

The crew watched in horror as she ignored their calls and marched straight towards the large, white stone. She was fixated on it, pulled towards it by an invisible force.

"Don't do it!"

Franklin ran to Robinson in an attempt to slow her, but it was too late. He stopped a few feet from her as she faced the altar. Finally at her destination, she froze with a wobbly nod and reached out to the slab in front of her. She placed both hands on the smooth, white surface and traced the carvings with her fingers. The group watched in horror.

After removing her hands, she turned and faced Dirk. She didn't react to his presence, nor was she affected by his questioning. All she did was walk towards the inner circle, sit cross-legged on the ground, and freeze in place.

"What the hell?" Franklin asked, his jaw gaping.

"You saw the look in her eyes" Dr. Rowens put in, and turned a wide-eyed gaze to Dirk. "She was terrified, obviously aware of something." She put a hand on Dirk's shoulder, and he turned to look at her. "So why didn't she answer? Why couldn't we stop her?"

Dirk frowned, patting Zoe's hand on his shoulder. "I have no idea. But we'll figure it out." There had to be something they could do for Dr. Robinson, something that might be different than what his scientists frozen aboard the *Ark* needed. She had come out of nowhere, from the oasis around the altar, and whatever it was which had led her back here was something they hadn't yet seen.

"We can at least wait here for a while longer," he said, glancing quickly again at Robinson. "See if she has any response to being here."

"Great," Franklin started. "So we just wait for the zombie to come back to life?"

Zoe folded her arms and glared at him. "Well, I can cut up your worm, now," she sneered. "Maybe it'll show us something." Franklin rolled his eyes.

"Good idea," Dirk said and led her to the flat work surface of a rock nearby. "Let me know what you need."

***

"There's nothing."

"What do you mean, nothing?" he asked.

Dr. Rowens stared down at the dissected worm and the pile of entrails through which she'd just finished sifting. "Nothing seems out of the ordinary. I don't get it."

"I sat here waiting for the thing to crack into pieces like a damn pistachio," Franklin interrupted. "It just bled a lot."

"Yes, unfortunately." Dr. Rowens ensured she inspected "Jim" thoroughly, despite her audience. "Everything seemed intact. The organs still functioned, the blood still pumped. The only thing is, its vitals spiked when I started to cut. It's like…"

"It could feel it. We are definitely not moving forward with the humanoids, if that's the case." Dirk would not willingly subject the humanoids to pain like that, especially because they still knew so little.

"As much as I hate to say it, I agree," said Dr. Rowens. "I didn't even really like doing it to this guy."

"We need to figure out exactly what's going on here. Anything that touches the altar becomes paralyzed but is still obviously alive." Dirk glanced around for the other cage, spotting it on the ground beside Franklin. "I need that other worm, Franklin."

Franklin raised an eyebrow and turned slightly away. "I'm not going to give him to you. God knows what will happen if he tries eating one of those stones."

"You're right. We don't know. And that is precisely why we need to do it. You know I don't condone any experiments like this, but given the circumstances, we have to make exceptions." Dirk paused, hoping Franklin would agree without further persuasion. "Franklin…"

Reluctantly, Franklin walked toward Dirk and slowly handed over the cage. "Don't hurt him."

Dirk put back on his thick gloves, making sure not to touch any of the broken, white shards. He didn't know whether the pieces still carried the same effect, but he wasn't about to risk it. Every precaution had to be taken until they had the slightest clue about what had happened.

He made his way to another rock with a flat enough surface to work on. He dusted the thick, red sand off and rested the cage on top. "Come on, little fella." Grabbing the two-headed worm from the cage, he placed it on the rock. He then sprinkled a few of the white stones in front of it and waited.

"Don't eat it, Frankie," begged Franklin in a chant-like whisper. He watched on as the worm slithered around the stone pieces, barely paying them any attention. "Maybe the two-headed ones don't eat stones?"

As outrageous as that sounded, and though he refused to admit it, Dirk wondered if Franklin was right. "Maybe he's not hungry. Show me where you found the other one."

"Who, Jim?"

Dirk refused to acknowledge the naming of a specimen, as he'd told Franklin numerous times not to do. "The other one."

The rest of the camp stayed put as Franklin explained that he'd found the original worm only a short walk away. With Alby dead and Ron restrained in a cage, Dirk didn't have any security personnel to spare. He decided it would just be he and Franklin.

After a few minutes, they arrived near the edge of P13-04. "What made you keep walking up here after you found the humanoids?" Dirk asked. He figured that once they found the humanoids and Korsakov ordered them to be caged, they'd just returned to the *Ark*.

"Korsakov told me I could explore a little more while he investigated the humanoids. It wasn't until I came back with Jim, there, that Korsakov said to load them up. I thought all of it was a little odd, but then I saw how beautiful they were and didn't really think much of it."

Dirk stood, his back towards Franklin, and looked out into the darkness. He still could not fathom why Korsakov would go against the first protocol, and Franklin's account further confused him. Question after question mounted without answers, or even clues.

"Here we are. This is where I found the little guy." Franklin pointed to a rocky area, much like the rest of the landscape of Santelli Minor.

Dirk was amazed that the man remembered it. Franklin made his way to the pile of rocks, lifting one that stood out from the group. It had a certain shine and color which Dirk did not recognize. The deep blue of the stone was highlighted by small crystals formed on the outside, its edges jagged at every turn.

"Strange."

"That's what I thought," said Franklin. "I mean, I thought it looked cool, but when I picked it up, all the little worms were underneath. I kinda forgot about the rock after that."

Dirk couldn't help but laugh at Franklin's ignorance. Despite his overwhelming size, Franklin was quickly enamored by any small creature, "cute" being a word the man used all too often.

Dirk took a moment to inspect the blue stone, ignoring the worms now burrowing into the sand after being disturbed. Stones were not his specialty. He always had an affinity for living creatures and had tended to ignore most other fields. This finding was better suited for Dr. Robinson, unfortunately. He'd have to confer with Dr. Rowens instead. He slipped the decent-sized stone into his backpack and turned his attention to the worms.

"Here, take a cage and grab a few." He handed the cage over to Franklin, who immediately grabbed three of the worms, one of which was by far the largest.

"Oh. Look at this one. I think—"

"Don't name him," Dirk said for what seemed the hundredth time. He bent down, grabbed two worms of his own, one just before it disappeared into the thick, red sand, and placed them in the cage. "Okay. That should suffice."

They made their way back to camp with cages in hand. Dr. Rowens still poked at the dissected worm, putting it out of its misery for her own sake. The doctors sat huddled around, discussing their own, non-scientific theories of what the altar really was.

Kuhn began to bark when he caught sight of his human. Rarely did Dirk ever leave him behind, but he didn't want to risk losing him again—or Kuhn eating the worms. Dirk apologized for any problems Kuhn may have caused, as he knew the dog's separation anxiety tended to lean toward the excessive.

"Let me out of here! I didn't do anything wrong!" Ron

yelled from inside the cage, pleading his case. "These things are creeping me out!" He sat huddled in the corner, avoiding contact with the humanoids at all costs. He'd been silent since his incarceration, and Dirk spared him only a glance at his sudden outburst.

"Dr. Rowens, please come over here." Dirk brought the newly captured worms to their makeshift workstation. "Now, let's try this again."

Shaking the cage, Dirk first emptied his two worms onto the rock, pushing them towards the broken fragments of the white stone. The first worm poked at the pieces, showing little interest before turning away and slithering down the side of the rock to burrow into the sand. Dirk's second worm sat without much movement, curling into a tight coil in defense-mode. "Well, this isn't working."

"Here, let me try. Leo will—I mean, this worm will totally eat it. Look at him!" Franklin reached into the cage to grab the bulk of the largest worm. He gently placed it on the rock and gave it a good luck pat on the head. "Go get 'em, Leo."

Within no time, the worm slithered to the shards of stone and swallowed each in a single bite. It continued around the rock, scooping up the pieces until all but a few were eaten.

"That-a boy, Leo. Knew you could do it."

Dirk shook his head at Franklin's instant bond with his new capture. "Now, we wait," he said.

Minutes felt like hours as the crew waited for anything—some semblance of an effect. The worm stopped moving and twitched. It looked like the same movements of the first worm, whom Dirk assumed to be "Jim", when Franklin had showcased its soil-eating tendencies. But this reaction was much more violent. The worm shook, coiled, then uncoiled as its midsection quickly grew to five times the size of its body.

"What's happening?" asked Franklin. "He's in pain!"

The crew watched as the worm passed an incredibly large stone. This wasn't anything like the soil the worms typically excreted. Rather, it came out as one solid mass. The stone crowned from the worm's backend, and Dirk immediately noticed the resemblance. He reached into his backpack, removing the jagged blue stone.

"It's just like the one they were hiding under, Franklin."

The worm continued to struggle, eventually forcing the stone out. It was much smaller than the stone Dirk now held, but the size was still incredible considering the size of the worm.

"What are these stones?" asked Dirk. "And how did this one get so large?" He couldn't imagine the size of the worm which must have made the one he held. His questioning was cut short by a low growl as the worm writhed in pain. It moved just a few inches, collapsed to half its original size, and died.

"Leo…"

Dirk placed the larger stone on the rock as Dr. Rowen disposed of the worm carcass. "Just another thing we don't understand," he said. "I think we should start heading back soon. Let's take a few more photos of the columns and we'll review them on the *Ark*. I'd like to at least get her," he nodded toward Dr. Robinson, "back to the *Ark* where it's safe. I can come back with a smaller crew to dig around the site, see if we can come up with anything else. This was enough excitement for a few days."

Dirk loaded the stones into his backpack and instructed Franklin to bring the worms back to the *Ark*. Dr. Rowens and the other doctors packed up camp as they got ready for their long trek back.

"Here, Ron, hold this," Franklin said, handing him the worm cage through the spaced bars. "They'll protect you from the humanoids. Hey, Dork Ferret, what are we going to do with these? Just leave them here?"

Dirk opened his mouth to answer, but was cut off. Dr. Robinson, sitting cross-legged by the altar, let out a long, piercing scream, and the worm cage clattered from Ron's hands to land at his feet in the humanoid enclosure.

Chapter 6

D irk ran to her aid, but before he could reach her, she stopped screaming and fell flat on her back onto the sand. He knelt beside her, making a futile attempt to pull her upright into a seated position. His head swiveled toward the humanoid cage when Ron bellowed in pain and fear.

"It bit me! Help…" His plea trailed off abruptly as he shuffled in among the humanoids and jerkily sat down to assume their frozen, cross-legged stance. Ron stared straight ahead, apparently as lost to his surroundings as his mute companions.

Franklin opened the cage and went to his fellow security member. "What happened?" he asked as he shook the lad none too gently.

There was no response, but the movement shook something loose from Ron's cupped hand. Franklin picked the thing up

59

with his gloves. It was one of the worms taken out from under the blue rock, one he hadn't named. Its top section was red with what he assumed to be Ron's blood. He turned around to face Dirk, who now stood at the open cage door, and held it out for him to see. Within seconds, the worm returned to its normal color.

"Apparently, pebbles aren't the only things the worms bite," he commented as he gingerly put it back in the small cage with the other captive worms. "It must have escaped somehow when Ron dropped it."

"Kill it," Dirk ordered with all the authority he could muster. He still thought he heard his voice crack.

"What? Why?"

"Can't you see? It's not the altar that's turning our people into human shells. It's the worms."

"That's dumb. I've been handling them all along, and they haven't bitten me."

"Maybe you don't look tasty to them," Dirk said, then was able to more coherently form his thoughts. "Besides, you've been wearing protective clothing all along, for collecting samples. It makes sense. Only some of the scientists touched the altar, yet all of them are now unresponsive. Even if they were wearing protection on the expedition, they changed into regular gear when they returned to the *Ark*. There must have been worms hiding in their clothing, and they were bitten as soon as they were exposed. Then it spread to the others."

Franklin set the worm cage on the ground and stared at it, unwilling to accept the idea that his cute little pets could be so dangerous. He shrugged and left it there, then walked through the open cage door where Dirk still stood. "Fine. I suppose it's a possibility, but I can't kill them. You'll have to."

The big man joined the group of doctors, who prepared to

60

start off on their trek back to the *Ark*. Dirk closed the cage door and looked around for something to use to crush the worms. He flexed his shoulders to relax the tension, then noticed that his upper back experienced a strong, tingling sensation emanating from the area where his backpack hung. He started to remove the pack, then heard shouting from the vicinity of the altar. He looked over just in time to see Dr. Korsakov emerge from the lush vegetation of the oasis.

The man pointed something with an oscillating blue light toward the sand dunes in the direction of their path back to the *Ark*. It emitted a steady hum, so loud that everyone within sight of it was forced to cover their ears. Everyone except Dr. Korsakov; he seemed immune to it. His face held no expression; he just stood perfectly still, holding out the object. Dirk reached into one of his multiple pockets and put on a pair of ear protectors to block out all sound, then approached his second in command.

"Korsakov! What are you doing?" he shouted.

There was no response. Dirk got close enough to see that the other man held the main remote key device for the transport pods. It controlled all the pods at once, meant to be used for mass maintenance and repairs. It couldn't be overridden by any of the individual pod keys but only by the main computer on the *Ark*'s bridge, and only within ten miles of the ship.

Dirk now realized why the other pods didn't work after returning to the ship with the humanoids. Korsakov had been controlling them from his main remote, preventing them from being used to return to the oasis. Dirk lunged at Korsakov and tried to grab the remote but was thrown back several feet by the oscillating blue light. He was barely able to keep his footing in the sand as he landed squarely on his heels. All the while, the other scientist made no move, no indication that he even knew Dirk was there or that he'd tried to attack him. Dirk backed away, took off his ear protection, and strode purposely to Franklin and the group of doctors, who had been watching from a safe distance. He approached Dr. Rowens and shook her violently by the shoulders.

"Do you know anything about this, Rowens?" he shouted in her face.

"No! Why would I?" she screamed back, angrily shoving his hands away from her.

"It's common knowledge that the two of you have been sneaking around, giving each other extra attention. You probably know him better than anybody. Why would he stay behind and block the pods?"

"I have no more idea than you do. We don't exactly have the kind of relationship that includes much brilliant conversation. It's more…er, physical," she said, blushing a little. "Besides, what we do behind closed doors is nobody's business but our own. I thought he was still hiding somewhere on the ship. We had a huge fight before he left for the last mission. He wanted me to go, but I didn't. I have enough to do to keep everyone on board vaccinated and healthy without running out on stupid little errands collecting rocks and plants. I only came this time because I wanted to find a cure for whatever has frozen up your scientists. In any case, he called me a one-dimensional, unimaginative moron. I told him if he ever came near me again, I'd cut his dick off. That was two days before he left, and I haven't seen him again until just now. I have no clue what he's up to."

Mollified by her obvious sincerity and the flash of anger in her eyes, Dirk backed off. Now that he'd recovered from his recent involuntary flight through the air, he felt the burning sensation in his upper back again—only now it was no longer just annoying. It was actively painful. He finally unbuckled the backpack from the front and pulled it over his shoulders, then dropped it to the ground in front of him. The pain in his back ceased immediately, and the pack glowed with the same blue light emitted by the main pod key. Thinking that the two blue lights must be connected, Dirk turned to watch Korsakov.

The man hadn't moved an inch, nor had the blue light changed its intensity. The entire group watched him for several minutes, no one voicing an opinion or offering a solution. Dirk kicked his backpack in frustration. An outside pocket flew open, and the blue rock he'd removed from over the burrowing worms rolled out. It too oscillated, then levitated to approximately the same height as Dr. Korsakov's hands. Then it literally rolled through the air and attached itself to the end of the pod key, adding its own pulsing light to that of the remote.

The two objects together made such an overwhelming hum that it had the entire group of humans, excluding Korsakov, scrambling through backpacks and pockets for sound-blocking ear protectors. Even then, they all had to run off to a safe distance to avoid the sound vibrations which made one's head feel like it would split down the middle. Korsakov was a small dot in the distance before everyone stopped running and formed back into a group, hoping for the safety of numbers.

"What do we do now?" Dr. Rowens asked quietly.

Dirk shrugged, head down, fighting off despair. *What can we do? What are our options?* he thought as he kicked the sand with one steel-toed boot. Just then, loud static and a lot of swearing emanated from his backpack. He stared it as though it had taken on a profane life of its own. Anything was possible, considering the total weirdness of today's mission already.

"Dirk. Dirk Forret! Where the hell are you? Come in…come in…anybody. We have a situation here!"

Hearing the familiar voice of the *Ark*'s pilot, Arthur Johnson, Dirk dove for his pack and dug around in it until he found his long-forgotten communication device.

"I'm here, Johnson. What situation?" he asked calmly, trying not to let his anxiety show in his voice.

"All five transport pods are leaving the ship. Are you calling them away with the main key?"

Dirk looked back at the tiny speck of his second in command. "No. I think Korsakov must be. He has the main key. I thought maybe he was preventing them from coming to us, but I think now he must be calling them to himself."

"Why?"

"I don't know. We can't get near him to take it away."

"Why not?"

Franklin and Zoe shared a nervous glance with him. "Long story. I have a feeling that whatever his reasons are, they aren't good ones. Is there any way you can block the signal between the master control and the pods?"

"I just found out what was going on. I'm trying to bring them back, but they're not responding."

"Have they reached the limit of the ship's force field?"

"I don't think so."

Dirk felt a surge of hope with a spark of inspiration and nodded vigorously at the radio. "Activate the forcefield. It's designed to withstand nuclear warheads, so maybe it'll block Korsakov's signal, as long as the pods aren't out of range yet."

"I'll try. I'll get back to you," Johnson said. The device went silent for a moment, followed by a loud whoop of triumph.

"It worked. They're all gathered together inside the field like a bunch of dolphins waiting for their feed of fish. What do you want me to do now?"

"Try to bring them back to the ship. I don't want Korsakov to get his hands on them. I have a bad feeling he may use them against us somehow." Dirk had been smiling at the small success, but that last thought wiped it off his face again.

"Why? What has he done?"

"Nothing except draw the pods out, but I don't like the way he's doing it. He's shutting us out. Have you tried getting them back into the ship?"

"Yeah. They're moving real slow, but I got them to return to their pod bays now."

"Lock all the bays until you hear otherwise from me."

"Yes, sir, doctor. Are you guys in danger?"

"I'm not sure. Maybe." Dirk glanced at Dr. Rowens, who at his words sighed and put a hand to her forehead.

"Should I send out the rest of the security guys on a rescue mission?"

"How? They can't use the pods. The minute you lower the force field, Korsakov will be in control of them again."

"What should I do then?"

"Sit tight until you hear from me. Over and out." Dirk sat down on the sand and pulled his pack toward himself, then put the radio in an outside pocket.

Franklin came to sit behind him. "It looks like things have changed," he said quietly as he nodded in Korsakov's direction.

Dirk glanced across the sand dunes and noticed that all the humanoids, including Ron, were now out of their cage and walking towards him and his little group of doctors. Korsakov walked behind the humanoids, pointing the pod key at them, controlling them the way he had apparently been controlling the transport pods. Dirk got instantly back to his feet and rejoined his group. Franklin followed suit. They stood together and watched the humanoids getting closer and closer.

Chapter 7

"Radio frequencies," Dirk said aloud, watching the scene unfold in front of him. Korsakov was using radio frequencies to control the entranced humans. The control key ran off those frequencies, and Dirk had read a few medical studies where humans with sufficiently low inhibition were susceptible to radio frequency influence as well. The trick was that the conscious mind usually overwhelmed the weaker signals, because, generally speaking, humans had more will than the average garage door or pod craft.

A peculiar set of events had made the perfect environment for Korsakov to first decide to steal the master key, then attempt to use it on the mindless humans bitten by the zebra worms. Had it been Korsakov pulling the strings when Alby was shot as well? Dirk shook his head; that was impossible. Making someone walk while essentially a zombie was one thing, but making them talk and operate a gun was impossible. That would be more like possessing someone than controlling their seemingly empty body.

There were too many pieces, and only Korsakov seemed to have any answers. Korsakov intently focused on controlling the humanoids and Ron, and then Dirk had an idea.

"All of you, stay here," he shouted to the team. They glanced nervously back and forth from the approaching group to Dirk. "I don't know what Korsakov thinks he will accomplish by doing this, but I'm going to go find out. I need you guys to distract him."

"What do we do? Are we supposed to fight Ron, too?"

"If it comes to that. Honestly, I'm not sure how much control Korsakov has over them. I'm hoping that this is some sort of weird bluff, some way to get his back."

"Get his back?" Rowen asked

"It's possible he's feeling unmanned, for some reason," he said pointedly to the doctor. The flush of her face was barely perceptible. "Honestly, I can't think of a single motivation for this insanity that would make any rational sense. Do whatever you need to do, and look out for zebra worms." Dirk put on his pack, hoping against hope his plan succeeded. He wasn't much for physical violence. Then again, he'd never been threatened with anything like this before, either.

He circled around through the sand dunes. It was difficult to walk through the shifting sands without losing his sense of direction, and he alternately checked his compass and peeked over the top of the dunes to find his way behind Korsakov. The shambling people were definitely slow moving, and Dirk made it behind them before they were anywhere near the others. His boot knocked against something hard, and he kicked up a large rock buried in the sand. Picking it up, he moved onwards. It was better than nothing.

With stealthy feet slipping up the dune, he crept up behind Korsakov. The man was a fair bit taller than Dirk, and when Dirk raised his hands up with the rock between them, still sliding down the backside of the dune, he only managed to crack Korsakov at the top of the spine instead of at the crown where he'd intended to strike.

The remote tumbled from Korsakov's hands, and he whirled around, teeth bared in rage. Dirk's eyes grew large and he took a step back. This was not Korsakov; this was something else, something filled with wild fury. He lifted the rock again and struck Korsakov on the forehead as the man bent over to retrieve the fallen remote. Dazzled, Korsakov grabbed his head, and Dirk launched himself at the prone form. Korsakov flailed and tried to throw Dirk off him. He outweighed Dirk but seemed more interested in the remote than in actual escape or harming the scientist, and so Dirk pressed his advantage by soundly voicing his rage at the bizarre situation with his fists to Korsakov's face.

Korsakov lay still as he lost consciousness. Dirk took off his pack and dug around for some rope. He bound Korsakov's wrists and put the remote in his backpack along with his own blue stone. That done, he checked Korsakov's vitals and sighed in relief at the strong pulse. He seemed to stir, then started to snore.

Briefly, Dirk glanced up and across the dunes at the controlled beings shuffling toward his team. The various humanoids in the group became disordered. Some of them were still walking, but not in the right direction, and some had stopped entirely. Others walked repeatedly into those who had ceased moving altogether. The entranced humanoids were no longer controlled by the remote, Dirk realized, and he saw that the blue stone had disconnected itself from the control key when Korsakov dropped it.

Without knowing what to do or who to listen to, most of the humanoids just sat back down.

That was easy, Dirk thought, but easy or not, he was going to get some answers. "I guess you can give me some answers when you wake up," he told his unconscious second in command. Whatever had caused him to act like this, it was over, and they could sort it out aboard the *Ark*. Dirk grabbed his communicator to report in but stopped as he stared at the oasis and the sight of his friends being surrounded by what looked like another group of the humanoids.

Dirk swore under his breath and looked at Korsakov, whose eyes were now open again. He stared at something behind Dirk, who followed the man's gaze and saw two of the hairy, scaly aliens behind him. Korsakov smiled at one and whispered, "My love."

Dirk's jaw dropped at the endearment, but he didn't have time to think of the ramifications of Korsakov's rebound alien romance. Something was wrong with Dirk's head... He wasn't alone inside his own mind. With a shock, he looked at the humanoids.

Not entranced by the zebra worms, their eyes were bright with intelligence. Intelligence and, Dirk thought, something else. Cruelty? They were completely foreign to him, and Dirk knew that he was missing some nuances to their emotions.

"Why did you attack and bind Rodney?" a petulant voice asked in his mind.

"Rodney?" Dirk said. "Oh, Korsakov." Dirk realized the look he'd previously seen on Korsakov's face before rendering him unconscious had made the man seem somewhat less...human. The man had been oddly distasteful before taking up with a telepathic alien lover and committing mutiny; he was an outright douche, now.

"Do you know what mutiny is? Do you know that taking control of people and using them to attack your shipmates isn't something we take lightly?"

"Now we will hurt you and take you to Mishrak. We will tie you up, because you hurt Rodney."

One of the aliens held a device—a stone weapon of some sort, emblazoned with brightly colored pictographs blended together incomprehensibly on the side. One of them Dirk recognized, though—a zebra worm. One of the humanoid aliens brightened as she sensed his recognition. *"In your language, you would call this 'Ray Gun'. We will hurt you, and you will come with us, or you will be worse than these others."*

Dirk's shoulders slumped. "No, don't do that. Do what you have to do and take me." The defeat was bitter in his mouth, felt like a dream. But really, what other option did he have?

Gleefully, she put away her ray gun. Dirk wondered if it even worked or if it had just been a ruse. He realized that what his team had thought were scales were in fact armor when the gun disappeared under what appeared to be some sort of flap. As the first blow came, he realized he might have been way too invested in his career.

The beating he'd been promised was more of a general roughing-up. The aliens appeared much more interested in untying Korsakov and giving him drinks from a strangely shaped flask. Whatever was in it seemed to revive the man, and he used the rope to then tie Dirk's hands behind his back. The others had vanished, and the humanoids marched him across the desert towards the oasis. Dirk strongly regretted not having time to check in and hoped that someone had a chance to tell Johnson what was happening out on the desert.

Korsakov retrieved the remote from Dirk's backpack and

directed the shambling, entranced victims of the zebra worms forward. He grinned smugly at Dirk.

"Korsakov, what are you doing?"

"I'm amassing an army."

"But...why?" Dirk could never imagine Korsakov having planned this for the future, despite having disliked him from the start. The man had talent and experience, was a strong leader Dirk had chosen to work at his side. None of that was reflected now.

"Why? Why wouldn't I?" Korsakov looked genuinely puzzled. The aliens exchanged a glance; it was quick but Dirk saw it. They were concerned by Korsakov's response. There was more going on here than it seemed.

"It's a little strange, isn't it? I mean, you just met these creatures and you've completely thrown out your career and your life. And you've never been very sentimental about your 'relationships'. Come on, it was anger, not sadness, when you and Dr. Rowan fought. This is out of character, even for you. It makes me think you're either acting under duress or you aren't yourself. What would you think if you were in my situation, Rodney?" Dirk used the man's first name, hoping to trigger a more human response in him.

The telepathic humanoids had apparently learned to utilize the strange powers of the zebra worms. Was it really such a leap to think they had mastered other forms of mind control as well? What had they stumbled into?

It was difficult to walk on the shifting sands with his hands behind his back, and Korsakov put a hand on Dirk's shoulder to keep him from falling over. He felt a surge of hope then; Korsakov had nothing to gain by helping these beings. He couldn't really be in love with one of the strange-looking things. There had to be some of the self-interested Korsakov left in there. Dirk hoped he was right; if he was, they might have a hidden ally wherever the humanoids were taking him.

They reached the altar area, cluttered now with footprints. The creature who had 'beaten' Dirk did something he couldn't quite see to the pictographs—the ones he'd thought were connected to Santelli's twin suns. A surge of greenish light emanated in a glowing sheet between the pillars.

"Where are they taking us?" Dirk asked Korsakov in a low voice.

The man's eyes were flat, the green light reflected in them. "Mishrak."

Dirk was lightly pushed through the green light. He flinched away from it instinctively, but all he felt was the slightest chill, like walking into an air-conditioned room. The desert flickered and went dark, then Dirk, Korsakov, and the two humanoids were in a room made of the same stone as the white altar. These creatures, which the team had assumed were primitive, suddenly looked a lot less so with the panels of equipment and blinking lights.

"What is this place?" Dirk asked while Korsakov herded the last of the humanoid-husks through the curtain of light.

"*It's a transportation chamber. We can travel anywhere on the planet using these devices. But that is not enough.*"

"You want to leave?" Dirk asked. "That's what this is all about?"

Korsakov smirked. "There's a lot more to it than that. Mishrak will catch you up."

Dirk didn't like Korsakov's smirk. The man obviously thought Mishrak would dazzle him into some sort of submission. Dirk thought that the aliens wanted off the planet—that they were using mind control to get Korsakov to head a mutiny. Whatever

73

had happened in the past to get Korsakov to hunt and trap the first of the entranced humanoids must have triggered the rest of this. Dirk wondered if Ron shooting Alby was a precursor of the same sort of mind control under which he suspected Korsakov to be.

He didn't have any longer to try to piece together this puzzle. These creatures were far more dangerous than anything he had ever encountered before or imagined, and they were only beginning to see the evidence of the power they wielded. One of the humanoid women hit him hard in the back, and he toppled onto his face, his hands helpless to stop his fall, and into a room with something at the far end which looked like a two-headed idol to some sort of exotic god. Rays of light were depicted coming out of its head in stylized, stone 'beams'.

A deep voice resonated within Dirk's brain. It was so strong that it blotted out all rational thought. *"You will bow before Mishrak."*

Chapter 8

Despite his struggling, Dirk remained helpless as two of the humanoids stripped off his clothes and unceremoniously hurled him down again in front of the idol, scraping his knees against the stone floor. He winced and instinctively tried to spring back up to his feet before a soft and incredibly strong hand pushed him back down. Quick, searing pain traveled up from his knees. He could already feel tiny droplets of blood growing and smearing beneath his skin and the floor as he contested against her strength.

Korsakov clicked his tongue. "It's for your own good, you know. No use in fighting it."

Dirk turned toward his second in command and grunted in protest. "Rodney, why would you—" A sharp crack to his forehead ended the question fast, and Dirk was pushed forward against the idol face-first. Even with the humanoid female holding him down,

Dirk managed to turn his head enough to open one teary eye.

Korsakov kneeled down, close enough that Dirk could feel the heat of each traitorous word just behind his right ear. "This is going to happen whether you like it or not."

Korsakov approached the guards, held up his key, and, wordlessly, they nodded back in response to some unspoken command. The female guard opened her mouth, and what flowed out was a beautiful, hypnotic cooing. For a moment, Dirk felt a warm calm melt over him before shaking it off and clutching at his composure. He watched her walk to one side of the room and wave her hand, after which a hidden stone panel opened with a soft grind, sliding out toward her. She reached into the dark and pulled out what appeared to be a glistening, plantlike substance.

Dirk was reminded of a species of seaweed called *Codium fragile*, known for working its way into shellfish beds, deftly attaching itself to the unsuspecting mollusks, and snatching the animals away. It was more commonly known as the "oyster thief", or by its more morbid moniker, "Dead Man's Fingers".

Korsakov's voice cracked. "Beautiful, isn't it? Every life on this planet is just...so damn beautiful. People back home couldn't understand this kind of beauty. It's..." Korsakov held up his hands and clasped his fingers together, "...connectedness. Zoe wouldn't even understand."

Dirk turned toward him as much as he could and swore he saw tears forming in his captor's eyes. Was this really the same man who'd been all threats and bravado just moments before? What had this planet done to him?

The plant, tenderly caressed in the female guard's hands, began to wave and flow slowly, as if the sound of her mesmerizing voice were waves in the ocean. Its tubular appendages swayed through the air, bowing submissively to a current of sound. Dirk tensed as she neared, but the other guard's hand on the back of his neck tightened, reminding him that escape was nothing more than a fantasy.

Without breaking her intonation, the guard placed the plant along Dirk's bare shoulder and down the back of his right arm. He felt the tubes lightly affixing themselves in place as they made contact with his skin. Another stone panel slid open to his left, followed shortly by more tubules set gently along the other side of his body. He tried to steady his breathing but found his terror making that difficult.

He didn't realize it at first, but the guard's singing had abruptly faded. His heart quickened as the hand on the back of his neck, no longer concerned about attempted escape, finally loosened its grip. Panic had already settled in, and then the strange plants wrapped violently around his arms, small barbs digging into place.

Korsakov nonchalantly leaned up against the wall and picked at his teeth with a fingernail. "Well, that can't be pleasant."

Dirk held back any sign of pain as defiantly as he could but inevitably broke down and cried out until his voice cracked and went hoarse.

Korsakov sighed and knelt beside him, running rough hands through the disparaged younger man's hair. His voice uncharacteristically softened. "Listen, I get it. I do. But this isn't about torture, Dirk, not at all. This is just a step in the process." He softly grabbed Dirk's face, forcing him to make eye contact, and whispered, "Didn't you ever want to be a part of something important? Make your life actually mean something?"

Dirk could see the earnestness spread across Korsakov's face. This couldn't be the same man he'd spent so much time working with on the *Ark*, could it? His mannerisms were all undeniably Korsakov's, but it just didn't make any sense. Why would he do this?

"We're going to need you to fall in line, Forret." Korsakov patted the side of Dirk's face and stood. He spun his finger in the air, motioning for two of the guards to follow, leaving Dirk alone in the room.

He sat in silence and tested the possibility of tearing away from the plants holding him to the spot. But any egregious movement he tried sent searing pain down each side of his body. If he eased too much to the right, the plants on his left side tore into him, and vice versa.

After realizing the pointlessness, Dirk glanced around the stone room and noticed a tiny movement near the bottom of the idyllic statue. Four zebra worms slowly inched their way from miniscule, pre-carved holes in the wall, which he'd failed to notice before, and moved intently toward his exposed body. He tensed, muscles twitching, and fought with caution not to move. "Oh, God. Oh, no." His voice gave a tiny echo in the empty room.

He watched, equally fascinated and horrified, as one worm stopped to wriggle around in a pool of Dirk's sweat and drool on the floor before quickly absorbing it into its outer membrane. Then it continued along with its companions. Two more worms took a bit longer with the small puddles of blood from his lacerated knees. They rolled around almost playfully, covering themselves in the sticky fluid. The final worm, however, seemed willfully determined to be the first to scale Mount Forret.

From watching their behavior, it seemed plausible that the worms had quite a finely tuned sense of smell, perhaps even infrared sensitivity. Dirk banked on pheromone detection and tried to work up the saliva in his mouth. He spat at the closest worm making its way toward his inner leg, but his aim went wide and caught the attention of another worm. Not the intended target, but he was on to something. He tried again and came closer this time, but the worm ignored it. One more attempt managed a direct hit. The worm stopped for a moment, but instead of indulging in the hasty gift, it turned back on course toward Dirk himself.

"Damnit! No, that should have worked." He tried again to work up a spit, but could only manage a few pathetic dribbles. Fear had dried him up.

The worm reached its objective and began its ascent up the inside of Dirk's calf and onto his thigh. He attempted to shake the little intruder off, but it held fast. This *was* going to happen.

"Heh." It started as a slight exhalation of amusement, then grew into a laugh that surprised him. The plants tightened their grip, but he was getting used to the pain. Regardless of his predicament, he just couldn't help but be impressed by the evolutionary wonder exploring the wide expanse of his leg, waiting for the right moment to chow down. When it came right down to it, they truly were amazing.

A quote from his schooldays came to mind, and he repeated it within the stone walls. "It may be doubted whether there are many other animals which have played so important a part in the history of the world as have these lowly organized creatures. Thanks, Charles," he added.

The worm circled and then reared its upper half, revealing a lamprey-like opening. A tear rolled down Dirk's face as he closed his eyes. The worm struck, and Dirk wondered what it would feel like to be a zombie.

Then everything went white.

There was the sound of metal being scraped vigorously

back and forth. Then, the loud hiss of water evaporating off hot, searing metal. Underscoring the noise was a cacophony of clanging, chopping, and sizzling. The smells hit him next; tomatoes simmering, olive oil heating up, basil, oregano, flour. He was in the kitchen of his uncle's restaurant.

He opened his eyes to a shining, flawless masterpiece. What was he doing here?

That's right. He was nine, and out of school for the summer. His parents had sent him to stay with his uncle to "straighten him out". He remembered the fear and uncertainty of being thrown into this world of metal and heat. No, that wasn't quite right. He feared it *now*, all of it—his uncle especially. A towering inferno of a man, Dirk's uncle seemed to disapprove of every movement, every word, and every thought his nephew had.

He was only nine years old, but Dirk had already fallen in love with the animal world, much to the eternal torment of his parents. They cared about his happiness, they honestly did, but they were constantly finding frogs, birds, and rodents in every nook and cranny of the house. They just couldn't fathom why Dirk wasn't satisfied with a simple visit to the zoo, where he could see any manner of exotic animals. "But it's not, like, *real* animals!" he had protested.

So they'd sent him to work with his uncle. The man was family, but could detach himself so quickly when in the kitchen. In an effort to break down the boy's insatiable curiosity, he wouldn't let Dirk refer to him as anything else other than *Chef* while they were at work.

His uncle had such control over his kitchen that he never needed to bark an order. Each of his chefs knew their role and never dared to stray. Despite being there under protest, Dirk was undeniably impressed by the symbiotic nature of the kitchen staff.

His uncle lurked at the far side of the kitchen, his presence unmistaken but not directly intrusive. He was a composer, silently directing his symphony.

"Order up, Chef!" The Sauté Chef, exotic and beautiful, set her dish aside. It was exquisite in its simplicity and perfectly prepared—sautéed *Capelli d'angelo* with aromatic garlic, fresh basil, and bright red tomatoes.

"Salad ready, Chef." Another woman with a brown ponytail, the Cold Foods Chef, placed a simple garden salad onto the counter next to the pasta. She looked sad, Dirk noticed, but she was so pretty. Something in him just wanted to cheer her up, pull her away from her duties, but he didn't dare interrupt any of his uncle's staff while they worked. To get in their way was tantamount to treason.

"Dessert up, Chef!" His uncle's Sous Chef next placed up an elegant pair of chocolate cakes, intricately decorated with white icing along the plate. It looked familiar. The Sous Chef turned to Dirk and smiled. "Why don't you lend a hand, kid?"

Dirk gasped. It was Korsakov.

"If you help us out, we can all get out of here that much faster."

This wasn't right. This isn't—wasn't—how he met Korsakov. Dirk backed away from his uncle's Sous Chef—no, Korsakov—and against one of the short boy fridges behind him. Korsakov's smile faded, and he moved on to his next meal.

Dirk looked up at the other Chefs and realized the pretty Cold Foods Chef was all too familiar.

"J-jenny!" he cried out.

Jenny gave him no notice as she continued on yet another salad. That was her name, right? Why didn't she answer?

The Sauté Chef now hummed to herself, and Dirk could

have sworn he'd heard that melody. It was warm and comforting—a song to soothe all the hurts of the world. He turned around to face her, just to be close to the source of that beautiful melody. He wanted to wrap his arms around her but held back when he realized that she was more than just exotic. She was one of the humanoids.

It was difficult for him to focus. Memories of his time on Santelli Minor crudely intermingled with what he knew to be real—this kitchen. He wasn't a zoologist, he was just a scared nine-year-old boy who wasn't allowed to go home and play with his frogs and bugs. And…Kuhn? No, he didn't have a dog. His father was allergic. They couldn't have one in the house, right?

He looked over to his uncle, who surveyed the kitchen. He would have some answers. He was in charge here. He'd know what to do. *Just trust in him.*

Dirk ran to him and tugged at his uncle's Chef coat. "Chef! Chef! What's going on?"

"Fall in line, Dirk."

"Everything's so weird here, Chef," Dirk protested.

Korsakov turned around again. "Dirk, we need you to get with the program here. We need to get out of here, and we can't until you fall in line."

Dirk looked up at his uncle, but the man's face had been replaced by a bulging mass of…boils? No, it was like a fungus. *Cordyceps*! It looked exactly like the *Cordyceps* fungus that invaded, infected, and sometimes controlled host bodies. How did he know that?

Dirk stumbled back and felt a pain in his leg. The worm! It was coming back to him. He knocked against the counter and bumped the plates. That wasn't pasta or salad waiting to be served; it was a bowl filled with zebra worms and a plate of the seaweed plant.

The Chefs all turned toward the sound of commotion, and Korsakov stepped forward. "Now, be careful with those dishes. They're for some very important people from back home."

Dirk examined the dessert plate and realized why it had looked so familiar. The cakes and icing were arranged just like the symbols found on the broken pillar. Instinctively, he picked up the plate. Korsakov and the humanoid chef held up their hands in protest.

"Now, that is something you *don't* want to play with, Dirk."

Dirk glanced at his uncle, then to Korsakov and his chef, and then to the still melancholy Jenny. Backing away, he hurled the dessert to the floor, smashing the plate and destroying the dish.

His "uncle" bellowed in rage. Korsakov turned toward his superior. "Chef Mishrak!"

Dirk awoke, sore and sweaty in the white stone room. The plants had withered and fallen off his shoulders, and a few of the worms wriggled on the floor in front of him. He smashed each and every one into a sticky paste.

They had used his memories against him. That summer had been the first time in his life he'd ever been made to follow someone else's rules instead of following his own way, and those bastards had used it against him! He knew, if they got off this planet and onto the *Ark*, they would do whatever it took to spread their will across any other life-bearing planet—even Earth.

Like hell would he let that happen.

Chapter 9

Humming the theme song from the good ol' Game of Thrones, that classic from the early 2000's, the blond ran an idle hand through his hair. Arthur Johnson had his legs kicked back against the yoke, eyes fixed on the ceiling. The steering instrument trembled indignantly but didn't budge. The ship was as still as ever, the lights of the piloting controls unblinking in their sleep mode as the rest of the ship's function lights pulsed around the bridge.

The day was as exciting as all the other days had been. Which was basically not very. This hadn't been what he'd expected at all. The pod and force field incidents had been troubling—thank the gods he'd been on the bridge when he received Dirk's radio call—but in the end, he was still stuck in the vessel, unable to go anywhere. The love of his life waited for him back on earth, the simple thought of it reminding him that he could have been watching the digitally enhanced 3D episodes, kicked back on his couch instead of the pilot seat in this narrow space. He couldn't remember the last time he'd seen a blood-bathed man dragging his own battered body across the battlefield, his last cries of despair echoing across the land.

There were crumpled Sudoku puzzles tossed on the floor, though each and every one had been completed with precise pencil markings. Though it was an old-school pastime, it still worked to engage the mind. Now, his brain had had enough stimulation from the puzzle, *thank you very much*. Boredom struck again as eagerness for some action arose. And it had barely been twenty-four hours since he had to adjust the force fields! Too many puzzles had already passed under his pencils, abandoned in favor of reminiscing about his time on Earth.

The only relief from all this, he thought as he lumbered out of the bridge, *is exercise*. To be specific, it was his practicing of the traditional, vigorous, ever-exhilarating Kung Fu.

It was a topic worthy of boasting, he was sure, but not a single member of the crew had heard the endless speeches of his fighting prowess which played repeatedly in his mind. Most of these spacey scientists and adventurous explorers knew zilch about the wonders of Chinese martial arts—had never had their eyes opened to it. He knew most of them would not be amused by his sudden shows of throwing kicks and punches at the air once he had the space, and he didn't have to deign to their opinions of him to stay in top fighting form. It was a must to retain such valuable knowledge, no?

The *Ark*'s small holodeck was a quick walk from the cabin; surely nothing would require his urgent attention now that the pods were secure. Johnson continued humming as he strolled along the brightly lit corridor. To the bored pilot, the empty holodeck was a blessing, and he wasn't about to question that. Pumping a fist in the air, he skipped into the white paneled room, and the door hissed shut behind him. He was here to work himself away from the boredom of the ship, and he took a moment to warm up before selecting a combat program.

As he did his warmups, his mind wandered back to his days on Earth, memories as clear as still waters. There he was, hair ruffled from a sparring session, pushing effort into every move. As exciting as it had seemed tossing kicks around and jostling with his partner, it soon, well, bored him. Not just in the moment of sparring, but for his last few months on his home planet.

What was the point of continuous practice and competing with strangers? It had been fun indeed, but it was just missing this...*bam*. There was no sudden spike of excitement, nothing unexpected. It had just seemed so bland. That whole pondering of his purpose in the vast universe was what had made him search for something else, something which wasn't a regime of thrusts and grabs. Just something out of this world.

What better option than to travel out to space? When the offer came around in his necessary yet completely unfulfilling career as a private jet pilot, he couldn't say no. He, Arthur Johnson, the powerful Kung Fu fighter, would be going *to space*. Up, up, and into the world of the unknown, and to explore new planets, no less. How was he to deny such an exciting offer?

But soon, even that couldn't fulfil his need for excitement. What was he supposed to do when he was stuck with the role of babysitting the ship? Frustrated, he began his routine in front of his invisible audience, missing the joy from the old days. Ironic, since he'd come here with the purpose of changing that.

Clonk. Something rang out from the corridor outside, as if an elephant had knocked on the metal walls of the ship. Johnson landed from his butterfly kick rather awkwardly at the sudden distraction. Frowning, he turned to the door.

The pounding sound repeated as he inched towards the closed door. It increased in volume, growing a little more frequent, all the way until he reached the door. Then the noise stopped, and he pulled his hand way from the door's open button, frowning. He waited a few more seconds for a repeat of the noise, but there was none, and he shrugged. Time to move past the warmup.

He tapped in a key code on the holodeck's control panel and waited for the selected program. He'd specifically created his own add-on to the combat programs which let the *Ark*'s computer randomize his sparring opponents. It always gave him something new, something unexpected, and he enjoyed the challenge of discovering his holo-opponent's tactics and weaknesses after it had already started attacking him.

The holodeck's lights faded, came back up, and Johnson stared at his randomized challenger. Feminine and furry, a humanoid glared at the shocked man. Screeching, she leapt at him, but he was faster. Whirling to his right, he crouched down before trying for a jump, his leg flying at the humanoid. She reached for his leg, as if thinking it could stop the agile human. Eyes wild, she successfully clutched his calf just below the knee.

Exactly what his human opponents would do back home. It wasn't conventional, to let one find a grip on your leg, to let them toss you. The beast in him was lured out by the delicious exultation flowering instantly, roaring for a good fight. Johnson swung hard, dragging the creature along before she had the chance to attack again.

Immediately, she let go, arms stretching out to target his upper body instead. He ducked a swipe, following that with a swinging leg to the humanoid's torso to cut at her balance. Shaking, the wiry, hairy figure seemed confused for a moment before somehow stabilizing herself. She lunged for him swiftly, snarling in fury. Unfortunately, he took a moment too long to think and was caught in an effective arm-lock. Gasping, he struggled, then realized he had practically trained for years to escape this grip. Twisting to face the creature's enraged grunts, he slid under like a slimy fish, suddenly twirling against the humanoid's body so he had her arms locked up behind her back, at his mercy instead. Raising an elbow high, he brought it down on the back of her head.

Well, she was as worthy as an opponent could be, here on the holodeck. With a jerk, the unconscious humanoid slid from his grasp and thumped to the floor. Her limp body lay face-down, back exposed to him. The quick fight left him panting and basking in the vigor of the brawl—short, but nevertheless something to get his blood pumping.

It took him only a few seconds before he realized how odd it was for the computer to have chosen this projection for him to fight. The *Ark* had been programmed to perform an introductory scan on every new organism that came aboard. Johnson knew the lab ran more advanced scans on the specimens brought aboard, and he wondered just how much information on the humanoids the *Ark* had picked up while the specimens had been held here. This had in fact been the first time he'd fought anything besides another human.

He hadn't exactly had the honor of observing them up close when they were captive, but the holodeck program had given him a well-simulated version, ripe for the peeking. It was definitely something he could ask one of the maintenance crew for the *Ark*'s internal programming to look into, and he may finally have some kind of assignment. Well, an assignment that didn't involve sitting around and waiting for nothing.

Turning toward the control panel, Johnson needed a double-take when he noticed a little squiggle on the ground glowing red. Squirming, the little light struggled towards him, its awkward movement a contrast to its angry glow. It moved through the humanoid's furry head, and the hologram flickered and vanished. The glow, at least, was real.

Bending down, Johnson peered at it. A worm, no bigger than his thumb, inched in a wavering line toward his boot. Something else to jot down in his mental notepad.

Grabbing one of his gloves from his pocket, he carefully edged it towards the worm. Its body wasn't smooth like earthworms and had stripes across its width. Not seeing any teeth or dangerous features, he cautiously reached out further, patting the animal to test its reaction before picking it up gently with his gloved hand.

It made no sound of protest, though what could he have expected from this seemingly frail worm? He cupped the worm carefully and opened the holodeck doors. The worm's red glow grew brighter as it turned about in his hand. When he stepped through, the holodeck doors hissed shut behind him, and he walked down the corridor, which now remained as quiet as it had been on his way from the bridge.

He knew that Dirk and the *Ark*'s medical team turned explorers were still out, running about in the desert sand. Things had seemed relatively back under control when Dirk had put Johnson on standby for his next instructions, but that had been over twenty-four hours ago and he hadn't heard anything since. Dirk would most likely commend Johnson on his foresight in handling the glowing worm with a thick glove and taking it where it belonged for now, until further notice. When the team returned, he'd tell Dirk exactly where he found the creature. But right now, it seemed the best idea to take the little thing down to the lab, put it in a cage or something, and keep it secure.

Chapter 10

Deep in the bowels of the *Ark*, something stirred. The slightest shift in the air around the larger cages in the depths of the holding area. The ones which had housed the serene, silent, and somehow sensual humanoids. Empty now, but for a single figure sitting Buddha-like, alone but unperturbed by the fact that one elegantly crossed leg stopped abruptly above the ankle joint. A soft rustle ran through its fur and gleaming scales, like an old-fashioned fan fluttered by a maiden aunt.

Then the humming started. At first, beyond the reach of human hearing, but enough to prick up the nervous, sensitive ears of Kuhn the Chihuahua, had he not been sixty miles away somewhere on the planet's surface. Gradually, it built, rising in volume and pitch until it seemed to physically fill the vaulted holding area.

Not that Matt Babbage, the junior security guard assigned

to patrolling the area every half-hour, noticed a thing. The harsh, driving Space Metal screaming straight into his ears would have drowned out a nuclear bomb going off in the next room, and his frantic air guitar and imagined drum solos with his flashlight were hardly conducive to a thorough examination of the inhabitants of the cages under his care.

He was just screwing up his steel-grey eyes to give the driving riff and chorus of "Black Hole Baby" his best performance when a penetrating buzz sounded through his headset, interrupting his illusions of inter-Galactic superstardom. He spun around and peered down the long corridor of cages to the main door to the vault. A blue light blinked insistently above the door. Someone needed to come in.

"Bloody 'ell," Matt muttered under his breath in a Devon accent as thick as clotted cream, undiluted by his two years at Space Academy. "Who's that, then? Can't be any of the science bods. They're all zombied out in the lab. Oi 'ope it's not that ball-breaker Evans checking up on me again."

His inner rock-god-renegade wannabe fought the insecure young lad from Taunton and lost. Matt pulled the ear buds out and trotted obediently down to the door. It was more of a noisy waddle than a trot, thanks to the clanging equipment clamped and hanging from his work vest and utility belt. Most of the samples behind bars ignored the passing clumsy figure, merely turning around to face the other way or sipping idly at their water feeders. All except one spectacularly ugly lizard, which didn't move a muscle but blushed a furious shade of bright flamingo pink as the guard approached the door.

Sweating slightly after his two-hundred-yard dash, Matt peered through the panel next to the door to see who it was. A madly gesticulating Johnson looked through the glass, then held

94

up a heavily gloved hand and signalled for his friend to open the door.

It was against protocol to let anyone but authorized personnel into the vault unless they were accompanied by a scientist. On the other hand, Matt owed the pilot more than a favour or two, thanks to his apparently unlimited access to various goodies from back home to relieve the boredom of interstellar travel—thanks to his contacts with the guys operating the wormgate.

He opened the door a crack.

"What d'yer want, Arthur?" he drawled. "I'm in the middle of my patrol."

"That can wait. No one's checking stuff like that right now, anyway," said the pilot, pushing his way in and grinning like a Green Celesian River Monkey. "I've got something you gotta see, me old Cabbage."

Matt sighed, opened his mouth to protest, then shook his head in exasperation and shut it again.

"Anyway, I'm being a responsible crewmember and bringing a specimen in for proper storage. Ta-da!" He held his gloved left hand up to eye level and opened it to reveal a neon-bright, red worm, squirming and wriggling figure eights in his palm. It seemed to throb and glow, like a heartbeat, and raised one end of its body—head or tail—as if to sniff the air of the vault.

"Where'd you find that little bugger?" asked the security guard, brushing the dark hair out of his eyes as he bent over the worm. "Juicy bait like that would catch a lot of fish in the River Tay, as my granddad used to say. If there were any fish left, that is. Or a river."

"Let's just say he came to me in a dream—or on the holodeck," Johnson replied with a wink. "But seriously, no idea where it came from. I figured I should play it safe and bring it in for proper storage. And while I'm at it, you can let me have a look at those sexy zen aliens I've been hearing so much about."

"Too late, mate." Matt shook his head. "They've all gone. The scouting party took 'em all when they set off for their jaunt yesterday."

"So what's that over there, then?"

Matt turned around to see a humanoid, one foot missing, sitting cross-legged in the cage. He scratched his head, confused. He was certain they'd taken all the humanoids and didn't remember seeing it only moments ago.

"Ooh, an alien cripple? That ticks even more of my fetish boxes." Matt really couldn't tell if the pilot was joking or not. "Come on, Matt, let me in to have a look. I won't tell if you don't."

Matt stopped short, torn between his instinct to follow the rules and the knowledge that doing Johnson a favor could give him access to something, anything, to relieve the endless tedium of space. "Aw, come on, Arthur. You know I can't do that. It's back there, in the restricted area. No one's supposed to go down there unless they've got the say-so from the head honcho."

"But where is the head honcho, Cabbage, baby? Off the *Ark* and sixty miles off base, up to god knows what, god knows where, with a bunch of doctors. Half the crew on board are vegetables, and the others are just hanging on 'til something actually happens. Who exactly do you think is going to snitch on you if— and it's a big *if*—they find out you gave your old buddy Arthur a sneak peek at one little-bitty crippled humanoid? And, by the way, did I mention how grateful I'd be?"

With his free hand, Johnson pulled on the top of a piece of paper so it peeped out of his breast pocket. It was a list Matt knew well—the informal catalogue of illicit treats Arthur was known to have access to from back home. You name it, he could get it—

porn of every imaginable kind, including some that went way beyond Matt's limited imagination; real hooch, the type that burned
as it went down; the latest in recreational drugs; vintage Cuban
cigars; even Scrabble sets. Everything a young man might need to
survive the mind-numbing ennui of outer space.

"Well…I was wondering when the latest 'Badger Todd and
the TB Army' sequel was out, and if I might be able to get a sneak
preview?" Matt ventured.

"Not a problem, my boy," Johnson said, and gently tapped
on the top of his paper to hide it again in his pocket. "Say the word
and it's yours, and I'll throw in a vintage Tetris game and an original Monopoly set, complete with the original top hat and boot."

Babbage shrugged indifferently.

"Or maybe I could tickle your fancy with the latest blue
crystal dream bulbs, fresh off the production line in Antarctica?
Latest thing in the clubs of hottest clubs off Terra del Fuego and
Auckland."

Matt's eyes widened before he recovered his composure to
hide his enthusiasm. "All right, then, but just for a bit. And absolutely no touching," he said, feigning reluctance. "And on our way
out, we deal with the fishbait you've got in your mitt."

Johnson grinned and patted Babbage on the shoulder.
"Good lad. You know it makes sense. By the way, what's with the
spooky humming?"

Matt shrugged—he was good at shrugging—and said
something about the air conditioning, then locked the vault door
behind them.

Sauntering up the long rows of cages, they paid no attention to the inhabitants, not even when the color-changing lizard
flashed a sick chrome yellow. They were too engrossed in a heated
debate about whether the ref had been blind or simply biased in

97

the weekend's semi-final game in the Zero Gravity Football League championship.

All talk of off-sides and visually challenged officials trailed off as they neared the larger cages in the restricted area. The humming was much louder, almost tangible. It seemed to shimmer in the air. As they reached the last cage, to look at the lone figure sitting serenely inside, all conversation ceased.

Johnson's usually cocky demeanour abandoned him as he stared at the humanoid, mouth agape. Whoever had said they were the most beautiful things they'd ever seen wasn't kidding. Silenced and mesmerised by the elegant alien before him, he barely noticed the movement in the gloved hand hanging by his side.

The silent figure still sat in the same cross-legged pose, facing forward. Its huge eyes and small mouth were shut but appeared somehow soft, malleable. It made no sound or movement but seemed to pulse with the oscillation of the humming filling the area. A gentle spectrum of pastel colors danced gracefully over its soft pelt, rippling it almost like a breeze.

Beside Johnson, Babbage stood like an idiot, mouth wide open and a strand of saliva bridging his lips, and felt himself slipping into a state of utter peace and contentment he had never known before. "Flippin' 'eck," he said. "I think I'm in love."

Unconsciously, both men now swayed softly in time to the hum's pulse, like seaweed in the evening tide. They stood stupefied in front of the cages, blissfully happy and utterly passive.

***

Five minutes passed, then ten. At fifteen, Johnson felt the worm in his gloved hand stir again. He brought his arm up, opened his palm, and looked down at the tiny creature, smiling the broad, beatific smile of a sacrificial lamb with no idea how much his martyrdom was going to hurt. As he watched, the worm squirmed and wriggled, then doubled in size like a child's balloon being blown up at a party. It filled the pilot's hand, and its phosphorescent glow intensified, growing brighter with every second, until the pilot had to squint to look at it.

Heat permeated through the thick protective padding of his glove. Fiercer with every passing second, it grew and grew, eating into Johnson's palm in exactly the way it shouldn't. Before long, the burning was unbearable, and he swore he could smell the feint scent of charred flesh.

He dropped the worm and ripped the glove off. Nursing his hand, he was surprised to note that there was no damage, and the intense, hot pain subsided instantly. At his feet, the fat red worm squirmed its way through the bars of the cage towards the humanoid, then climbed its way, leech-like, up the elegant folded legs to settle like a beloved pet in the humanoid's lap.

The humming grew by a semi-decibel, though Matt and Arthur were too entranced to notice. Colors ran faster and faster across the humanoid's fur. Its large, avocado-shaped eyes snapped open to reveal jade-green orbs with a slitted, cat-like pupil. They stared directly at the pilot, boring down into his very soul, if he'd had one, and rendering him utterly helpless but still standing.

Babbage collapsed into a gibbering heap beside him.

The hum rose again, this time accompanied by a loud rustling as the humanoid's soft scales heaved, sending flowers of refracted light around the room. The noise seemed to take form, like a song hidden in the wind blowing through a forest. The figure raised a slender, long-fingered hand and stroked the glowing red worm nestling happily in its lap. Johnson glanced briefly down at the humanoid's legs, noting that it lacked the human equivalent of a foot and thinking in a dream-like state that the disfigurement seemed to lend the thing that much more power. The hum became words inside Johnson's head, soft and persuasive and not to be denied.

"We've been expecting you."

Chapter 11

D r. Zoe Rowens winced when yet another twig whipped her arm, leaving a harmless but quite bothersome scratch in its wake. It was more annoying than painful with each extra scratch. Regardless, she had stopped complaining about it hours ago when, after a few wise-ass remarks about her not getting along with nature, Franklin had offered to lend her his coat. The worst part was that it hadn't been a joke; it had been an honest, selfless offer. *Typical Franklin behavior, all knight-in-shining-armor, the bastard.* If there was something she didn't need right now, it was to play 'lady in distress'. She could take anything at this point, but not pity. Not from him.

And yet, she couldn't help but take comfort in his attitude. At least something was normal. Or almost.

They were a day into the jungle, making their way back to

the *Ark* by means of an alternate route, the joy of having recovered one of their own seriously dampened by the loss of their leader. Morale was low among the crew, and although Franklin had been doing his best to act his usual self with all the bickering and chauvinistic crap, Zoe saw that this affected him more than he let on. He had abandoned a friend to ensure the safety of the crew, had taken on the burden of being the one who made the choice. Dirk was one, they were many, most of them unarmed and without training in combat. They had had a hard time as it was, breaking the circle around them long enough to make retreat an option; he wasn't going to risk taking them further into the enemy's field just so they could rescue the zoologist.

Thankfully, Franklin's men seemed to trust him, and they didn't waste time in getting everybody away from the site as soon as possible. They had even picked up Dr. Robinson.

Zoe spared a glance for the woman walking behind her. She walked unaided already, which was a good thing. Her skin had recovered some of its color, but her eyes were vacant in a way that gave Zoe the creeps. That, and the fact that she still hadn't spoken. The anthropologist had regained consciousness shortly after they had traveled a mile or so away from the oasis, but she seemed to be too much in shock to speak or react to any of her surroundings. Zoe hoped she would snap out of it soon. She was at least able to dodge obstacles while walking, for now, but if they ran into trouble, she would need to be as lucid as possible. Zoe felt like the only one who recognized the importance of that.

Somewhere behind her, someone asked for a 'shift change'. During the fight, one of the doctors had managed to knock Ron down to keep one of the security staff from actually killing him, and now they carried him in a folding stretcher they had brought with all the other portable medical equipment. Groups of two had begun by taking turns carrying it for an hour or so, but now it was all they could do just to hold on until they were too exhausted to continue. Then they passed the torch to whomever was willing to take it next.

Everyone was tired. Franklin's orders had been clear. "No stopping until we reach the *Ark*." And while nobody liked it, they all had to accept that he was right. Each time they stopped for rest, they gave the enemy an opportunity to catch up. That was, of course, without assuming that the humanoids had already contacted another group to intercept them if they happened to pass nearby. They had no idea of the creatures' positions, and Zoe had never felt so helpless.

She found herself praying that Ron would wake up soon. She barely knew the man, but in a place surrounded by enemies, every ally became a brother. And all the time he was down, not only would he be a burden, but it also meant they had one less soldier.

She quickened her pace to catch up with Franklin, who had moved to the front of their column as the hours ticked by. She passed a few gloomy guards, finally came up beside him, and they walked side by side in silence for a few minutes. She found she really didn't have anything to say to him, and he didn't seem particularly interested in starting the conversation this time. She didn't like this. Not the silence, but the fact that after all that had happened, just when she thought she had gotten over it, moved on, just when she thought she could take care of herself, she was almost instinctively seeking his company once again. She didn't like that it made her feel safe.

But then again, who wouldn't feel safe walking beside almost six feet of Gallic strength—clad in combat fatigues and sporting enough firepower to take down a small ship—in a situation where a monster could suddenly come out of nowhere any moment? Add to that the hunger, the exhaustion, the stress, and yes…maybe those were perfectly good reasons for wanting to be near him. That thought seemed to relax her.

"So…" She sighed. "What's the plan after we get to the *Ark*?"

Franklin looked startled by the sound of her voice, as if he hadn't been expecting to hear her speak. "Oh, that. Yeah. Dunno, really. Protocol states that in case of emergency, the Chief of Security takes charge of the ship. But I don't feel up to handling this kind of shit. I was thinking we have a meeting with the rest of the staff, and then…" His features twisted in a pained scowl. "I think the safer option's to go back home. We can try to find a cure for the scientists there. We're practically at war here. Our forces are not prepared for this. We can report the situation, and they can send a special team from Earth. Real military, I mean. Enough people with the right equipment. Leave it to them to find out what the fuck's wrong with Korsakov, and…" He didn't say it, but then again, he didn't need to. And rescue Dirk. If he was still alive.

Zoe nodded. She had to give it to the man; maybe he wasn't very brilliant, but he knew his stuff when it came to security. And when it came to what exactly they weren't equipped to handle. She looked up at his face—the tired lines, the worry. Something softened in her. She grabbed his hand. "Ray, I—"

Then the wind changed.

Franklin heard it a fraction of a second before it hit his face. He turned on his heels; it came from behind them. The gust was dry and cold and fast, a sharp contrast to the jungle's warm, damp breeze. It froze everybody in their steps, and that was before the sand came.

It started with a few grains, carried by the wind like a trickle, tickling their faces and causing one or two of them to sneeze. Then it blew heavier, as if there wasn't wind anymore but only a thick mass of moving sand, like a bizarre school of flying fish slithering through the air like a serpent. Everybody ran for cover when they saw it coming, memories of sandpaper adding to the mathematics of a nightmare. Franklin watched in horror and disbelief as it swallowed those behind him, one by one. He watched them disappear: Soldiers, medics, the stretcher, Dr. Robinson. It was so close now. He shut his eyes.

But when the storm hit him, it didn't hurt. When it finally reached him and Zoe, it was instead a caress, as if whoever controlled the phenomenon had decided to slow down and let them feel it. It was far less solid than it seemed but much more rigid. He could breathe through the storm, but the sand didn't get in his mouth. It was as if each particle knew exactly where it was going and wouldn't be diverted from its path unless there was a true obstacle.

And then it was over. As abruptly as it had started, it was over. When he opened his eyes, the sand had returned to the ground. "The fuck?" he breathed.

Not three seconds had passed when the top layer of sand stirred again. This time, though, it condensed upwards, forming what at first seemed to be a thick pillar. The sand shifted, swirled. Some of it fell to the jungle floor again. It then took a humanoid shape—nothing like Santelli's humanoids they had seen so far, but a basic standing representation, with two arms, two legs, a torso, and a head. It was just a simple pattern, like an empty canvas.

It turned to face Franklin, and as it did so, it changed again, adding details. It shifted and morphed, flipping through different combinations of sexes, builds, hairstyles, clothes. He knew them all; it was like a catalog of the people he loved. He lowered a hand to his gun, a trickle of cold sweat ran down his back.

"Don't…" the sand-being said. "No need to fear, Ray." He heard Zoe's surprised gasp; the being was mimicking her now.

Franklin growled. "You bastard…you killed Alby!" he shouted, losing his cool. "You made Ron do it!"

The thing held up its hands. "You are mistaken, Ray. It wasn't us but the Sons-of-Mishrak who entered your friends mind."

Yeah, of course, Franklin thought. "Why should I believe that? *You* were the storm that appeared, not the other creatures."

The thing slowly nodded. It did everything slowly, and that only infuriated Franklin even more. "We were, in fact, there. Not to harm, but to prevent. To warn. We tried to communicate with Dirk before the Sons-of-Mishrak forced us out of their territory. It took us too long to comprehend his mind—too many images there we weren't used to. But we have learned, and now we warn you. We need your help."

The forest was suddenly too quiet. Help? No, he had been right. He couldn't handle this kind of shit. His men stepped forward, weapons drawn. Franklin held up a hand to stop them; if this thing decided to stop playing friendly, he wasn't sure they would be able to fight it.

"Help?" said Zoe. "Help how?"

"Against the Mishrak. Its sons. They are consuming us. And they want to consume you, too."

Chapter 12

"I need you to get out there and rip his damn head off! You hear me, Franklin?" shouted Coach Dean as he pointed to the Stallions' Quarterback.

"Yes, Sir!" Franklin responded through the burn of lactic acid now drenching every one of his muscles below the waist.

"The rest of you punch a hole for this big sumbitch to get a clear sack! Now, Grizzlies on three!" bellowed the Coach.

Fired up with the promise of victory, the team counted and broke for the final down of the Oklahoma All State Championship game. The Grizzles had been pegged as the underdogs in this fight. The Stallions' Quarterback was a senior named Benny Doss, and it was well accepted that he was bound to go pro straight out of high school. He had the foot speed and agility of a gazelle but also boasted an arm that could throw a football like it was shot from a cannon. Benny Doss was one of those gifted, once-in-a-lifetime, total-package athletes. Doss singlehandedly won the majority of the Stallions' regular season games. Against all odds, the final game of the season had come this close on the last play. The Grizzlies led the score, but the Stallions had possession of the ball and were less than ten yards from the other team's goal line. Doss wasn't sweating this play at all. None of the other teams in the state had an answer for Doss, except perhaps for the Grizzlies.

Ray Franklin was an unprecedented case in the team's history. He had been a varsity starter for the Grizzlies' defensive line by his sophomore year. This came as no shock to anyone, as the boy had towered over most of his classmates, already six-foot-two tall and weighing two hundred and eighteen pounds. Franklin had propelled his team to claim their first regional title that year. And then he had another growth spurt to start his junior year at a gargantuan six-foot-nine and weighing two hundred and thirty-one pounds. The rest of the Grizzlies had dubbed the lineman "Franklinstien" by Homecoming.

In this game, Franklin's mere presence on the field had eliminated any of the Stallions' hope for a running game. He could effortlessly push through any two, and sometimes even three, of the Stallions' offensive linemen on his own. Franklin had gotten two good runs at Doss this game, but the Stallions' Quarterback had made the pass the first time before Franklin could reach him. The second time, Franklin had charged the other team's MVP, and Doss had fled out of bounds.

Now it was all down to the next few seconds. Franklin took position on the field with his teammates. He felt his heart pulsing in his ears and the salt in his sweat stinging his eyes. Franklin felt the touch of short-cut, cool, green grass beneath his fingers while he crouched in wait on the football field. He heard the roar of Grizzlies and Stallions fans alike as they cheered on their respective teams. Franklin heard Benny Doss call out the last play of the game. He remembered the snap of the football, but that was it. The next thing he remembered about that day was regaining consciousness in the hospital.

"There you are, champ," said Franklin's father, brimming with pride. Franklin looked about the hospital room and saw the rest of his family, his coach, and several of his teammates gathered behind the doctor.

"It's good to see you awake so soon. You played one fine football game," said the doctor. Most of the people crammed into the room nodded and murmured in agreement. "That last play gave you a hairline fracture on your collarbone. You'll heal up from that just fine and should be back to a hundred percent by the time school's out for the year at the end of the month. You also took one hell of a knock on your head, so we're going to keep you for the night, just to play it safe." The doctor's explanation was calm and collected.

"We won?" Franklin asked in a groggy haze.

"We sure did, son! That Quarterback sack you had—" Franklin's father's words were cut short as Franklin's mother stared daggers at her husband. "Anyway, you rest up, son. You have a summer full of celebrating ahead of you!"

Each of Franklin's visitors slowly trickled out of the room one by one. Franklin couldn't sleep that night. Not only did the throbbing in his shoulder and head keep him awake, but something stuck in the back of his mind—some memory of what exactly had brought him to lay in this bed which he felt he had to recall, but everything was a blank. He lay awake into the far hours of the night, and when he could no longer stand the repetitive drone of the machines monitoring him in his room, he let himself out and went for a walk. Franklin wandered the dim and flickering halls of the slumbering hospital like a ghost. Other people saw him there, but nobody really noticed him.

Somehow, he found himself drifting through the halls of the trauma recovery ward. He found that bizarre and perplexing, as though some unseen force had guided him to this place and directed his feet to move on some predetermined path. The sound of sobbing caught Franklin's attention above the white noise of the hospital. He was drawn to the source of the tears, a room that read 'Benjamin Doss' on the door. Franklin lurked outside the room and listened, guilt burning in his ears.

"Mr. and Mrs. Doss, the surgery was a total success. We fit your son with two prosthetic vertebrae and performed a spinal bypass. With intense nerve therapy and physical rehabilitation, Benny should be able to walk again in a year's time." The doctor's voice was thick with both hope and concern as he tried to reassure two devastated parents.

Franklin never played football again. From that day on, he only wanted to get away. He wanted to escape from the wrong he had done to another person and the life he had forever altered. He wanted to leave it all behind—his school, the town, and state in which he lived. If Franklin could even get off of this planet, he would.

Chapter 13

The dark, slightly orange circles beneath her eyes were beginning to show. It was going to take more than a quick touch-up of her makeup to get the rings to subside this time. Major Heartly folded her compact mirror and returned it to its designated pocket in her flight suit. She checked the timer on her left wrist. It flashed three red zeros, just like it had for the last ninety minutes. It was past time for her medication, but the Major hated dosing up while on a contract. The Dirk Compound always made her feel foggy, and the Company paid her to keep her mind sharp and focused. Those were about the last two things she felt right now. The Major figured she could gut it out for another forty-five minutes before her hands began to shake too violently to conceal it from the rest of the retrieval team.

Forty-five minutes should be more than enough time to get

Grewder's report and apprise Corporate of the situation on the ground, she thought. The Master Sergeant's A.P.C had just returned to the dropship, and Grewder would be hauling his massive frame into her quarters at any moment to deliver his report. She hated talking business in her private quarters, but she couldn't bring herself to face any of the other crew right now. Major Heartly looked at the bruises on her left breast, made by the needle each time she dosed, peeking out from the lace of her bra. All she wanted to do at that very moment was slam that syringe into her chest one more time. Her fingers began to undo the snaps on her flight suit's right thigh pocket where she kept her injection wand. Forty-five minutes could be a long time to wait.

The door to her quarters whirred as it slid open to allow the massive bulk of Master Sergeant Grewder into the room. Major Heartly quickly pulled the zipper of her flight suit back up below her chin before she swiveled her chair around to address him. The Master Sergeant stood at attention; his hand began its path to a salute, but then he stopped himself. It was an old habit, she knew, but Heartly had admonished Grewder several times for continuing to salute despite now being a member of the Private Sector. Most of the Company's retrieval teams were composed of ex-military and maintained the trappings of enlisted life from even before the Great Upheaval, but not Heartly's team. The Major was a top-notch professional, even carried a stateswoman-like sense of etiquette, but she loathed military ceremony.

Heartly caught herself before she let her eyes fall to the scars and poorly-healed burnt flesh littering the right side of Grewder's face. She faced that same challenge not to stare each time see saw the man. She attributed it to the fact that her mind refused to accept just how horrific the Master Sergeant's wounds were. No man or woman should have been able to withstand what

112

Grewder had and lived another day. The phenomenon of the Master Sergeant's resilience propelled Heartly's imagination into conflict with reality each time Grewder was present.

The man held out his hand, firmly grasping a data pad as he spoke. "Reports from Recon Teams One and Two, Major," he said with the usual difficulty the burns on his face afforded him.

Major Heartly had become accustomed to Grewder's slow and labored speech over the course of the dozen or so Retrieval contracts the Company had assigned them to work on together. The Master Sergeant was an acquired taste for sure, but Heartly had found she could depend on the man to perform well in the areas of the job which played to his strengths. Fortunately, with Grewder standing six feet nine inches tall and weighing just shy of three hundred pounds, the Company didn't require the man to present with much in the way of eloquence.

"Still no update from the Consultant aboard the *Ark*?" asked the Major.

"No, Ma'am. She has been M.I.A for the last forty-eight hours," the Master Sergeant responded.

"This is cause for concern," she said, barely raising an eyebrow. "Corporate gave assurance that the Consultant was agreeable to all our client's needs, including strict autonomy from the crew. If she's gone rogue, it will make the conference call at nineteen hundred hours with the Home Office and our client's Rep very unpleasant." Heartly took the data pad from Grewder and briefly scanned the information contained on the device. "What the hell is this?"

"Just what is says there. Beasley from Recon Team Two was K.I.A." Grewder droned.

"I see this, but how did it happen and why is this the first I'm hearing of a Retrieval Specialist K.I.A.?"

"I was there with Diller and Scott when it happened. We had eyes on the *Ark* research team while they were playing with their little science experiments just outside the altar site. From out of nowhere, a dust storm kicked up, and then just like that, Beasley started spouting gibberish. Next thing we knew, he put his sidearm in his mouth and pulled the trigger. They actually think one of their own did it instead. Put the poor bastard in a cage. Then the storm scrambled up our long-range comms," the Master Sergeant grunted.

The Major was unaware that her right hand now rubbed her right temple. It was a nervous habit that presented when she was stressed and overdue for her medication. Heartly took a few moments to process the information in its entirety before speaking again. "Well, this is a wholly different matter."

"Ma'am?"

"This incident was the result of a self-inflicted wound, and Beasley was still probationary. This is not a K.I.A. It's a K.I.A. Accidental."

"So, what's the difference?"

Heartly removed her hand from her head and glanced heatedly up at the Master Sergeant, trying hard not to stare at his scars again. "The difference is that there is no one at fault, no assignment of blame, and above all no liability to the Company."

"Corporate liability or not, we're down another man on the ground," Grewder huffed indignantly. He quickly turned his head to hide the bit of drool that slipped from the torn skin at the corner of his mouth.

"Well, this job is not for everybody." Her tone was almost playful as she pushed back several locks of dark blonde hair that had fallen across her face.

"Yes, Ma'am. That's a fact."

"You said the *Ark* team ran tests at the alter site. Are they still at the same coordinates?"

Grewder swallowed, the burns on his neck rippling in effort. "As I said, Ma'am, the sandstorm scrambled our comms and the surveillance drone connectivity has been out for the last twenty-seven hours. There's another type of interference—the team's current location is still unknown."

Major Heartly's stomach heaved in a suddenly intense urge to rip open the pocket at her thigh for the injection wand right then, no matter the present company. "I presume you'll have that rectified shortly." Her voice carried more antagonism than she intended, but it gave the desired effect. Grewder nodded. "Have Diller jack into their data stream. If they find out anything worthwhile down there, I want to know what they know."

"Understood, Major."

Major Heartly returned her attention to the data pad in her hand and took in the rest of the information. "It looks like Recon Team One has a favorable report."

"Yes, they indicate a positive confirmation of the specimen aboard the *Ark*." The Master Sergeant could not restrain the smile that transformed his burned, scared face into a truly demonic visage.

"It's clear they have no idea what they possess," said Heartly.

"How's that, Ma'am?"

"If those people on the *Ark* knew what they had, there is no way they would still be planet-side. They would have scrubbed out and been long gone by now."

The Master Sergeant grunted. "Shall I order the team to engage?" The smile on his face broadened with the promise of combat.

"No, not yet," Heartly said. Her words instantly crushed the smile on Grewder's twisted face.

"Why stand down? We know where the specimen is. Let's go in and get it."

"It's not that simple, M.C." She forced her lips into a tight line and pressed her faintly shaking leg into the floor. "We cannot afford a direct assault with the crew of the *Ark*. Those are hard orders from Corporate. Our client has paid for the Full Discretion package, and that is what we will provide. If we go in loud, it could expose the Company, and more importantly implicate our client. It's a no-go." Her words clearly upset the enormous Master Sergeant.

"Speak freely, Ma'am?" Grewder asked curtly.

"Go ahead, Grewder," Heartly said with a sigh, bracing herself for the outburst about to ensue.

"This is all a giant load of horseshit. They got nothing but civilians and lab coats, and we're standing down. I could go in there myself and be gone with the specimen before any of those softies got their heads out of their asses."

"I know you don't like it, but it is what it is, and the client will get what the Company promised," Major Heartly stated. She never liked bickering with Grewder. He was so wonderfully one-dimensional that it was often difficult to get him to see a contract from a wider perspective. Her patience for the Master Sergeant was fast wearing thin. Heartly's fingers twitched intermittently now, and her skin temperature spiked beneath her flight suit. If she pushed off dosing much longer, there would be no hiding her shaking hands, nor the inevitable heavy sweat. She could not let Grewder see that happen.

"If the client is worried about implications, why don't we just retire all of the *Ark* crew and scrap that hunk of junk once we extract the specimen?" asked the Master Sergeant. Even his marred face could not hide his macabre hope that a full-scale slaughter would be accepted.

"M.C., come on. The *Ark* is a one-of-a-kind vessel, and there is some serious capital tied up in that so-called 'hunk of junk'. If it or its crew went silent, there would be more questions than you, I, or any one at Corporate Headquarters would care to answer."

"Begging the Major's pardon, but Ma'am, this sackless kind of garbage is not my style. If the Company wanted soft and gentle, they made a damn piss-poor call sending me to this dusty rock."

Major Heartly folded her arms across her chest to keep her hands still. Several moments of silenced passed as she formed her response, searching for the best method to send Grewder on his way. "I know that, M.C. As much as I can admit loving to watch you play one-man army, hard and fast are not how we get to handle this one, and you are just going to have to deal with that. When we get home, book yourself another cage brawl or get a couple of hookers to slice up—whatever you need to do to scratch that itch. I don't care. Right now, I need you here, focused on the job and acting like a professional Retrieval Specialist. This means that you are going to do as you are ordered. This is not up for debate or further discourse. Am I understood, Master Sergeant?"

Grewder stood to full attention and let out a deep, animalistic growl as he barked his response with the command of a battle-hardened veteran soldier. "Yes, Major! What are the Major's orders?"

Heartly took some time to think of the best approach for retrieval of the specimen. She had been so preoccupied with convincing the hulk of a Master Sergeant against his desire to go head-to-head that she had not formulated a subtler plan for extraction.

"Pick three men for your team. Once it goes dark outside, your team will take the second A.P.C. and leave it outside of the *Ark's* short-range radar with a driver. Randolph and Post in Recon Team One will hold their position and spot for you. Under cover of personal cloaking devices, you and the rest of your team will have to travel by foot for the remainder of the distance to the *Ark*. You will breach the *Ark's* perimeter and tap into their radar, sync up the A.P.C.'s profile to their database, and then mask it. Once that is accomplished, the A.P.C will head to the *Ark* while you and the rest of the team locate and secure the specimen. When the specimen is in your possession, you will retreat to the A.P.C, retrieve Recon Team One from their position, and all hands rally at the dropship. We dust off and meet up at the Company ship in orbit and head for home. Contract complete, simple."

"Simple, yes, Ma'am," Grewder said with a dour expression. His voice said 'simple', but his tone said 'boring'. "I understand we are not to engage the *Ark* crew, but what if the application of force becomes...unavoidable?" he continued.

"I will be on comms and optics the whole time, and I will advise the team on the application of force should that contingency become *unavoidable*," the Major said with a sarcastic tilt of her head and purse of her lips at that final word.

"Understood, Major."

"You are dismissed, Master Sergeant," Heartly said, clenching her forearms so tightly that she felt as though her bones might snap at any moment.

"Ma'am."

The Master Sergeant turned his sprawling back to the Major and left her quarters. It was all Heartly could do to sit upright, but she forced herself to wait just a few moments longer. She heard the cabin door lock shut, and Grewder's heavy, tromping footfalls faded into silence. When she was certain she would not be disturbed, she quickly uploaded and transmitted the reconnaissance reports on the data pad back to Corporate.

The very second the transmission was sent, Heartly ripped open the pocket that held her injection wand and pulled down the front zipper of her flight suit with enough force to nearly tear the sturdy metal clasp from its teeth. She slammed the wand's needle into her breast and proceeded to push six cubic centimeters of sweet, neon-orange, liquid bliss directly into her bloodstream. The Major fell back into her chair and let her eyes fall shut as her hands rested peacefully in her lap.

Chapter 14

The futility of his efforts to break free from the white stone prison slowly fed the insanity creeping into Dirk's joints, body, and mind. Already exhausted from the 'experiments' conducted by native plant-life and creatures, a mockery of his recent yet distant life, he began to find the unchanging scenery of his makeshift cell equally as tiresome and maddening. *It must have only been two, three days. So why does it feel like months?*

"I'm okay."

He whispered these words like a mantra, a meditative expletive so he could hold onto whatever shred of sanity remained. The more he tried to recall the odd experience of twisted memory, the more he realized the worms seemed to have depleted him of the actual details, learning whatever they could about him and morphing his version of that time in his uncle's kitchen. And for what purpose? What purpose could his life's memory serve them? What were their plans?

"I'm okay."

His whisper became a quiet voice this time, to let them know that he was not going to give up. They would not capture his mind so easily. Although, the question repeated itself—where had his mind gone? It felt somewhere in between the tiny cracks of the white stone, through the holes in the wall out of which the worms had crawled. It seemed to be anywhere else beside his own head and that damn statue before him. The statue of Mishrak was more than just an idol, more than an object. Perhaps it *was* Mishrak. *No. Don't let your focus turn to him.*

"I'm okay."

It was a statement now, through sudden tears and in hopes that some of his mental pain would flow out with the salty water, that it might disappear into the cracks of the white stone. How could he even see anything in here? Where was the light coming from? From the holes? The worm holes? A smile ran across his face. The worm holes in the white stone. He chuckled lightly, then giggled like a child, then laughed with a covered mouth, then bellowed until his laughter filled the room. The room suddenly seemed to grow brighter. At that moment, he noticed the light came from the idol's two sets of eyes. Frustration and rage took hold of him.

"You can't get to me!"

He yelled now, but the statement felt like a lie from which he would garner no strength. There was little energy left in his mind or body. His spirit remained but it felt distant. It seemed spirit would do him good no longer. What was spirit anyway? Intangible waves of thought, unguided hopes, which amounted to nothing helpful. That's what he needed now. Help.

Then he heard a familiar and terrifying noise—movement from the holes in the wall. Light scratching filled the emptiness of sound in his white prison; perhaps a new creature approached to finish him off. He could not handle fighting the sentient seaweed again, even if he had not shaken the fronds off, much less some completely new attacker. If death came for him now, Dirk only wished for it to be quick. He thought he deserved that at least, even amid the fleeting thoughts of his crew and regret that he could not reach them. He slumped against the wall, too tired to fight.

He was, however, surprised to find sand pouring into the quiet room instead of death. He did not understand why, but this raised his hopes and even his posture. The sand ran in from every hole, forming little piles beneath them. The thought of being buried alive crossed his mind, but Dirk quickly vanquished the assumption. This, for some reason, did not feel like a threat, or at the least did not seem malevolent. Then the sand stopped.

A feint breeze flooded through the holes and hit Dirk's nose like a dream of freedom. With his eyes closed, a smile once again crossed his lips, this time from joy and even hope instead of growing madness. Dirk sat up with energy he had lost and opened his eyes to a sight he could not believe. The sand seemingly moved of its own accord, as if it had a mind of its own. It formed beautiful patterns, some recognizable like concentric circles and Archimedes spirals, some new and completely unique.

Something then entered Dirk's mind. It did not force its way like whatever power had put him in the trance, but felt benign, cooperative, and sensitive to his concern. Then it felt blissful. The sand, meanwhile, constructed itself into a vaguely human form, then unmistakably became a native humanoid figure. Fear and hate flooded Dirk's mind, and the sand figure wavered before him, telepathically feeling his pain, past and present.

'*Please, we do not represent the Sons-of-Mishrak, those who imprisoned you. We represent the Sons of Life, who fight against annihilation.*'

Dirk believed the sand. He felt that the figure was not lying to him within his consciousness, but his rational mind, now present with his renewed energy, begged him to seek proof.

'*We understand your mistrust. We are here to help you, for we are now undeniably united in purpose. This is our home, what you call Santelli Minor.*' The figure collapsed into a pile of lifeless sand, then raised and formed pictures as the voice spoke in his mind. '*Our home's primal history resembles yours. Centuries of chaos, and centuries of calm. Our two suns forged this planet into an unforgiving, harsh place. But this did not deny life. It only encouraged a stronger form. As evolution inevitably creates sentient life, we were born alongside plant and animal, and we knew this from the beginning. Yet our communication evolved necessarily to be different from your own. The first five thousand years of our ancestors' sentience was spent through sandstorms and lightning storms. There was no quiet to develop spoken communications. There was no clarity to develop written communications. Within their shelters, they spoke through vibrations and thought, and this is the way it has been since.*

'*When the storms ceased, our ancestors emerged, masters of consciousness and thought. They developed scales to fight the sand, and fur to fight the cold of the night. It was the only way they could have survived, and survival was the only life they knew. The next two hundred years, as our lifespan is roughly one hundred fifty of your years, was difficult for the noble and aged members of our ancestors. The comfort of our new, tranquil home made them uneasy. You do not have a word that fully encompasses what they felt, but 'boredom from lack of fight' is the beginning of the idea.*

Several hundred of them took to the endless desert in search of combat and struggle, and it is said that when they could not find it, they sacrificed themselves to end their emptiness.

'The majority of our people who preferred peace and tranquility remained a single tribe. The young took up farming and developed the ability to communicate with plants and animals through thought. Slowly, we enmeshed with our environment and created what you would call tradition and culture, although we came to call it life. Your people have a craving to categorize and label which we lack. That is simply your way.

'Our home was peaceful for a long time. We do not keep strict record of the passage of time so we do not know for certain how long it has lasted, but we do know that less than a year ago, in your years, that peace ended. In some of our young, the feeling of boredom and purposelessness resurfaced. They only sought to fight, to want to survive instead of thrive—an old need that remained in our makeup. When they began hurting their kin for sport, we decided to banish them. This was a crucial mistake.'

The narrative lasted a minute at most, the words of the sand-being washing through Dirk's mind instead of being spoken. With each new thought, the sand formed crudely detailed images of its history, rising and falling in what would have been almost imperceptible changes had the being not entered his mind as well.

'Somewhere, where the endless desert meets the forest, they found something buried that should never have been found. We do not know what it really is, but it is most likely a remnant of those who took their own lives. It calls itself Mishrak.'

Dirk shuddered at the name as it filled his mind. He dared not look past the sand to meet the gaze of the idol beyond.

'Your fear is well-founded. The idol you see now has filled our youth with violence and purpose. They named themselves the

125

Sons-of-Mishrak. This is the first time any of our people diverged and gave themselves a new identity. They have not communicated their true purpose, but from their actions, it can only be assumed they wish to annihilate us, the Sons of Life, and to move from our planet to find the chaos they crave elsewhere. We know at least this much from that which they have created with newfound persistence, and what they have made of our home. From pure, malicious will they change the plants and animals on a fundamental level from peaceful to violent. They pervert their own consciousness so they may manipulate what you call DNA and repurpose it for destruction. You have experienced this firsthand, but you do not know how far their reach extends. We have seen it in your past. The fires of Japan were but a spark compared to what they have planned for countless species of our universe.'

Having felt what they could do with simple worms and plants, Dirk had no doubt of their potential once the Sons-of-Mishrak had an army behind them. How could anyone stand against that power?

'We are the only ones who can stand against that power. They know this, and if they defeat us, there is no civilization that may stand against them. Once we encountered their weapons, we delved deep within ourselves as a tribe, as a people, and sought aid. This world, our home, felt our distress and answered elegantly, gifting us the ability to command the winds. This is how we fight the Sons-of-Mishrak, and this is how we seek the assistance of you and your people. We are united in purpose, which is a stronger bond than you can understand.'

For the first time, Dirk spoke aloud. "What can *I* do against a force like that? My crew, the *Ark*…we're explorers—researchers. Not warriors."

A deep rumble, which seemed to reverberate from the

planet's core, entered the white stone chamber and interrupted the answer Dirk so badly wished to hear. The humanoid figure re-appeared in the sand. *'Time is against us. We must be quick.'* Then it disappeared back up through the holes in the white stone wall.

***

Sixty miles away, the deep rumble was a quake, and felt like it might split the planet in two. Grewder and his team waited quietly in the tree line, the *Ark* in sight and relayed back through surveillance drones.

"Originating seismic activity confirmed as coming from the *Ark*," Grewder whispered into his comms unit. He turned to Randolph, who pulled the long-range binoculars from his eyes and nodded curtly. Grewder returned to the relay pad in his hands. "Oh, ho," he said, the scars of his face stretching into a grotesquely grim smile. "Here's comes our brave little explorers."

"From the altar sight?" Grewder's man Hinkle suggested. He raised his own binoculars to have a look. "Total count…fifteen crew members, two gear transporters… Master Sergeant, the count is one short."

Grewder grunted. "Those amateurs were bound to find trouble in the desert. It doesn't matter." He watched the enclave emerge from the desert and sprint toward the shuddering ship. Raising his comms unit, he dialed in one more time. "Dropship One, this is M.S. Grewder. Rendezvous confirmed with Recon Team One. *Ark*'s exploration team located, in transit by foot toward the *Ark*. Remaining members assumed to be onboard. Specimen also assumed onboard and active. My men and I are cloaked, initiating Phase Two. Over and out."

Chapter 15

D irk felt a moment of panic as the benevolent sensation left him alone once more in the white stone room, bereft but stronger after the sands' momentary presence. For the first time, he coherently considered the danger facing the *Ark*'s crew, the universe, and all its lifeforms. He was again assailed by the visage of the pillar. *A totem of some kind,* he thought, keeping his eyes averted from the statue of Mishrak.

He felt stronger since his contact with the sand, but he now found a growing awareness of a certain draining within himself. He concentrated on the feeling, quietly speaking the mantra, "I'm okay." To his utter horror, he became suddenly, wholly conscious of the differences in his brain, the fragmentation. His mind was being shared with something…millions of somethings, wriggling frantically through his bloodstream. He also realized that he shared their sentience as well.

Dirk felt the tangible withdrawing of his physical energies. *The worm bite…* he realized. The little alien worm was a parasite, and then it all made sense. *So this is the army*, he thought, and saw in his mind's eye the larvae greedily absorbing nutrients from the oxygen-rich plasma of his blood, starving the tissues and adding to the buildup of carbon dioxide. Every heartbeat pumped the silent killers through his circulatory system, and for this cognizance, a particularly violent assault on his mind ensued—one he fought desperately.

"I'm okay," he barely whispered to the empty air. He shakily resumed the position he had taken before the sand-being had come to him. The assault on his mind overwhelmed him, demanding his obedience and weakening his body. His knees buckled and he fell hard on the rock-strewn floor. Pebbles bit into the tender flesh, but Dirk never felt the pain. He was no longer there.

The room spun dizzily and became a lecture hall, and he was in a memory five years ago where he had first seen Jenny as he lectured at her university—her dark hair falling around her shoulders and the slight blush on her face as she raised her hand. He had immediately sensed the intelligence behind the sparkling blue of her eyes, an arresting comparison to her dark hair and light skin. She was beautiful.

Abruptly, Dirk was nine years old again and back in his uncle's familiar kitchen. He turned to run and the Cold Foods Chef still had Jenny's sad face. He was stopped in his terrified tracks as he saw her beautiful face morph with the bulging, running mass of boils—the *Cordyceps*.

Jolted back into adulthood, he realized Jenny was calling to him from far away, desperately pleading for help. *Jenny!*

The thought exploded through Dirk's consciousness. It was

enough to release him from the paralyzing tug of the larvae swimming through his body, and he realized what had happened to her and the rest of his research team. He could see the larvae at maturity, eating their way through musculature and vital organs…taking the life of the host who bore them.

Dirk was terrified, and as the deep rumbling came again, it barely registered. He jumped up and paced the cold white room. As he did so, he felt his strength returning. It seemed odd, but a glimmer of hope was born. Then he ran in place—hard—and as his breath quickened, he felt his body strengthen and his mind clear.

"I am okay!" he shouted, running a circle around the room. Even the pain quickly diminished. Dirk slowed the pace to a light jog and chanted in a childish, sing-song tone, "You can't get to me! You can't get to me! I'm okay!" He realized he was on the verge of hysteria and he drew in deep draughts of air, attempting to calm his thoughts. Trying desperately to concentrate, to figure out what could be done, he continued the physical exertion, slowly pacing himself.

Dirk almost instantly found the increased polarity of his thoughts and senses, and he cried out in surprise and triumph. As he regained his strength, he became more aware of the growing force inside him. The words—he could access their sentience now, their memories and objectives. The more he focused, the more sluggish and confused he felt the larvae become. Although he hesitated to touch this newfound knowledge, he was all too aware of the fact that he needed to somehow use this understanding if he was to save his friends and colleagues.

Concentrating, he noticed a shift in the air…and sensed the war beginning inside of him. The breeze, at once a soft caressing waft and an ill gust blowing all around him, kicked up dust. He felt the benevolent host enter his mind, swirling and swift with a feeling of peace and friendship. It completely opposed the entrance of the divergent sentience, which felt like a violation—like the rape of his body, mind, and spirit. The alternating struggle for the power of his mind shot white-hot pain through his body, and he knew he had to stay active to help strengthen the benevolent sentience. He suddenly knew that if he were to lose his strength again, it would give the Sons of Mishrak only more power.

***

Matt Babbage lay unconscious on the floor as the glowing zebra-striped worm hopped from the lap of the horridly smiling humanoid and inched slowly toward his motionless, outstretched hand.

Johnson thought the humanoid repulsive, the smile more like a grimace, and raised his boot to squash the worm in one fluid motion before it reached the helpless security officer. His hands immediately flew to his head as he both felt and heard the screech in his mind, coming from the crippled humanoid. The thrumming of the ancient song had ceased, and Johnson felt increasing pressure—palpable rage within his mind. Physically paralyzed and captivated, he watched as a radiant red light illuminated within the enlarging slits in the jade orbs of the humanoid before him. The silence was absolute and not even the wildly pounding, terrified sound of his own beating heart reached Johnson's audio faculties. He saw what he registered as surprise on the humanoid's face and at once he was released. He fell to the floor, writhing in pain but free from the creature's grasp. Arthur Johnson was a strong and capable man, and he knew they had to get the creature off of the *Ark*. His mind worked clearly even if his body had weakened. He was certain that somehow it was the humanoid affecting the group of scientists slowly dying aboard the ship.

The humanoid hummed peacefully again, those horrible eyes closed and the pulse of the fur barely audible as the pastel dance of color dimmed significantly. Johnson gained his feet and ran as quickly as he could to the nearest emergency panel. He slammed his palm hard against the A-1 Emergency button, their highest alert, while also opening the cargo bay door to allow access for the security crew still aboard the ship. Immediately, he returned to the cage, bolted the door, and lowered the observation panels, cinching them down.

As men filled the corridor, a low trembling began beneath their feet and quickly intensified to a mind-numbing vibration, accompanied by a shrill squeal that threatened to deafen anyone within earshot. It escalated until the floor below them bucked and rolled; it felt like an earthquake inside the room. Cages split and slid, the men of the detail went flying in every direction as the *Ark* rocked and jumped, but the cage held. The cargo doors opened and Johnson lowered the immediate force field around the ship, but not the extended field. As he did so, the thrumming inside the cage increased, and he fumbled and panicked.

The security men quickly jettisoned the cage and its humanoid occupant from the cargo bay while Johnson sputtered crazily about lights and worms. The hydraulic cargo transport attached to the bottom of the cage slid swiftly across the coarse red sand, guided by Evans, the acting security supervisor. The cage began to glow, heat waves rolling off it like a mirage in the desert. The hydraulic transport suddenly spewed smoke and halted just inside the extended field.

"Got to push it out of the extended field!" Johnson called. He started down the cargo ramp at a full run, followed by the four-man security team. The men could hardly touch the outside observation barrier but they pushed at it anyway. Johnson punched at the remote rheostat on his right forearm and lowered the extended field long enough to shove the cage through, then recalled the field at the highest strength possible from the remote rheostat.

He ordered the crew back onboard immediately. Evans shouted and pointed toward the desert, where the fifteen-member exploration group rounded the fore corner of the *Ark*. Johnson let them inside the extended field and yelled for the returning travelers to enter at the forward hatch. Then he ran for the cargo door. The team hesitated in confusion and uncertainty, and an explosion knocked them all, including Franklin and Zoe, from their feet. The repercussion caused the *Ark* itself to quake, rocking back and forth in her moor even through the extended and perimeter force fields. The cage outside the extended field imploded, throwing speeding projectiles of metal and rock in all directions. Fortunately, nothing penetrated the protective shield.

Master Sergeant Grewder and his cloaked team were not as lucky. Outside the force field, they approached from the tree line on the stern of the mighty *Ark*. The containment bars of the shattered cage, reinforced with Dirk's energy field, remained intact with the humanoid still trapped inside.

Bodies scattered in varying positions on the ground inside the outer force field, and by the time they regained their footing, another tremor shook the land around them. The group could clearly see the glowing red of the humanoid's eyes.

Johnson got to his feet, yelled hysterically not to look at the humanoid, and sprinted for the cargo door. Evans had no more hesitation and the entire team followed at breakneck speed. Johnson was the first one there, and he ran immediately through the corridors for the bridge—the only place from which he could access the emergency field protections.

Another deep tremor shook the *Ark* so hard it knocked

Johnson from his feet and he went sprawling, sliding down the corridor toward the door of the bridge. He pulled up on the wall, placing his hand over the auto print ID panel, and fell in as the door swished open. Arthur Johnson, pilot of the *Ark*, trembled. He opened the forward hatch and protected it with a dense antimatter shield as the bedraggled crew ran into the safety of the *Ark*.

* * *

Master Sergeant Grewder and his cloaked team were knocked awry as they approached the stern of the *Ark*. Grewder's comms unit vibrated persistently while he gained his feet. His men had been closer to the second explosion and not shielded by a force field; he could barely hear for the ringing in his ears. "What?" he yelled into the comm.

"Report," came the one-word command from Major Heartly.

"Hinkle is down, likely dying. He took a barrage of stone and metal to the face." Grewder had taken the same dust and debris into the tender scarring of his own face and it was quite painful. He said nothing about that. "I guess they discovered *something*. They have set the specimen inside a containment cage outside the *Ark*, and the drones are picking up full emergency precautions. All layers of force field, including anti-matter shield, at full strength." He laughed gruffly and then coughed.

Major Heartly's sigh was just barely audible. "Abort Phase Two. Place the containment units over the cage, engage the homing device, cloak and extract the specimen. Rendezvous with Team One and return to Dropship One immediately," came her barking voice.

"Aye. Grewder, out," he answered and turned off the comms.

Later, with his mission successfully completed, Grewder

handed Heartly the data pad and she read carefully. Hinkle was lost but his body had been recovered, no evidence left behind. The insider on the *Ark* had been with the fifteen who returned that day, but she seemed catatonic. She had likely been bitten and Major Heartly doubted the woman would be of any further use to the Company. That was unfortunate. The extraction had proven far easier than she'd expected, and the commander of Dropship One enjoyed a pleasant conference call with the Home Office later that day. It almost seemed too easy, Heartly was now focused on getting the humanoid home, without any further incident. She knew what she was doing was a risk, but all that prestige and money appealed to her adventurous side. Still she had a niggle that what she was doing was wrong, but pushed that feeling deep down away from her rational thoughts. She was sure if she stayed strong and focussed, everything would work out as planned.

***

Dirk lay on the ground, a battle for life raging inside him. He faded in and out of consciousness, still fully aware, but the pain had worn him down. The benevolent spirits, the Sons of Life, were outnumbered in this place and in his body, and the Sons-of-Mishrak had been buoyed by some outside power.

During the rare moments in which Dirk could think, he believed it might be some power found in the totem of Mishrak that fought the benevolent cause within him. As he felt the battle lines shift, he heard a whisper on a soft breeze that caressed his mind. Somehow, he knew this was a secret and it was important. He saw an image as the voice whispered, but he could not understand the words nor comprehend the image. His mind and spirit had been ripped and torn apart beyond their breaking point.

'The white stone...the white stone.' He heard a faraway echo, and the whisper grew louder. *'The white stone kills the*

worms, the larvae...but the starstones...the worms leave the star-stones. They will change you...change you...forever...'

All was silent. There was no more pain. Dirk thought he might still be unconscious; he had ceased any physical activity hours before, the pain had been too great. A breeze stirred the dust where his face met the cold stone floor.

'It is the only way to save your life...and you must live, Dirk. You must live to help us fight.'

He awoke in the darkness, the breeze caressing his face. The sand had flown back in through the worm holes and now shifted about the room in varying colors. The humanoid figure reappeared in the swirling sand.

'Time is against us. We must be quick.'

Dirk heard the urgency in the disembodied voice and sat up. He was so thirsty and so weak, he could barely stand.

'Pulverize the stone and eat it, Dirk. It will taste sweet and it will save your life.' He just stared silently at the shifting sand, hollow-eyed. *'It will save your Jenny, too, but it will change you...'*

Dirk blinked and grabbed two white stones from the floor. He hammered them together and was surprised when they flaked easily. He broke the flakes in his hands and put them in his mouth. They were delicious and gave him some relief from the dryness in his mouth. He didn't stop eating the crumbled rock for some time until excruciating pain hit his stomach and he felt he was being ripped apart. He screamed in the darkness of the white stone room until he could scream no more, and the world went black.

When he awoke, he was no longer in pain and he sensed the larvae no longer swimming inside him. He felt whole and healthy. He opened his eyes wide, and it would have frightened him if he could have seen the radiant blue light emanating from behind those eyes. Dirk Forrett had changed...

Chapter 16

For the first time in what felt like eons, Dirk's mind was all his own. The Sous Chef from his uncle's restaurant was not Korsakov, he was not telepathically being spoken to by the Sons of Life—for that fleeting second, everything stood still.

But the instant that moment passed, his thoughts were flooded with questions and uncertainties.

From his own cluelessness regarding the status of the remaining crew, to the fragments of facts wildly thrashing around in his mind, he could not deny the overwhelming feeling of defeat. With his extensive list of accolades and prizes to his name, Dirk had always managed to come out on top. It was not as though he were invincible—Franklin could break his hand in a handshake—but rather that he could always manage the vast amount of information surrounding him in any situation. He could compart-mentalize and quantify until a clear, logical answer presented itself. But now, as he sat alone in the cold, stone space, victim to the deafening howls of his evident failures and ignorance, it was nearly impossible for him to sort through his thoughts. Though his physical body may have been purged of the worm larvae and was now capable of completing a marathon, he scrambled to repair his mental state after the exploitation of his memories.

Taking a slow, deep breath, Dirk closed his eyes. No matter how appealing it seemed at the moment, it would do him no good to sit and wallow in despair; that much was clear. There was no telling how much longer he would be in solitude and have the op-portunity to just *think*. Silence and the chance to confront his thoughts were the two things he needed, for they were how Dirk Forrett always prevailed—how he soothed his own frazzled brain.

Whenever he had experienced issues with the creation of the *Ark*—it was never smooth sailing even after its completion—or whenever he had fought an internal struggle regarding his own personal life, he used reason and rationalization to come to terms with them. Every problem had an answer and, luckily for him, he had a blind stubbornness that prevented him from ever declaring a puzzle "too tough". He had not gotten where he was in life by sur-rendering to his own sense of defeat. Even in his anxiety and slight terror of the current state of affairs, he would make things work.

He had to; praises and honors were wasted on him if he amounted to nothing more than a white flag.

So he had to concentrate.

His first priority was to focus on the concrete, to consider what he knew to be the truth.

The zebra worms, which normally turned dirt into soil, turned the white rock found at the altar, and all around him now, into a blue, crystalline rock—starstones, the Winds had called them.

After consuming the white rock, the worms ballooned, excreted starstones, and died. Eating the white rock powder had theoretically done the same thing to the larvae inside his own body as it had to Franklin's full-grown, experimental "pets".

This much made sense to him, but with the Wind's whisperings of the Sons-of-Mishrak's ability to invoke violent intentions, Dirk had to question what actually happened to the worms. Did the white stone of the altar chemically react with something within their bodies that caused them to bloat and produce starstones? Or was it something much larger than that, something more spiritual—a purging of some ancient evil? As a man of Science, he would never have considered the latter to be an option, with no physical evidence existing to support that theory, but he could not deny the voices that had spoken to him in his head. The Wind's caress and encouraging words could not have been a result of the insanity which had previously consumed him, nor could the foreign, inexplicable hum of new power he felt within, like a jumpstarted warp drive core.

He wondered, then, how it was the zebra worms had become such harbingers of not only physical but mental violence. He had been shown that the Sons-of-Mishrak could instill such behavior in a creature, and Dirk could only assume that some of the humanoids were responsible for evoking that change. Whether or not this was an age-old tactic he had suddenly come to disrupt, or a new discovery for the Sons-of-Mishrak, he remembered well the two humanoids who had been with Korsakov and forced him into this room.

Gingerly cracking his knuckles, he remembered the look those humanoids had shared when Korsakov claimed they were amassing an army for the heck of it. Even if they were on the 'same side', their intentions must have been different. The Sons-of-Mishrak aimed to achieve primitive survival and war, but what about Korsakov? If he were bitten by a worm, his actions would have been explained, yet he wasn't paralyzed like the others. Then again, in Dirk's own butchered and transposed memory sequences, Korsakov told him to help so they could "get out of here that much quicker". Had that been a message? Or just part of the hallucination?

Dirk groaned.

There were too many variables, too many unknowns. Every piece of solid information he had led immediately to hypothesis and estimations. He was all for puzzles, but there was not enough time. He could not bet the lives of his crew on "if" and "potentially". The only facts which never changed were what the zebra worms did and how the white stones changed them. He had seen them ingest one thing and excrete blue crystal rocks with his own eyes; he had done it in his own body and that, he supposed, would be another fact—

Time seemed to freeze and Dirk found himself holding his breath.

Eating the powdered rock and turning it into starstones within Dirk's body had obviously killed the larvae. But the very real reality was that a new compound had just been formed within his own bloodstream, something he did not have the time to properly examine. What did these starstones really do? How would this ultimately affect him? The only real experience he'd had with the blue stones was having carried it from the altar in his backpack—and having to drop it quickly for the burning sensation through his pack. Though he tried not to dwell on the incredible pain he'd gone through after eating the white rock himself, he couldn't help but wonder what kind of physical trauma awaited him with the starstones having formed as a part of his internal ecology. What would they do to the human body? Right now, he felt better than just okay, but would he survive the change much longer? How would it affect those around him—his crew and other humans? What did that mean for him and Jenny—

Jenny.

The Winds had told him that the powder would help her, too. The unknown consequences of the starstones made Dirk anxious, but if he could save her, he would not pass up the chance.

She was the one who greeted him with a smile every morning.

She was the one who believed his plans would succeed when others had not.

She was the one who dared to befriend the renowned genius.

She was the one who had never abandoned him, even when he yelled and shouted, showing his worst side, during the *Ark*'s construction.

So he would not abandon her, or Franklin or Zoe or the rest of the crew. There were times when he was sure they all regretted joining the *Ark*—that thought had even crossed his mind when he received a wedding invitation from a grad school buddy—but they had travelled the universe together. They deserved more than his own self-pity.

Cautiously opening his eyes, Dirk focused his attention on his hands. He had always considered himself a peaceful, morally-minded scientist. His work in laboratories and libraries led him to have gentle, precise hands. He was an intellectual—a nerd in its most stereotypical sense. He was brains-over-brawn, a reasonable guy without a hero complex, that kid who got picked last in gym class. He was the guy who got a callous here and a papercut there, not this man whose hands now were dirtied, scraped, and bruised. This man now was a fighter.

The humanoids could make soldiers and with them evoke war and conflict. They could raise an army of mindless pawns. Mishrak could incite the twisted parts of the heart to bend to its liking, but it would be just that. *Bending.* Never would they be able to create willpower. They could only destroy it in other creatures, for willpower was not *created.*

Willpower was *ignited* from a desperate, blazing, impenetrable need to prove something. To be something.

Humanity, with all its faults and convoluted emotions, was not something to be underestimated.

Blue eyes burning with an inhuman fire, Dirk rose to his feet.

Chapter 17

Jenny could feel that she was sitting, and sometimes she could hear voices. Mostly she heard those voices calling her name. They shone a light in her eyes as well, but that was…elsewhere.

The worms had taken her mind away, but she wasn't gone. Not completely. She sensed the others sitting cross legged in the sealed speciman lab on the *Ark* but had no understanding of the gravity of the situation.

Her mind was many lightyears away, distracted by the memories being re-lived by the now millions of worm larvae squirming and wriggling through her bloodstream; they were waiting to reach critical mass. It was hard for them to find humanoids who didn't know the dangers of their bite, as it was the most vital part of their reproductive cycle to get into the bloodstream. Soon, there would be more larvae than Jenny's bloodstream could hold.

They would break through the blood vessel walls, consume her muscle mass until they were large enough to survive in the pupae stage outside of their human host.

Much like the ancient Earth tale 'The Arabian Nights', the worms had to distract until they met their objective—their lives in exchange for Jenny's. She would be lost in their tales as they triggered her with what would one day be called the 'Scheherazade hormone'—a chemical the worms released that was akin to a hypnogogic television show, and it raced through all the victims of the zebra worm's bite.

Jenny was no different. She saw the light the doctor flashed in her eyes, heard her name, but she transposed it into the memory of which she was her own victim. She was blissfully unaware of the invasion of her bloodstream and believed herself to be back in graduate school. It was five years before her first mission on the *Ark*, and she attended a guest presentation by her hero, Dirk Forrett.

"You'll find, as you travel the galaxy, that there is nothing more exciting, nothing more thrilling, than the discovery of a species never before known to humankind. With every ocean trench delved into and every forest or jungle thoroughly explored, for over five decades, humanity had nothing left to discover. It was only with the launching of New Odyssey and the first human mission to reach the frozen oceans of Pluto and his moon Charon that we discovered the first new plant and animal life for nearly sixty years.

"I was a much younger man on that mission. It was my first, and the mission I will always remember. The discoveries we made in those five years away from Earth were profound. The specimens we brought back with us became the building blocks of new medicines, military and technological developments. That was, in its own way, the first '*Ark*' that ever returned to Earth."

The class was silent, entranced by the legend of a man who, all before the age of thirty, had been the first to discover the Giant Finite Amoeba. That specimen contained an enzyme which had ended all abnormal cell growth and inflammation in humans. It wasn't a cure for all disease, but it put an end to even the most obscure and deadly of cancers. It had ended chronic pain caused by injury, trauma, or stress. This man, barely out of grad school, had discovered, classified, and named the giant amoeba, which was the size of a child's palm. The amoeba's distinctive characteristic was its vivid neon orange color, which was also the source of what was now called Dirk's Compound. Once all its properties were thoroughly analyzed, it was quickly synthesized and regulated.

With few side effects—long-term use could tinge the skin orange, some elderly patients had scattered reports of possible breathing difficulties, and less than one percent of patients reported an allergic reaction of a vivid orange rash, only unattractive and uncomfortable but never fatal, that was soon called Dirk's Disease—and a remarkably marginal chance for addiction, Dirk became a fast hero on Earth. His findings and assistance with the rest of the mission soon made him one of the most respected Galactic Researchers and Planetary Zoologists in the galaxy. It took only his presence to immediately entrance the audience of his lecture now.

The thought 'entranced' made Jenny's body, far away from Earth, stir the briefest of movements, then she remained still again as Dirk's voice continued. A close look at her eyes with a microscope would have revealed that the larvae swam in her ocular fluid; she was deep, deep under the spell of the zebra worm.

"When we returned to Earth," Dirk continued. Jenny looked up from her notes after momentarily having lost her train of thought, returning her attention and her heart to Dirk once more. "…we returned to a new world. That is something you must prepare yourself for when you leave on your first long-term mission. When you return, things are guaranteed to have changed. These are times unlike any other. Even when I had returned from that first mission, the Revolution had begun, the Great Uprising had already ended, and life had returned to "normal". But when the New Odyssey's crew returned, life as we know it now was anything but normal to us. Light speed travel had been trumped by Atomic Travel, and suddenly, the galaxy was our oyster. While we tootled back with our little menagerie, just barely at light speed, others had already left the solar system and ventured into the galaxy."

Dirk smiled disarmingly, the shadows of his traumas dissolving in his charm. "Of course, while I was away for five years, Earth had gone through almost as many decades. You were probably all just babies during the Great Uprising."

The class laughed. Jenny laughed with them, and her eyes filled with stars and the idea of flying through them with Dirk at Atomic Speeds. That fantasy had brought her to the field of Intergalactic Research, and now her hero was standing before her, speaking almost as if only to her. Her heart raced, she raised her hand, and Dirk looked up from his introspection.

"You there, in the cute t-shirt."

Jenny blushed; her t-shirt had a Japanese puppy cartoon on it. "Um, yes. I was wondering, do you ever hire research assistants right out of graduate school?"

He smiled and his eyes bored into hers. "Leave me your resume and grade card along with your report assignment, and I guess we'll find out."

Jenny couldn't believe that he'd agreed to give her credentials a glance. She hugged her notebook to her chest and smiled, locked onto his gaze. "I will."

Dirk looked around the class. "That goes for the rest of you, as well. You never know where you'll meet the next great explorers! I'm not making anyone any promises, but the only way to succeed is to try."

He spoke to every student, but to Jenny Adonna, his words were far more intimate. She had to finish her report tonight, and it had to sparkle and shine above all the others. She *had* to be Dirk Forrett's next assistant.

In the *Ark*'s laboratory, Jenny's face was slack and emotionless. Even though she and the other entranced worm victims had been locked away in there before Dirk's team had departed, there was no reason to do so. They weren't going anywhere. As far as she was concerned, Jenny wrote her paper for the first time again while her body starved to death. No amount of supplemental fluids could replace the amount the worms consumed directly from her veins. While she relived writing her reports, followed by her first tentative responses to Dirk's impressed reception of her work, Jenny's body slowly died. She vividly relived her very first mission, that time remarkably as Dirk's personal assistant out amongst the stars, completely unaware of the cold, sterile walls around her and the heat of parasitic life within her body.

There was nothing the *Ark*'s medical team could do for her or the other victims—at least, nothing within their current realm of knowledge. The few doctors left aboard the *Ark* did not have the capacity to find the source of the trance, had no previous experience with this type of biological phenomenon, and the victims became more emaciated by the day. The doctors had tested for everything they knew how to test, but even Dirk Forrett's own remarkable discoveries for Earth medicine had not prepared them to deal with unexpected medical disasters of Santelli Minor. This was something new, and it grew in Jenny and the other victims at a rate that would have terrified their shipmates had they only known.

Chapter 18

"Move, move, move," screamed Franklin.

As the group came over the last ridge towards the *Ark*, Franklin could see the chaos enveloping it. He knew he had to get the group within ten meters of the ship's hull or they all risked being locked out once the force field and anti-matter field were activated

Franklin turned and noticed Dr. Robinson flailing behind. He ran back, hauling her over his shoulders and screaming at the others to keep going. As they passed the humanoid's cage, it imploded, sending them all face-first into the sand

The force caused Dr. Robinson to be thrown from Franklin's shoulders. He crawled to his knees and made his way to her, pulling Zoe along with him

Evans rushed from the ship and helped Franklin to his feet.

Together they picked up Dr. Robinson, making it just inside the perimeter before Johnson activated both shields again.

Franklin spun around to make sure no one was left behind and noticed something warm trickling down his face. He wiped it with the back of his hand and saw that it was covered in blood. *Something from that cage exploding must have hit me*, he thought.

"Franklin, move your ass!" Zoe yelled, grabbing his bicep and pulling him towards the ship.

The team clamored up the ramp, Evans hitting the button repeatedly to close it behind them. With the click of the door shutting and the vacuum seal afterwards, the welcomed silence was eerie, all anyone could hear was the person breathing beside them.

Franklin pulled himself up and addressed the group. "Anyone requiring medical attention, get to the medical bay, now. Zoe will take care of you."

He looked over at Zoe, who nodded back, a look of fear still evident on her face. She scanned the group and her eyes fell on Dr. Robinson, slumped on the floor.

"Help me," she shouted, scrambling over to Dr. Robinson. The woman appeared to be unconscious and had a nasty gash on her cheek.

More flying debris, Franklin decided. Evans helped Zoe carry her to the medical bay, and a few others from the group trailed behind. "Security," he said to his team, "you need to watch Ron twenty-four-seven in case he tries to hurt anyone again. I don't want him kept in the medical bay, keep him isolated and restrained in his room."

All of a sudden, Johnson flew into the cargo hold.

"What the hell happened?" Franklin asked.

"Where's Dirk?" Johnson shouted.

Franklin put his hand on Johnson's chest to slow him down.

He looked over the remaining group. "Get cleaned up, everyone, and meet in the cafeteria in an hour."

"Might need to heed your own advice," Johnson retorted, glancing at Franklin's temple.

Franklin realized just then that he was still bleeding. Turning on his heels, he made his way through the ship and down to his quarters. The stillness of the ship reminded him that half the crew were still in a trance and that he was no closer to getting them out of it.

Slamming his hands down on the bathroom sink, Franklin could barely look himself in the mirror. The last four days had been a nightmare, even by his standards. He cupped his huge hands underneath the hot running water and splashed his face repeatedly until the water in the sink swirled a crimson red. Grabbing a towel, he wiped the back of his neck and then pressed it to his temple. He never thought he would think it, but he did. *What the hell would Dirk do right now?*

With the towel still pressed to his temple, Franklin made his way to the medical bay. Zoe was still treating Dr. Robinson when Franklin arrived at the door. She explained to him that the doctor had been falling in and out of consciousness, babbling the same line over and over.

"What is it? What is she saying?"

Zoe let out a long sigh, and Franklin put a reassuring hand on her shoulder. "Let's take a look at you and I'll fill you in," she said, pointing to Franklin's bath towel.

She led him into her private office and opened a surgical pack. Franklin sat on the edge of her desk, anxiously awaiting her response.

"Hold still, it's pretty deep." Franklin winced and Zoe began to stitch the massive slice at his temple. "I really don't know what to make of it," she began. "She keeps saying, 'They're coming for the humanoids.'"

"They?" Franklin stuttered.

"That's what she keeps repeating. I mean, we've only just discovered them, so apart from our crew, who else knows about these creatures?"

"And do they know what the damn creatures are capable of? Why in the hell would anyone even want anything to do with them? I mean, they have Dirk, for Christ's sake, and Korsakov."

Zoe finished up and put a small amount of antibiotic ointment over the stitches. "Anything else I need to look at?" She cast her eyes over Franklin's long, muscular arms. Times like these he would have given anything to wrap her up in them again.

Franklin held her gaze for a few seconds, then glanced at the floor. He should never have let her go all those years ago. Too proud to admit he was wrong, by the time he realized it, she had left on another mission.

"I need to talk with Johnson," he said. "I'll see you in the cafeteria soon." He squeezed her hand and walked to the bridge. As he made his way, security brought Matt Babbage in on a stretcher.

"We found him unconscious where the humanoids had been caged," the security detail reported.

"Keep him next to the doctor until he regains consciousness. When either of them are coherent enough to tell me what happened, let me know. I also want a full sweep of the ship for any more worms. Do not, and I repeat, *do not* let them bite you."

***

Johnson tinkered inside one of the panels under the console, wires strewn all around him as he tried to regain control over the pods. With the master key in Dr. Korsakov's hands, he had to re-route control of the pods to his localized console on the bridge. He heard footsteps, and when he looked over, a pair of size-fourteen boots stood next to him and he knew Franklin had arrived.

"I need to see all surveillance videos of the last thirty minutes," Franklin barked.

"Um, kind of busy here, if you haven't noticed. I really need to regain control over the pods—that is, if you ever want to use them again and maybe, I don't know, go find Dirk!" Johnson's sarcastic tone lingered in the air.

Franklin pulled Johnson out from under the console by his ankles. "Listen here, pipsqueak. I don't have time for games. I need to see what happened when we were running back to the ship. Why did you push out an empty cage?"

"It wasn't fucking empty. That humanoid cripple was in it." Johnson jumped to his feet and assumed a Kung Fu fighting stance.

Franklin only bellowed a laugh. "Well, do I spy someone whose been keeping a secret around here? Before you go all Sha-olin Monk on me, you might want to use those fighting skills to help me get the others back and get the hell off this planet."

Johnson dropped his arms and made his way to the surveil-lance console, staring at Franklin the whole time. As much as he would have loved to drop him on his ass, he knew there were other priorities above his pride. Searching through the surveillance foot-age, he filled Franklin in on what had happened in the cargo bay after taking the worm back from the holodeck. After several minutes of searching, he found the footage of the men pushing out the cage containing a humanoid.

Franklin stared in disbelief. "But we took them all back. How did we miss one? Stop the tape there!" he barked. "Okay, inch it forward, bit by bit. There, do you see that?"

"See what?" Johnson frowned over the footage.

"From what I've witnessed of the humanoids, they don't have the strength or power to break free from one of those cages. We had them specially constructed with Unobtainium, the strongest metal in the known universe. For a species that loves mind games, it just doesn't add up." Franklin paused, then pointed to the screen. "Then, see here, two small explosions, both very precise and calculated. The cage breaks apart, flying debris blocks our view for a moment. Look, there's the humanoid in the sand facing the ship, and then..."

Shocked, Johnson remarked, "It's gone!"

"Exactly," Franklin sighed.

Taken, cloaked, then moved—both men were thinking the same thing. The humanoid didn't break the cage; someone else had. Why would someone or something want a humanoid? Whoever it was, they obviously had no idea what those things were capable of doing.

"Look, Johnson, I don't have all the answers yet. You need to get one of the pods working so we can make our way back to Dirk and Korsakov. I'll round up the crew and see who wants to come back out with me. Keep the force fields up. No one leaves this ship without my permission, got it? Whatever took that humanoid could still be out there."

"I'm on it, Franklin."

***

Man this shit is getting crazier by the minute, Franklin thought as he made his way to the cafeteria. He bumped into Zoe coming out of the medical bay.

"Any change with the doctor?" he asked.

"No change, still feigning in and out of consciousness, still repeating the same thing. She doesn't seem to be under the human-oids' control, but I'm running some blood work to see if I can find anything that may explain why she was only 'temporarily' affected."

"Zoe, you remember when the sand-being said the Sons-of-Mishrak wanted to consume us?" Franklin had to take the chance now to ask her advice.

"Yes, vaguely. It all happened so quickly. Why?"

Stopping just short of the cafeteria door, Franklin spun Zoe around to face him. "If they want to consume us, then how are we meant to help the sand-beings? What if the Sons-of-Mishrak have already killed Dirk and Korsakov? We can't even help the crew onboard, let alone those still out there."

"We can't give up, Franklin. Dirk wouldn't give up, and I won't let you, either. The answers are out there, we just have to be brave enough to find them. I believe in you." Zoe stood on her tiptoes and kissed Franklin on the cheek.

He wrapped his arms around her waist, pulling her tightly to his chest. "I'm sorry for everything," he whispered into her hair.

"I know. Now let's go get Dirk."

They walked the remaining corridor to the cafeteria, abruptly stopping just short of the door. A faint whimper came from behind one of the wall panels. They bent down and crawled along the corridor, listening for the source. Zoe pointed to a small air vent, and Franklin pulled a small screwdriver from the emergency tool kit he always carried. As the last screw fell to the ground, Franklin removed the grate and was greeted by the wide, glistening eyes of Kuhn.

"Kuhn!" Zoe shouted. The dog was covered in sand and shaking. Zoe gently lifted him out, cooing his name over and over.

"Well, I'll be damned! That's where the little bugger got

to." Franklin laughed.

"Looks like we have one more member for the away team," Zoe said, beaming.

***

Major Heartly retired to her sparsely decorated quarters. With the precious cargo now safe and secure in the hold and her shift for the evening finished, she sat down at her desk and started planning the final flight trajectory back towards the rendezvous point.

She wished to leave the orbit of Santelli Minor as soon as the forecast meteor shower was over. By her calculations, it should pass them by in three hours' time.

Rubbing her temples, she couldn't help but wish this was her last run. She had promised herself it would be, that she'd take herself 'offline' after this mission, head to a planet retreat, and sort herself out. She'd made that promise more than once, but the money was way too tempting and it lured her back in, again and again.

Pouring herself a synthetic whiskey, she stared out into the blackness through her small window. *Who am I kidding?* she thought, having burnt all bridges with her family after the terrible accident that had claimed her father's life. She'd decided to leave the family business and never look back. Now here she was, cash-rich but emotionally dead, ferrying toxic cargo around for the "Company"—a lucrative employer who would take her out should she ever cross them.

Checking her watch, she noted the meteor shower should be starting soon. As if on cue, the ship suddenly started to vibrate violently, throwing her against the wall. Her glass crashed into the desk as she tried to steady herself, cutting into her hand.

The button on her intercom flashed red. The ship felt as

158

though it was starting to tilt in orbit as she pulled herself up onto the chair. Pressing down hard on the intercom button, she barked, "This had better be life or death. I'm off the clock at the moment."

The crew knew better than to ever disturb Major Heartly in her private quarters unless it was an emergency. "Major," came the voice of a junior engineer, "we need you on the bridge ASAP. We've got power surges coming from the cargo hold, and they're taking the engines offline. Dropship One's being pulled into the planet's atmosphere."

"Get Master Sergeant Grewder to meet me there in five minutes. Activate Level 4 Alarm, now!"

Chapter 19

G asping for air, his hand struck out from beneath the soaking wet sheets, searching for the glass. Clawing it towards him, he gulped down the rust-colored liquid made from rotting Coiniver berries. He clutched the empty glass to his chest when the liquid sizzled in his stomach, causing him to cry out in pain. Soon, the highly toxic substance circled through his body, bringing with it a euphoria that slowly washed over him. Rolling over, he fell out of the bed onto his knees. *After all these years, she's still here with me, no matter how hard I try to forget her.*

A nightmare that would not let go. It clung to him like a dead spirit not yet crossed over. No matter how hard he tried to lock it away, the memory always escaped—she always escaped—to remind him of that day over and over again.

***

Two magenta Lyla-jean hummingbirds danced around the branches of the blue Elephantus tree on the planet Castellina. Sean Grewder looked around at his colleagues scattered about with the Elders of the settlement and couldn't help but grin. Breathing deeply to soothe his nerves, he waited in anticipation for his bride-to-be to join him, palms to palms and souls to souls in their hand-tying ceremony.

Amber had been his trainer in Military Academy. Drawn to her 'take what you want' attitude, he had found a kindred spirit with the same drive and determination as himself. It wasn't long before her extra intuition had taken on a whole new meaning and they had fallen in love. The danger and excitement of not getting caught only heightened their passion for each other. After graduation, they'd decided to try a long-distance relationship, which allowed them to focus on their respective careers without distractions. Eventually, enough years passed for them to truly go their own ways.

"I will always love you," he'd said at the end of their last conversation.

Then six months ago, fate had intervened and they found themselves reconnected on an operation protecting Castellina from faction renegades. Their mission was to restore calm and provide security for the native population, and no more than twenty-four hours had passed before she had snuck into his cabin. This time, he would not let her get away so easily.

As they sat upon the rocky outcrop overlooking the Aquidian jungle below, he had known it would never be more perfect than this.

"Amber, there will never be another heart that I wish to beat beside mine," he said, looking in her hazel eyes.

Before he could continue, Amber had jumped into his arms,

planting kisses all over his face. "Why wait?" she giggled. "Let's do it here in the settlement, the way the Castelli people have done for thousands of years," she whispered in his ear.

With barely a week of planning, the day had now arrived. The moon and sun were rising and setting in unison when Amber appeared from the small hut at the end of the bridge. Sean gasped at how beautiful she looked. Her long dark hair fell in waves around her shoulders, the ends just kissing the top of the gold-beaded joining garment she wore. The hummingbirds twirled around her as she made her way along the bridge and a light breeze danced through the valley, picking up the loose petals from her bouquet and swirling them up over her head.

Suddenly, the breeze intensified, leaves from the trees stripped from their branches and whirling all around them. Amber looked up into the sky behind Sean and screamed.

By now, he could barely see for the leaves thwarting his view. Whipping around to see what had caused his bride's fearful cry, he could not believe what he saw.

"Run," he shouted at the group. "Get to hiding, now!"

People fled in all directions, the wind and dust creating mayhem. He pushed through the group and ran towards Amber, who was hunched down, gripping the railing of the bridge.

A renegade patrol ship came straight for them from above. Tripping and falling as he clamored along the bridge, he grabbed her arm and pulled her towards the hut. They were almost there when the ship discharged its weapons, throwing them both inside the hut and knocking them unconscious.

He awoke to the smell of smoke and a heat so intense it pinned him to the floor. Struggling onto his elbows, he crawled towards his bride, the heat and flames becoming more extreme the closer he got. As he reached Amber, the roof of the hut came crashing down and then there was darkness.

Two weeks later, the world was still black as he came out of the coma. Bandages covered his whole face, the horrific burns he sustained now intrinsically a part of him. When he was told Amber had perished in the fire, he did not care whether he saw the world another day. All he had ever loved was gone forever.

***

Pulling himself up from the floor, Grewder walked to the desk and opened up the small drawer on the side, careful not to glance at his reflection in the mirror hanging above. Pulling out a small, black velvet bag, he tipped it slowly into his palm. A single gold bead rolled out. Picking up the bead, he rolled it between his fingers, and one tear slipped down his scarred cheek.

Now a lost soul with no true path in life, he'd gone off the grid and left the academy. It was then the 'Company' had found him. That's what they did; they preyed on the weak who had nothing left. It was the only way they knew they would get the loyalty they so desired.

Everyone who had ever meant anything to him had died that day in the attack. He had died that day. He was just a number at the Company, and that was just the way he liked it.

So it hardly rattled him at all when the ship lurched and rumbled and the emergency light on the intercom flashed out at him across the small quarters.

Chapter 20

The 'Humm D Jeep Extreme' jolted and jived along the dirt road towards rural Imboomba, two hundred miles west of Ron's training camp. Tearing along the familiar old road, he reminisced about all the exciting times he had there as a child growing up. Each electrified black steel gate he passed denoted another childhood friend's place where they spent the summer running wild, honing their hunting skills on poor unsuspecting frogs, and gazing up at the sky every night, wondering if they would ever make it up to space. Sometimes, he pinched himself, unable to believe he had finally fulfilled his childhood dream and been accepted onto his first space mission with the famous Dirk Forrett to Santelli Minor. He had made the long journey home to tell his parents the good news and show off his new set of wheels.

Breaking hard around the last bend, the back of the car

started to lose control, causing Ron to quickly turn the steering to the right. Ron started laughing; he had forgotten how sharp that last hairpin was and thought about how many cars he had wiped out into that scrub.

Screaming to a halt in front of his parent's gate, he waited for the dust to settle before cracking open the door. His parents always joked that they could see him coming before they heard him.

Ron jumped out and surveyed the surrounding landscape. His parents' ranch-style property once sat in a lushly forested valley with a tinkle of a river running through it. They bred Sturgoose—a genetically modified goose that yielded twice as much meat as a normal goose—and people travelled from other planets to taste their delicate meat. That was before the government discovered what lay beneath this fertile land. First, the river stopped flowing, cutting off the blood to the farm. Then the trees began to twist and wither, the crops perished, and the Sturgoose grew sick and died. Ron's parents refused to budge; they were the only ones who had not sold out and now their property sat precariously on the edge of a two-mile-deep pit surrounding them on three sides.

Ron punched in the code for the gate and jumped back into his Jeep. *Maybe this time I can convince them to move,* he thought as he drove towards his frantically waving mother.

He opened his arms to embrace her. Standing a foot taller than her, he bent and kissed the top of her head. As an only child, it was always a celebration when he returned.

He felt a nose prodding at his jeans, trying to wedge between them. Bending down, he scratched behind his old dog's ears. "Hey there, Star, old buddy."

"Where's Pop?" Ron looked around the yard, then back to his mum's face. "What's wrong? What's happened?" He touched her shoulder.

"Your father's been taken ill. Come, he's inside waiting for you."

Ron's boots thudded ominously up the wooden staircase towards his parents' bedroom. He knocked softly on the door before opening it slowly. His father sat in his favorite high-backed, green leather chair, gazing out the window. A single line of trees was all that segregated the back of the property from the vastness of the mine beyond.

"I only ask one thing," rasped his father. "When I go, bury me on this land. I need to be part of what I created and worked so hard on all my life. That way, when they take this land, my soul will remain here forever."

Ron gulped and squeezed his dad's hand. The pressure from the mining company had finally taken its toll; there was no fight left to give. Ron promised himself there and then that he would always fight for what he believed in, no matter what the odds.

The following day, Ron grabbed the shovel from the garden shed and struck the golden-colored earth between the trees. The more times the shovel struck the ground, the faster he dug until he fell to his knees sobbing. He was relieved his father was no longer in pain and that he had been able to share with him the greatest achievement of his life so far. But it was more than losing his father—it was also losing his childhood home. He loved coming back here during his training. It grounded him, showed him how far he had come. He scooped up a handful of the soil and let it slowly fall between his fingers before picking up a small red rock. Putting it in his pocket, he continued to dig until the tears on his cheeks were no more.

**

Ron awoke with a jerk. His left eye wouldn't open and he had no idea where he was. As he tried to raise his hand to his face, he realized his hands were bound to either side of the bed. He slowly let his aching head fall back down while he tried to remember how he got there. He recalled being tackled to the ground, *But for what?* he thought.

Hearing footsteps coming towards him, he froze in terror. He recognized the voice as Franklin's, talking with someone—a woman, maybe Dr. Robinson?

"When do you think he'll wake up?" Franklin sighed. "Do you think he's under the same influence as the others? Keep an eye on him and let me know the minute he wakes up. I need to know what happened!"

Franklin's boots twisted on the floor, thumping away from Ron. He felt soft hands on his wrist, taking his pulse. He didn't know what to do—had no idea what had happened in the last few days. He remembered trekking out to the altar, he remembered a dust storm sweeping down upon them, and then nothing. His mind was blank.

He attempted to speak to whoever was beside him, but all that came out was a barking noise. His throat was so dry, as though he'd been eating sand.

"Shh, Ron, just relax. I will get my kit and have a look at the cut on your temple." Zoe squeezed Ron's arm, not knowing why she felt this overwhelming urge to protect him and not let Franklin know he'd woken up yet.

"Take a break, boys. I'm going to stitch up Ron's gash while he's still unconscious. Don't worry. If anything happens, I'll be sure to let you know," Zoe barked at the security detail.

Ron heard her footsteps disappear down the hall. Opening his right eye slowly, the florescent light of his room caused it to start watering as he wondered what the hell had happened.

Chapter 21

Dropship One was going down. Rotating around itself at an accelerating speed, it would only take a handful of minutes for Santelli Minor's atmosphere to tear it apart.

"Grewder, what the hell's going on? What happened to the engines?" Major Hartley, still unaware of her injured hand, yelled at the intercom console. Despite the vibrations, she stood over the pilots, studying the screens above their heads. Not receiving a response, she turned to the junior engineer, who stood by her side waiting for orders. "Didn't I tell you to get Master Sergeant Grewder here? Where is he?" she growled.

"He's not responding, Major."

"So? Get him here! Now!"

After the engineer stormed out of the bridge, Hartley approached one of the cabin's triangle windows to look outside. The planet's dusty red surface slowly filled her field of view, along with a bent piece of metal sticking out from what she presumed to be the wing. Even if Dropship One was one of five all-new drop-ships ordered by the Company, with experienced crew, decorated pilots, and the only one equipped with an APC, Hartley knew she would not survive such an uncontrolled atmospheric entry. The smell of burning rubber increased her sense of urgency.

"Grewder!" She punched the intercom, smearing it with blood.

"Major, the controls aren't responding and the engines are still offline. All shields are down. If we don't evacuate soon..." The copilot, drenched in sweat under his helmet, turned briefly to look at her.

"Are you telling me that we can't handle a simple meteor shower?"

"I'm not sure this is about the meteor shower, Ma'am."

"Major, we can still save this baby. We only need to get her power back on. Just give me a minute," the pilot added. Suddenly, another vicious vibration caused the overhead monitors to crash down on the floor, missing Hartley by a hair's breadth. "Of course, if you want to evacuate, it's up to you, Ma'am," the pilot added after checking his own broken multi-function display. The only thing still functioning at the cockpit was a smiling Earth-on-a-spring toy with hands and a little polka-dotted umbrella shading the North Pole, which kept bouncing uncontrollably—a gift the pilot had bought for himself before boarding the ship, as a re-minder of how far he had truly come.

Hartley knew they were running out of time, but she didn't want to abandon the mission before making sure there was nothing else she could do. Going back alive without the shipment meant no payment. The Company would never trust her again, may even ensure she never worked again. *Grewder had better be dead. There's no other excuse for disobeying my orders*, she thought, struggling to keep her balance between the two pilots as the drop-ship took heavy damage.

"Oh, no. Look!" The pilot pointed at a wide piece of debris, very much like a giant sponge, heading straight towards them.

Hartley moved closer to the windscreen, unsure of what to make of the object. "Prepare for impact!" she yelled, then rushed to buckle up in the empty crew chief's seat behind the pilots.

Instinctively, pilot Bosler broke the little open umbrella off the Earth-on-a-spring and held it as a shield in front of his face. He had always wanted to do that.

***

On Santelli Minor, a portly lizard had just finished drinking from one of the small lakes scattered in the oasis when a bright flash in the sky caused it to look up. It blushed a neon pink. Uncertain of its safety, the lizard crawled clumsily under the rotten log it had momentarily abandoned to quench its thirst and disappeared from Korsakov's sight.

Korsakov smiled at the alien creature's behavior. Had it noticed him, crouched among the vegetation a few feet away, the otherwise naturally pale green reptile would have blushed its snout at him, too. Korsakov got to his feet and looked up to the sky. All that was left of the sudden light burst was a thin grey cloud, barely visible and dispersing quickly. Without contemplating the event any further, he proceeded through the oasis.

Walking along the lake in the opposite direction of what he'd heard others call 'the altar', Korsakov looked for signs in the sand. Before long, the shape of a bear formed before his eyes. Immediately recognizing the pleasant memory, he breathed a sigh of relief and kept on his way.

Korsakov hoped the faith he'd put in the sand-beings had not been misplaced. From the moment they started presenting themselves to him in the form of past memories, he felt they'd been guiding him on the right path. In return, he cooperated with them in their fight against the Sons-of-Mishrak and had not hesitated to lure Dirk, or capture him in the transportation chamber, when they had asked it of him. The sand-beings had communicated to him that Dirk was their last hope against their common enemy, and that without the *Ark,* there could be no salvation. Korsakov knew that once the process was over, Dirk would acquire powers previously unknown to him and would become almost a whole new living being.

Stepping upon a worn, round slab which gave way to his weight, Korsakov took the time to think over his actions while he waited for a response. He had disobeyed orders and taken initiatives without informing his superior, but there was no time to explain, and intelligence had informed him about possible insiders among the crew. The risk was too great to have acted in any other way. Back inside the stone chamber, he had told Dirk that he was amassing an army, and that had been true. Only, he wasn't amassing an army for the violent, manipulative, and idol-worshipping species, as most surely thought. Now, as he stood face to face with the leader of the Sons-of-Mishrak, Korsakov was grateful the being could not read his mind.

***

Inside the beaten yet sturdy *Ark,* Franklin had everything under control. Zoe's unexpected support and reassurance that they would find Dirk had given him a huge boost in self-confidence. Of course, he was terribly worried about Dirk and Korsakov's disappearances, but he felt powerful enough to save the day for the first time since he became the *Ark*'s Chief of Security. Finally, all his hard work and loyalty had paid off. Hell, he'd even stopped swearing as much, and even Zoe had mellowed towards him. When they'd found Kuhn together, Franklin sensed things were finally turning around for the better.

All I have to do is grab a few men, get Dirk's ass back to the Ark, and...well, just bring things back to normal again. Easy. Dirk can pick it up from there, Franklin thought as he observed how Johnson added his final touches to the pod. Johnson had only managed to rewire the smallest pod of all, which took a crew of four in a tight cabin. Not exactly Franklin's size.

"...and she's ready! Earthquakes and explosions may slow me down, but I always get the job done." Johnson presented the pod to Franklin, who scratched the wound on his forehead over the bandages. "You shouldn't be doing that, you know." Johnson pointed a finger at him.

"Are you flying this thing?"

"I'm the *Ark*'s pilot. *The Ark's*. I'm not going anywhere, my friend." Johnson patted the pod's frame. "Most guys around here can fly a pod. You're on pods all the time. What's the problem?"

"It's small."

"And?"

"It has no windows." Franklin frowned.

"This version doesn't need any windows. It has those little state-of-the-art Nano-displays that show you—hey, don't tell me you're claustrophobic? Are you? Big guy like you? Really?" Johnson laughed, but Franklin wasn't amused.

"Fine, whatever. Good job, Mr...Karate newbie." Franklin started to leave the cargo hold.

"It's Kung Fu, actually!" Johnson spoke up. With his back to Johnson, Franklin raised two fingers as he kept walking "And that doesn't even mean anything, but nice try!" Proud of himself, Johnson switched on the pod's floodlights and engaged in a Kung Fu fight with his own shadow.

Without Dirk giving new orders and Johnson busy with the pods, Franklin found the bridge nearly abandoned. He had just returned from the cafeteria, where he had informed everyone onboard about the missing commanders. It hadn't been easy, but everyone saw that Franklin's squad and Johnson's skills could keep them safe.

Franklin had arranged for Evans to gather ten of the best guards in the living quarters so he could handpick the search and rescue team, but the procedure was taking longer than he'd hoped.

"Sir?" Evans came rushing in, getting in the way of Franklin's thoughts.

"Is it time?"

"Dr. Rowens needs you at the medical bay. She said it's an emergency."

"Why didn't she call me directly herself?" Franklin was already hastening his way down the *Ark*'s corridors, Evans chasing after him a step behind.

"I don't know that, Sir."

"Is she okay?"

"She's fine. I was in there collecting medical supplies for the mission, as you ordered, and I think she was changing Dr. Robinson's dressings. She told me to come get you."

To Franklin, the *Ark*'s hallways seemed suddenly much longer than they actually were, and he didn't think twice before pushing and shoving anyone who happened to walk along the same path. Once they reached the medical bay, Franklin was relieved to find that Zoe was indeed all right, although he had to slow her down because she spoke way too fast.

"It's Robinson! She's stopped repeating the same words over and over and says... Listen!" Zoe dragged Franklin by his upper arm, bringing him closer to the catatonic doctor's face.

Dr. Robinson lay on a medical bed with her eyes half closed. Bandages were wrapped around her head, although they were loose enough to allow her to move her jaw. She spoke slowly and quietly. "Call Franklin...need to talk Franklin...Zoe...call Franklin..."

"She's been calling your name for the past few minutes. Try talking to her." Zoe encouraged him to pull up a chair and sit by the bed, which he did.

"Uh, hello?" Franklin asked reluctantly.

"Call Franklin..."

"I'm Franklin."

"Need to talk..."

"Okay, I tried." Franklin jumped up off the chair. "Maybe we should give her more time. Call me if anything changes. I've got a crew to gather. Dirk needs me."

"Sit down," Dr. Robinson ordered in her usual up-and-about tone, taking everyone by surprise. Even though Franklin felt his blood freeze in his veins, he obeyed and exchanged a nervous glance with Zoe. "We're trapped. There is no escape. We can't leave this planet."

"What? How do we know she's not just drugged?" Franklin asked Zoe over his shoulder, but Dr. Robinson spoke again before she could reply.

"Remember New Odyssey? My very first mission to Pluto and Charon?"

"No..." Franklin stirred in his chair, feeling he should have known the answer.

"The Giant Finite Amoeba?"

"Dirk's Disease."

"Never liked that name. Remember what I wanted the disease to be called instead? It was Jenny's idea." Franklin shook his head and smiled sheepishly, scratching the bandage on his head. "First time you showed me the worms, you called them 'cool shit'," Dr. Robinson went on. Franklin remained silent and seconds went by before Dr. Robinson spoke again. "Franklin, this is Dork Ferret."

"It's Dirk! He's alive! Where are you? We're coming to get you!" Franklin jumped to his feet. "But, how the hell are you—"

"You can't save me, Franklin. I'm using Robinson as a conduit. I can't talk for much longer, or she's going to die, and we need her alive. Listen, we all have to stay here on Santelli Minor. No one may leave the planet."

"Why?" Franklin's excitement was gradually fading.

"We're running out of time. There is something we need to do, and I'm going to need you on this."

"Sure, Dirk. Anything."

"We must destroy the *Ark*. We have no other choice, do you understand? Trust me, Franklin, it's the only way. Prepare the crew. I've got to go." Dr. Robinson's eyes closed and the muscles on her face relaxed, her breathing stable for the first time in days. Now she looked asleep instead of half-awake.

Silence fell upon the medical bay. Nobody could believe what had taken place right in front of them. Evans was left speechless while Zoe approached Franklin, who shook his head in disbelief.

"Destroy the *Ark*? How...how do I prepare the crew for this? How do I tell anyone they can't go home? There's got to be another way. Maybe Dirk's wrong this time. *If* that was Dirk." Franklin brushed Zoe's hand off his shoulder and stormed out of the room, leaving her and Evans behind with their gazes still fixed on Dr. Robinson.

Chapter 22

Heartly looked around the bridge of Dropship One. The crash landing on the planet's surface had left the ship in a slightly uneasy condition, but the collision with sponge-looking object still attached to the ship—whatever it was—had probably been the only reason they'd survived the sudden descent through Santelli's atmosphere.

"We all okay in here?" Heartly coughed out, not really expecting anyone to be able to hear her to respond but just hoping for a comforting answer. She got nothing in return. Standing shakily, she tried to walk around. The crooked floors and walls bent beneath the weight of her footsteps. She made her way slowly and carefully to the front of the ship, where the main plasma window lay still intact. If she could break through, it would be her quickest and easiest method of escape. Before she managed to leave the bridge, she found Bosler impaled by a lever on the control panel. He was very much dead. Heartly just hoped she wasn't the lone survivor on the ship.

Heartly didn't have to wait long for proof of something else alive after the crash. She had to make her way through the cargo hold to get it to the front of the ship and searched for any signs of life along the way. Inside the cargo hold, she found the charred cage that had previously housed the humanoid specimen. Bodies lay scattered around the empty shell, all dead. She examined the cage and noticed a few strands of fur and even a scale hanging onto the broken glass edges.

She was meant to bring the cargo from the planet to the Company, and now she hadn't even gotten off the planet—and not for a lack of trying. Now, that thing was somewhere out there, maybe even still on the ship with her. It could have possibly escaped the wreck somehow and made its way in any direction across the planet. The only thing Heartly did know was that she had to keep her wits about her because she was sure the creature was dangerous.

Heartly made it to a long hallway, at the end of which a light shone out to her. The light came from Santelli's sun falling through the window; she could make it with ease. The ship rumbled and shook as if a giant rocked it back and forth. Heartly fell hard onto the wall, which was now the floor. As she started to stand, she noticed her hands were tinted orange.

"No, no, no. Not now." Even if she made it to the window, she would go into withdrawal within the hour and her condition would be worse by the end of the day. But if she went back for it, not only would she endanger herself just by remaining on the ship, she would also be operating under a drugged fog in this life-and-death scenario. The lights flickered for a moment, then went dead again.

Heartly turned back. It was a long way to her quarters, but she would be in a lot more trouble if she didn't get the Compound. She'd brought enough of Dirk's Compound to last her for a few weeks more, which, considering her current situation, was the only silver lining she could see at the moment.

As she walked through the ship, she didn't find a single person still alive. She found plenty of bodies, but none of them with heartbeats. She became acutely aware of all the sounds surrounding her, trying to make out any grunts or groans of a potential trapped crewmate, but all she heard was her own footsteps and the groaning of the wreckage.

Heartly entered the stairwell, which would take her to crew's quarters. The ship, being on its side, forced her to climb along using the guardrails in order to make it to the next hallway. As she rolled out into the next corridor, she heard a loud crash followed by the sound of scurrying feet. She quickly looked around until she found a loose pipe. Ripping it off of the wall, she held it firmly in her right hand, then made her way slowly through the hallway. It was at this time that Heartly wished she hadn't been so adamant about having the last room on the left for her quarters. Luckily for her, when the ship turned over, it put her room closer to the ground, so she wouldn't have to climb up into her room and she merely had to jump down to leave.

When she opened the door, something leaped out at her. It scratched and clawed, but she automatically shoved it away and stepped back. She stood up, ready to swing her pipe at whatever had tried to attack her, but saw nothing. Whatever it was scampered away without a trace. She shook off the attack and returned to the door of her room. Steadying herself on the doorframe, she dropped in and landed with a thud in a pile of her things, which had fallen down in the crash-landing.

"Damnit. I should have thought this through a little better," Heartly growled as she dislodged her twisted ankle from in between the legs of her bedside table. She tore through the pile of junk collected at the bottom of her room, looking for a black case with two red lines on it.

"Need a hand?" Heartly snapped around to see Grewder standing in her doorway, feet above her. He seemed to have added a new scar to his face. "I know most people wouldn't say they're happy to see my mug, but I imagine you might be right now."

Relief lifted some of the weight from her shoulders, but she kept it at bay behind a lack of expression. "Why am I not surprised?" she said. Nothing seemed to ever stop the man. She couldn't help but crack a tiny smile.

"I might be able to answer that once we're actually out of here alive, Major," Grewder said.

"Yeah. I, uh…I just need to find something before I can leave," Heartly said. She hadn't told anyone about her use of Dirk's Compound since working for the Company, and she didn't plan on starting now.

"That stuff so your skin isn't orange? What is it, Dick's Solution?"

She blinked at him. "Dirk's Compound. How did you know?"

"It's hard not to notice it," Grewder replied. He seemed to have no opinion of her addiction one way or the other. "Is it in a black case?" Heartly nodded. "Under the clock."

She turned the clock over and there it was. She clutched it to her chest and squeezed it slightly. "Let's get out of here."

"I've read about some of the shit that happens to people who can't get a hold of that stuff when they need it. I hope you got a lot," Grewder said.

Heartly glanced at him and gave a curt nod. She walked to the bed, which was bolted to the floor, and used it to climb closer to the door. When she had gotten to the top of the bed, she extended her hand and Grewder grabbed it, yanking her out into the hallway with one swift tug.

"I think, at this point, our best bet is still to head to the front window. If we can break the glass, we can be out in no time," Heartly said.

"We'd never be able to break the plasma."

"I was hoping something in the cargo hold would help out with that part."

"Not a chance. Those windows are designed so nothing gets out and nothing gets in. A steel pipe ain't gonna do jack to that thing."

"So what do you suggest?" she asked. Her Master Sergeant just shot her an apathetic glare. "That's what I thought. Isn't there a plasma weapon on board somewhere? Don't you have one?"

"Not any more. Lost it in the landing. You tend to lose things when you're tumbling hundreds of yards."

"Maybe it cracked in the landing. Maybe there's a weapon still useable here. The window's still the closest exit by a mile." Heartly tried to speak with confidence but hadn't even managed to entirely convince herself.

"Maybe. If we want to get off this ship before dark and find a safe place for the night, that's our only option."

The pair made their way down the hallway and back to the window. "What happened to the specimen and your crew?" she asked.

Another violent shake gripped the wreckage, this time showering sparks on them from the shattered lights. Grewder reached out and gripped Heartly's wrist as she lost her balance. "You gonna make it?" he asked.

Heartly shook off his grip and refused to meet his gaze. "As long as you tell me what the hell happened in the cargo hold."

Grewder grunted. "No clue."

"Use your imagination."

He glanced at her for a few seconds, then stepped over a pile of wiring. "When the engines started having issues, I went down to the cargo hold to check on the crate. Some of the crew had been monitoring the specimen's movement since we'd brought it aboard. Told me it'd been swaying but seemed pretty subdued. As soon as they'd finished explaining, the ship jerked and some kind of explosion opened the cage. The thing didn't budge, but as soon as my guys moved to surround it, they dropped dead."

"It killed them?"

"Maybe, somehow. The damn creature never lifted a finger, but my men died instantly with no other force or injury. The fear in their faces was something I've never seen…"

Heartly turned to look at him, noticing the twitch in one of his memory-glazed eyes. She cleared her throat, and he turned to her again as if he'd never stopped talking.

"I've faced death with these boys before, but this was something different."

"How come you aren't dead?" Heartly asked, trying hard, even despite Grewder's knowledge, to keep her orange hands from shaking.

"I don't know. It didn't come after me, just stood up and walked away. But it got a good look at me before it left. I know it sounds like a wad of bullshit, Major, but I heard it in my head." Heartly turned to meet his gaze. "Told me to remember this."

Heartly decided to ignore the tiny shudder moving the giant of a man. "Well, it attacked me."

"What?"

"It pounced out of my room. No clue how it got in there in the first place, but when I swung at it, it disappeared. And it makes me wonder why the sudden change in strategy."

"Your guess is as good as mine," Grewder replied. "The Company didn't tell me anything about it, either."

When the pair finally reached the plasma window, they found it wholly intact and without a scratch on it. They rummaged through the wreckage for a plasma weapon, but to no avail.

"So what do we d—" A shriek cut her off. An ungodly howl shook the pair to their bones. They covered their ears but the shriek did not decrease in volume or dissipate. When it ended, they heard a thud hit the ground, followed by the shattering of glass. They looked up to see a hole in the plasma window, and when they approached the hole to glance out, all that remained was a trail of odd footprints leading from the wreck. "Never mind," Heartly finished. "I know what we do next."

"What would that be?"

"We go after that thing."

Chapter 23

Franklin strode down the corridor leading from the medical bay, having instructed Zoe to organize moving all the affected crew there from the lab so they could be closely monitored.

The change in Dr Robinsons status made all the affected unpredictable. He needed to know if one of them has another outburst of information.

He walked aimlessly but with purpose, unsure of where he was going. His mind whirled in conflicting thoughts and emotions. Had he really just spoken to Dirk? Was he being tricked? How was he supposed to blow up the *Ark*? He was supposed to protect it, not destroy it so they could never go home. Did the *Ark* have a self-destruct? Could he get back together with Zoe?

The last thought stopped him in his tracks. Of all the things he had to think about, his personal life was the lowest priority, but the thought had just entered his mind of its own accord. In annoyance, Franklin shook his head as if the very act could force the last thought out. Taking stock of where he was, he considered his possible courses of action. If he was to believe Dirk's words through Dr. Robinson, there was only one course of action—and it was, technically, a direct order from the expedition leader. If he believed.

Did he? Did he want to? By believing it, he would be stranding the whole expedition on this planet. "I need to find Johnson," he said aloud, the sound of his own voice seeming to shake him out of his temporary state of shock. "Oh, great. Now I'm talking to myself. Next I'll be hearing things that are completely impossible. Yeah, that already happened."

Laughing at his own facetiousness, Franklin made his way toward the bridge, where he hoped Arthur would be finishing the communications work needed to get that tiny pod moving again. He needed the help of the ship's pilot if he was going to destroy the *Ark*. With his mind seemingly made up, Franklin felt as if a weight had lifted from him.

When he entered the bridge, he heard Johnson swearing from underneath the very same console as before. "I'm guessing that just fixing the pod isn't enough?"

"I'm a bloody pilot, not a technician. I thought we were good to go, but the *Arks* comms is still not functioning right," Johnson muttered as he pulled himself out from under the console and stood to face Franklin.

"Hey, don't blame me," Franklin replied. "It was your idea. Look, that doesn't matter right now. We have something a lot more important, and I need you to back me up."

Johnson's retort froze on his lips as he saw the seriousness of Franklin's expression. "What's up? What's happened?"

190

Franklin paused before answering, getting his thoughts and emotions in check. With as calm a tone as he could manage he said, "We need to destroy the *Ark*."

"We need to *what*?" Johnson barked, staring at Franklin and seemingly trying to ascertain if the head of security had been either joking—badly—or was under some sort of influence.

"Arthur, calm down. I've just had a major shock and—"

Franklin didn't get the chance to finish the sentence before Johnson shouted, "I need to calm down? You've just said we need to destroy the *Ark*, and you want me to be calm about it? Are you bloody *insane*?"

It wasn't really a question and Franklin understood the implication. He let Johnson rant on for a few moments before he spoke again. "Arthur," Franklin began calmly, "look at me." He paused, waiting for Johnson to make eye contact, the shorter pilot looking up at the tall man. "I'm not insane, I'm not drunk, and I'm not on any illegal substance. I'm asking for you to listen to me for a moment and I'm asking for your help."

Johnson looked at Franklin, deep into his eyes, noticing the very serious, if somewhat shaken, expression on his face. "What's happened?" he asked finally.

"Dr. Forret—Dirk—has just gotten a message to me."

"How? I thought he was missing. I've been trying to get this bloody pod moving, as you told me, in order to go looking for him, and now you tell me he got a message to you. How?" Johnson, realizing he had just repeated himself, stopped talking.

Franklin sighed and sat down on the nearest seat. After what seemed an age, he spoke slowly as if to convince himself as well as the pilot. "Dirk spoke through Dr. Robinson." Franklin paused, raising his hand to stop Johnson interrupting him with what he was sure were numerous questions. "Dirk used some form of telepathy—don't ask me how. And before you ask, yes, I'm sure it was him. I just know. He told both Dr. Rowens and myself that we need to destroy the *Ark*, and he sounded—sorry, the voice of Dr. Robinson sounded as if this is time-critical."

Johnson stood mute. Franklin watched as a series of conflicting thoughts and emotions reflected on Johnson's face. *Not much of a poker player*, Franklin thought, then berated himself for his usual flippancy at a time like this. "Damn, this is stressing me out just as much as you. Maybe more," he said. "I'm the one who heard the instruction and I'm trying to figure out if I've gone insane or not."

"You look too bloody sane for my liking," muttered Johnson, eying him.

"Thanks." Franklin allowed himself to grin. "I think."

Johnson sat down facing Franklin, his face an open map of his thoughts on the situation and his consideration of all the variables. Franklin stayed quiet, giving the pilot a moment to think.

After a few minutes, Johnson looked up and said, "We need to get the chief engineer up here. I'm a pilot and I know how to keep the *Ark* in good condition, not how to destroy it. We need someone who knows how everything works."

"Does this mean you believe me?" Franklin asked.

"Yeah. I believe that you believe what you're saying," Johnson replied. "It doesn't mean I have to bloody like it," he added, more for himself than for Franklin.

Johnson stood and Franklin watched him walk toward the flight control and open a secret compartment on the decking below his chair. Curious, Franklin joined him as the pilot removed a small device.

Johnson turned, facing the approaching Franklin. "What's that?" Franklin asked.

"An iTransmit," Johnson said. "Never leave home without one."

Johnson handed the black, rectangular device to Franklin, who took it gingerly and with a disproportionate amount of reverence. "How did you manage to get one of these?" he asked.

"Do you really think I would travel to the arse-end of nowhere without some means of contacting home?" Johnson asked.

"But they cost a fortune." Franklin could only stare at the pilot.

"Worth every penny," Johnson said. "It may save our hides, if we're lucky."

The iTransmit, produced by one of Earth's few remaining mega-companies, was the height of cutting-edge technology. Unlike its predecessors, the mobile (or cell) phone, it didn't use conventional technology like radio waves or subspace. Instead, it used the principles behind quantum physics and literally defied reality. The exact science behind it was a closely guarded company secret, and any attempts to reverse engineer the device would be met with catastrophic failure. One really did not want a device that played around with quantum physics exploding without warning.

On the plus side, the iTransmit could call from anywhere in the known universe to anywhere else, and even great distances caused absolutely no time delay. It was a marvel of modern technology and cost the same as a small continent. How Johnson ever managed to own one was beyond belief, but Franklin had never been happier to see one.

"We don't *have* to be stranded," Franklin said aloud. The grin he received from Johnson made him realize he had just stated the obvious, but at that moment, he didn't care. His own grin matched that of the pilot, and suddenly, things didn't seem quite so bleak.

"Just because we can call someone doesn't mean this is going to be easy," Johnson said, breaking the tide of optimism emanating from Franklin.

"What do you mean?" Franklin asked.

"Well, for a start, it's going to take a fair bit of time and money to send someone out here to come and rescue us. That's if whoever we call is inclined to come out here in the first place," Johnson replied.

Franklin considered that fact. It made sense. They were about to destroy a very expensive project and that wasn't going to make people happy. That thought brought him back to the problem at hand. "Let's worry about that later. Right now, we need to get the right people together and sort our current problem out. Getting someone to rescue us might become a moot point unless we figure out what's happening right here, right now." Johnson nodded and placed the iTransmit device into one of the many pockets of his flight suit. "Just keep that thing safe, all right? It's our life-line and probably our only one unless Dirk has suddenly developed some other skill we don't know about."

Johnson nodded and grinned at Franklin's attempt to lighten the mood with his reference to the project leader. "Will do, and I'll grab the chief engineer."

Franklin added, "I'll get my team together and explain the situation before we tell the rest of the crew. We might need them to stop a panic. Someone might not take to the idea of destroying the *Ark* as well as you did."

With a final nod to Franklin, Johnson left the bridge to make his way down to engineering. Franklin watched him go, feeling a lot better than he had only half an hour ago. He had an ally, he hoped. Now he needed to do his bit and hope that his own security teams didn't mutiny when they heard what needed to be done.

Leaving the bridge, Franklin strode toward the security center with his last thought running around in his mind. He really didn't want a mutiny from his own team, but what about the rest of the crew?

***

Korsakov turned back toward the oasis as a breeze stirred the sands. He paused, straining to hear if the voice existed in the breeze. He heard it, barely above a whisper, but couldn't discern the words. He tried to slow his breathing and strained to hear the voice. The whisper in the breeze came to him louder than before but barely louder than the breeze itself. '*He comes.*'

Not sure if he heard correctly, Korsakov wondered exactly who. The co-leader of the Sons-of-Mishrak he'd been meant to meet here?

'*He comes.*' The voice in his head was louder this time, the breeze stronger and whipping up the soft sand.

'*HE COMES!*'

Korsakov jumped at the strength of emotion behind the voice seemingly shouting inside his head. The breeze suddenly became a sharp wind, the sand flying wildly into the air. He turned toward the altar, a blue glow now resonating around it. The glow grew brighter. Suddenly, it exploded in a blinding flash of light, the wind cracking like a whip. Then, silence.

Blinded by having looked directly at the altar and the flare of light, he opened and closed his eyes, blinking away the tears and trying to see what happened. He heard movement where the co-leader of the Sons-of-Mishrak stood but still couldn't see anything.

His sight clearing slightly, Korsakov turned back toward where the altar rested. Although not clear, he thought he saw something crouching, trying to stand. Blinking rapidly to clear both his sight and to force away the tears, he tried to see what exactly was going on. Then, in a voice he could never mistake, he heard a curse he never expected.

"Oh, *shit!*"

Chapter 24

Freedom. Glorious, happy freedom. Honest, life-affirming freedom. She was free. Finally, after all this time, she was free. The knowledge of the facts sang through her body like a choir of heavenly angels as she loped across the dunes. The energy of her joy spurred her forward at reckless speeds, but she didn't care. After a countless age of imprisonment and servitude, she had her life back. All the times she had silently begged for death, all the times she had raged against her confinement, and all the times she silently wept in her helpless cage of flesh, she never thought she would taste sweet freedom again.

The harsh, coarse sand scraped the soft pads of her hands and foot as she bounded carelessly across the desert. The hot, dry winds tore at her fur as the two suns slowly dipped toward the horizon. She could taste the baking air in her lungs as she drove her body forward. Finally, in the dark shadow of one of the dunes, she collapsed. Her arms and legs still twitched from the effort she had demanded of them.

Her vision dimmed as the exertion took its toll on her. But she did not care. The joys she felt in her soul were worth any price.

***

Heartly trudged across the dry, open desert with the Master Sergeant. She glanced over her shoulder and looked at her ship in the distance. It still sat in the center of the strange, spongy mass in which they'd crashed. It would be hell to try to get it space-worthy again, if they could even salvage anything. Hopefully, they could smuggle themselves and hitch a ride on the *Ark* if it came to a worst-case scenario. But if they could bag the specimen and get the hell off this demon planet in their own ship, she'd have far less to worry about.

As she staggered through the sands, she absently scratched at her neck. The shakes had started to ease off; maybe she could postpone taking a dose for a while. She touched the hard plastic case in her pocket for reassurance. On the bright side, at least she had enough Compound to last for several weeks. As Heartly was lost in her thoughts, she didn't realize that her companion had stopped walking until she ran into his back.

"What the h—" Heartly started to say, but was silenced when she saw the look on Grewder's face. He motioned toward the dune ahead of them, but she could not see anything important. He jabbed two fingers at his eyes and then toward the shadow of the nearest dune. It took her a second or two to realize that the tracks had stopped. She squinted against the setting twin suns and stared into the shadows. It was there. The specimen looked like it was sleeping, or maybe resting.

The Master Sergeant pulled his stun pistol from its holster

and adjusted the lever on its side. She saw him crank it up to its highest setting and guessed he wasn't taking any chances. He motioned for her to stay here and keep quiet. She nodded her understanding as the big man turned and slid silently down the sandy hill. He crept closer to the sleeping humanoid as he pulled a pair of restraining cuffs from his belt. Hopefully, they'd be able to capture it alive again and this time keep it from killing anyone else.

***

Grewder crept right up to the specimen. He guessed it had run itself to the ground and passed out from exhaustion. Carefully, he extended one of the cuffs toward its wrists. The C-shaped plastic restraint would snap shut as soon as it met flesh. With exaggerated slowness, he finally touched the creature. The plastic device made a buzzing noise as the plastic band snapped out and closed the circle. The humanoid's eyes flew open.

He stared into the laser blue gaze and froze. The world seemed to instantly become silent. Nothing moved around them; the shifting grains of sand hung suspended in midair. The first few stars of the night twinkling in the sky seemed to have dulled. He saw the major hiding on top of the dune, but her hair blown by the wind was frozen in place. Grewder looked back at the humanoid and stared into its strange, glowing, azure eyes.

"Sean," Amber said, looking up at him.

"What? You can't... How can...?" He gazed down at her.

"It's okay, Sean. I can explain. Just don't hurt me," his fiancée pleaded.

Grewder looked down at the woman lying in the shadows. It was her; everything about her was perfect, except for her eyes. As Amber looked up at him, her eyes glowed a bright blue. He was confused; how did she get here? How did he get here? Where were they? The restraining cuffs slipped from his numb fingers and into the desert sands. This was a lie, a trick, an illusion. Part of his brain screamed at him, but the rest of him didn't care.

"Oh, Sean, what happened to your face?" She reached up and ran her soft fingers against his ragged, tortured flesh. A shiver raced down his spine at her touch, and he could feel the warmth of her skin. The familiar smell of jasmine mixed with the hot, dry desert air. Cold, icy claws of sorrow tore at the insides of his chest. Of all the wounds he'd ever suffered in combat, this was one that could never heal.

"You're not real. You died. I watched you die," he said through gritted teeth, his eyes burning as he looked at her.

"I'm sorry, I don't want to hurt you. I just want to help. I have so much to make up for," Amber said as she leaned her head against his chest.

Grewder's fingers slowly encircled Amber's neck. He began to squeeze, but only to the point before it would become painful. "I should snap your neck right now," he told her. The promise of violence hung heavy in his sad voice.

"It's the least I deserve, Sean. You don't know how much damage I've done. How many people I've made suffer because of my arrogance. If the stranger had not freed me, I would still be a slave. Killing me would barely scratch the surface of my sins. When she was alive, she loved you so much. I wish you had taken a different path after your futures parted," she said, looking up at him as his fingers closed tighter around her neck.

"*You're...a...lie*!" he growled at her and began to squeeze. She only smiled at him, and suddenly his mind filled with all of their experiences. He felt every second he had loved her all over again. Every secret smile, every hidden glance, every intimate moment flooded through him like an apocalyptic avalanche. It made him suddenly taste the sourness he had allowed his life to become.

He had boxed all the wonderful memories up and shoved them deep inside of his soul. He had punished himself countless times for being so weak instead of cherishing the brief beauty they had had together. He'd buried his love for her the same day he'd buried her body. The injustice he had inflicted upon himself was now laid bare for him to see.

"I'm sorry, Sean. I know how much it hurts. I know how much you loved her. But I need your help now. The danger here is beyond your understanding, but I want to make amends. I want to make it right. I want to help you heal," Amber told him.

Grewder looked down into Amber's eyes as a storm of emotions poured through his soul. He wrapped his arms around her, pulling her to his chest, held her tight, and wept. The scent of jasmine flooded his nose. It was her scent. The smell he would always associate with her. They stood together for a long time until finally she looked up at him.

"Will you help me, Sean?"

"Whatever I can do, I'm yours, body and soul," he told her as he leaned down and their lips met.

The major would have found the whole scene totally unbelievable if it wasn't for the fact that she was almost dead. She lay on the crimson-colored sands at the top of the dune, the little black case opened to reveal a small army of useless, shattered glass vials. Their powdery orange contents fluttered away on the dry desert winds.

Heartly was happy to accept the cold, dark embrace dragging her into the shadowy beyond. She didn't care anymore; let it all end. As she slowly sank into the twilight oblivion of death, she welcomed it. The final step on her journey through life. No more cares or worries from this point on, nothing but peace and tranquility. Just as she was about to slip past the boundaries of this world, a hand plunged into the freezing waters and grasped her wrist. Its warmth flowed into her and seemed to strangely snap her into awareness of the situation. The Major was not ready to die yet. She had a job—no, a duty to fulfill. She grabbed onto the only thing anchoring her in the realm of the living and clung on for dear life. A strong hand pulled her from the freezing waters of death.

Sean watched as Amber sat with Heartly's head in her lap. The major did not look good. Large, orange sores had appeared on her skin. He had read somewhere that the compound was made of some type of fungus, and if you didn't take regular doses, the fungus germinated in the body. He held the Major's hand while his dead lover seemed to pray for her. Amazingly, as he watched, the angry, orange blotches slowly receded until they were nothing more than slightly discolored skin. When almost all of the growths had disappeared, Heartly suddenly sat up, taking in a lungful of air.

"Major, you're alive," the big man said with a smile.

"I didn't...what...who?" the woman asked, looking around. She saw the Master Sergeant sitting in the sand next to her, holding her hand. When she looked behind her, she saw the humanoid kneeling there. She reached down to her holster to pull out her sidearm but found it empty.

"It's okay, ma'am, she's friendly." Heartly looked into Grewder's eyes; they were lit with a blue glow.

"Grewder, have you lost your fucking mind?" she said, crawling backwards through the sand away from them.

"You don't need to be afraid, Major. She's not going to hurt us. She's explained everything to me." The man reached out and took the creature's hand.

"It's gotten in your fucking head, you idiot." Heartly picked up a half-buried rock from the sand and threatened the two with it.

A look of sadness crossed the thing's face as it cast its eyes toward the ground. It half looked at the Sergeant as if it spoke to him. The look of happiness slowly drained from the man's face and he turned back to the Major.

"She said, if you want to kill her, go ahead."

"What kind of fucking trick is this?" Heartly said, brandishing the rock. "Grewder, you saw this thing slaughter the men without a second thought. And now you're on its damn side? Has the whole bleeding universe just gone crazy?"

"No, Ma'am. Amber gave herself up willingly. The only thing she's asking is that we help her."

"That's a negative, Master Sergeant. We're securing the specimen and taking it back to the ship. We're not helping this thing."

"Understood, Ma'am. But I must point out that she saved your life," Grewder said as he held the creature's hand, trying to comfort it.

"What in the nine hells are you talking about?"

"We found you almost dead, Ma'am. It looks like your compound was damaged in the crash and you were unable to dose." He motioned toward a half-buried, black plastic container. The memories of just before she passed out filtered back into the Major's head. She vividly remembered the terror of opening the black case and seeing all the little ampoules smashed. She'd tried to call out to Grewder but had lacked the strength to make even the smallest whimper. Finally, the pain had ceased when she'd blacked out.

"You can't...how did...you..." The Major's words wouldn't

come out right. She couldn't think of what to say that wouldn't sound completely stupid. Her brain seized up at the thought of this monster saving her life.

"Please, Ma'am, help us save the Earth. Help us destroy the evil unleashed here."

Heartly stood and paced back and forth in the sand as she ran her fingers through her hair, trying to organize her thoughts. "How do we know we can trust it?"

"I trust her, Ma'am. Do you trust me?"

"Honestly, Master Sergeant, no. But what choice do I have? What does it need us to do?"

"She needs our help to get back to her ship."

"She? This thing has a ship?"

"Yes, Ma'am, but she made herself forget where the key was so the evil couldn't use it to get off the planet."

"Hum. Well, Grewder, it looks like we just took another contract."

Chapter 25

His vision slowly cleared, and Korsakov realized that the figure before him by the altar was Dirk. He let out a sigh of relief but was alarmed when his friend looked up at him and their eyes met. His captain now had striking blue eyes, and even in the bright light, Korsakov could see they glowed.

Behind him, he heard the grunting of a humanoid he had been puppeteered to meet. The creature took a few steps toward Dirk, angry at being taken by surprise yet also curious, tilting his head side to side as he took in the unexpected appearance of Dirks eyes.

Dirk looked past Korsakov toward the Son-of-Mishrak and smiled. The humanoid's large eyes glazed over and his face contorted into a number of expressions, the last of which was pure fear, before his eyes rolled back into his head and he fell to the ground in a deep sleep.

"That won't last long," Dirk said, "but it should give me the time I need." He stepped forward toward Korsakov and rested a hand on his shoulder. His eyes showed sympathy, but Korsakov didn't have time to wonder why. "I'm sorry, Rodney."

Before he could even register that Dirk had spoken, he sensed his friend in his mind, telling him to relax. He felt him sifting through only his most recent memories. One by one, he was forced to remember his actions as he relived the past few days.

***

They began with the memory of the first encounter with the humanoids, the one that started it all.

Korsakov stood on the rocky outcrop, staring in amazement down at the oasis that seemed to have suddenly appeared before them. Behind him, a few of the scientists talked excitedly amongst themselves, speculating on the kinds of things they could discover in this part of the planet.

"You wanted to examine those holes in the ground, right Jenny? On the other side of the hill?" he asked

"Yep!" Jenny said enthusiastically from behind him.

"Good. I'm going down to have a look around, and I'll wait for you to join me once you're ready."

"All right!" Franklin smiled wide, kneeling down to help gather Jenny's equipment for her.

Korsakov turned toward the other scientists and nodded, letting them know they could follow Franklin. Jenny took a step toward him with a smile

"Thanks, Rod."

Seeing Jenny's face sent shocks of emotion through Korsakov's mind, and it took him a moment to realize these emotions came from Dirk inside his memory.

Korsakov headed down the hill and into the thick growth of foliage. It was quiet here and smelled of rich life and wet soil. He came upon a clearing within the trees, where a large white stone stood in stark contrast to all the green, set between two large pillars and encircled by other smaller stones. He stopped, having come suddenly face to face with a group of three humanoid creatures covered in fur and a shimmering coating of what looked like scales. They stared at him, unblinkingly, with large emerald eyes. A small voice echoed in his mind, and he had an overwhelming sense of kindness and trust.

'We are the Sons of Life.' The voice spoke in his mind, and Korsakov's eyes grew wide. The voice sounded female. *'You must leave here immediately. It is not safe. The Sons-of-Mishrak are coming.'*

"We're just scientists on a peaceful expedition to study the wildlife on the planet," he said slowly, wondering how these new beings understood both his speech and his thoughts. "We're not here to hurt anyone."

'You may not be, but they are. The Sons-of-Mishrak—'

'Are here.'

Korsakov spun on his heels. A sheet of green light spread between the two pillars near the single white stone, and three more humanoids stepped out of it. The female who had interrupted their conversation snarled and attacked the three others with which he'd been speaking. In a matter of seconds, a fight broke out, and he tried to back away from them unnoticed. He opened his mouth to call out for Franklin, but his foot found a jutting rock and he fell backwards. As he hit the ground, bruising his arms and legs on the rocks beneath him, his hand landed on something squishy.

Almost immediately, a sharp pain shot through his hand

and up his arm. Looking down, he saw a small, striped worm inching away.

"Hello, Daddy." Korsakov looked up to see a young boy of six staring down at him curiously. "Why are you on the floor, Daddy?" The sand and altar had disappeared, replaced with Korsakov's screened-in porch, his in-ground pool sparkling in the background.

This can't be happening, he thought. *Not Robin. It's not Robin.* He squeezed his eyes shut, desperately trying to block out the sound of the hellish nightmare into which he'd fallen.

"Can I go swimming, Daddy?" A loud splash forced his eyes open, and Robin floated motionless on the surface, the water turning deep red from the blood pouring out of his cracked skull.

"No! No, no, no...please..."

Korsakov jumped to his feet and the pool was gone. He stood on the scorching sand, two suns blazing overhead. The Sons-of-Mishrak tapped the ground and three worms came up from beneath the rocks, biting the humanoids with whom he'd first communicated. Their eyes glazed over and they sat cross-legged by the white stone, unmoving.

'You are strong.' A male voice spoke into his mind this time. The three humanoids who had won the fight looked at him, impressed. Voices from over the dunes drifted on the wind, and the three exchanged glances. The female stepped forward, and suddenly it wasn't a strange, furry woman. It was Olivia.

"Liv...I thought...I thought you left me," he said, uncertain. He knew it couldn't possibly be her, but the sadness in her eyes, the loss and the grief and the hopelessness—it couldn't have been anyone else. He shook his head, trying to rid himself of the cursed vision, but she refused to disappear the way the image of Robin had.

'How could you let him die, Rodney? How could you lose our baby boy?' Her tone was sharp and accusing, even in his mind

"It was an accident. You know that.

'You broke me, Rodney. You could make up for it, you know. If you just do one little thing for me, I will forgive you. I'll take away the nightmares.'

Without question, he nodded. He would do anything to stop the horrible visions haunting him whenever he saw a family together or a swimming pool.

'Take these to the Ark, *Rodney. All four of them. They need to be there. Then come to me by the altar.'* She reached a hand out and brushed his cheek lightly, wiping away his tears. He looked over to the four humanoids who sat on the ground, cross-legged, staring into the distance. The fourth one, who had left her companions to join those sitting, looked up at him and winked, and he realized she wasn't in a trance like the others. She reached down by her legs, where he saw one of her ankles ended in a stump where a foot should have been. She grabbed a small worm from beside a rock and tucked it under her fur, then reassumed the catatonic position. The two remaining Sons-of-Mishrak walked off toward the pillars, disappearing in the sands.

"Korsakov? Is that you? What the—"

He turned around to see Franklin inspecting the entranced humanoids. The others on the exploration team followed closely behind Franklin, and Dr. Robinson came to inspect the white stone. She said it appeared to be some sort of altar, and Korsakov couldn't find it in him to say anything about what he'd just learned. He ordered the humanoids to be taken aboard the expedition pod and brought to the *Ark* for examination. Franklin tried to argue, but Korsakov put his foot down and would not stand for disagreement. Once they were loaded onto the pod, he slid back into the sands and walked to the two pillars. A green light flashed between them, and he disappeared after the humanoids.

***

He found himself in a white stone room with a two-headed idol in the back. Within his mind, he felt Dirk's recognition of the memory, of the ritual the doctor himself had experienced, as Korsakov relived the same process.

Stripped of his clothing, he knelt on his hands and knees before the idol. The male humanoid stood by the pillars in the back of the room. The female, who still appeared as Olivia, opened her mouth and cooed melodically. She went through the motions of pulling out the strange plants and placing them lovingly on his shoulders and arms. When she stopped her singing, she smiled down at him.

Mishrak will guide you.

Then she left, followed by the male humanoid, leaving him alone in the room with the pain of the plants digging their barbs into his skin.

From four small holes carved in the wall came four small worms inching toward him. He struggled as they drew closer—until he realized they had no interest in him, only crawling toward the sweat-drenched soil in front of him. A movement caught his eye, and a lizard darted out from a corner. The small lizard stopped for a moment, eyed a nearby worm, and in two quick movements swallowed it whole. It charged after two more worms, swallowing them in the same fashion. The fourth worm had wiggled its way onto Korsakov's arm, and the lizard didn't hesitate. It jumped onto his arm and bit down on the worm, sinking its teeth into a mouthful of human flesh as well.

Wincing in pain, Korsakov glanced down at the small beads of blood forming along the bite. A warm sensation rippled through his body and he yawned, suddenly very tired. Was the lizard venomous? A gust of wind blew into the room, and streams of sand danced on the breeze, swirling into the form of a native humanoid.

'The toxin will wear off soon, Rodney. It has killed the worm larvae in your blood. Now we require your aid.'

Visions swirled in his head, and he sensed Dirk's understanding of his memory in the back of his mind. He seemed to fast-forward through the memory, through the explanation of the blood feud and the Sons-of-Mishrak.

'You must become one of them, Rodney. Gain their trust. Get to Mishrak. We will guide you. We shall give you a gift to ease your troubles.'

Sand swirled around his head, clouding his thoughts. When the presence pulled back, a tangible shield remained in his mind.

'Mishrak cannot enter your mind, nor can his followers. You are under our protection, human. Fare you well.'

Korsakov walked to the pillars in the back of the room. The green light shone once more, and he found himself standing with the two humanoids by the altar.

***

"You are changed," the female said aloud, confused. Her fur rippled in a light breeze.

"It was the will of Mishrak," he told her.

She bowed her head and walked toward the tree line. "Follow."

She led him deeper into the oasis, through the thickening, lush forest. Korsakov could feel Dirk's surprise in his mind through the replay of the event. Even with two suns, only a few faint rays broke through the canopy to reach the forest floor.

They soon came to a large clearing. In the center sat another giant white stone, much like the one back at P13-04, except this one had a large crack coursing from the top and spreading down to the center of the stone. The symbol of two circles surrounded by rays was carved into the rock, but the crack split it in half. The trees around the stone shot high into the sky, and at the tops sat round structures resembling house-sized clay jars. Some were wider than others, and some were as small as walk-in closets.

The two humanoids took him up a wooden ramp and over two bridges to a large building. They sat inside at a long wooden table lined with benches.

"You have been chosen by Mishrak. You will do his bidding," the male said. A look passed between the two humanoids, and Korsakov could tell they spoke silently to each other. A flash of anger crossed the male's face, but the female spoke despite the continued looks they shared.

"Mishrak sees all, as does the Company. The army is forming. Our companion sits in your ship now. Once it is clear, you can use your pod key to summon the smaller ships to our village. That is your duty. It is the will of Mishrak."

It took all of his willpower not to convey any emotion across his features as he listened to the humanoid speak. He was afraid for his friends and wondered if they were searching for him. He quickly thought of a plan. If he could get in good with the female, the male's discontent would make no difference. Maybe he could even plot them against each other in the future.

"I have seen the truth." He concentrated on speaking confidently and with purpose, hoping they believed him. "My mind is clear now, except I still see my beautiful Olivia standing before me. Does that bother you?" He asked the female humanoid, with as much conviction as he could muster.

The female seemed shocked, but a small smile formed on her lips. "That is acceptable," was her only response before she tossed an annoyed look toward the male. "Come, I will show you to your quarters."

They walked over a few more bridges and up a rope ladder until they reached a small building. Korsakov was shocked to see Dr. Robinson inside. She sat in a trance, staring at a wall. He couldn't tell if she currently experienced hallucinations or if she had been bitten by a worm.

Dr. Robinson didn't move at all for the two days they stayed there. On the third morning, the female humanoid entered the small structure, carrying Korsakov's backpack. He had completely forgotten they had taken it from him the day they put him in the white stone room. Inside was the master pod key to the *Ark*'s exploration pods. He remembered putting it in his bag as they'd left the *Ark* to explore P13-04, knowing they could use it to call up a second pod if they ran out of space in the first one.

"Come now, Human of Mishrak. It is time to call the pods." With that simple statement, she turned and left. Dr. Robinson silently rose from her place by the wall and walked out the door.

He stood to follow her, but not before promising himself that he would not harm his crewmates.

***

After a short walk through the jungle oasis, they reached the tree line. Dr. Robinson walked out on her own. Korsakov looked at the female humanoid questioningly.

"She is of the Company. Traitors cannot be trusted with their own minds." It didn't seem to make sense, but he nodded and looked through the trees where she had walked out into the open. He couldn't see what was happening, but the humanoids he traveled with all seemed to be listening very closely. "Go now."

He took a deep breath and walked into the light, pressing buttons on the control key to program the pods to come to the oasis. To his surprise, Dirk stood by the altar with some of the doctors from the *Ark*. He almost had to duck as a bright blue object flew toward him. It attached to the control key like a magnet, and the battery meter on the device jumped from halfway depleted to fully charged.

Korsakov noted the humanoids coming out from between the trees and saw the looks in their eyes. He figured they used the radio frequency from the remote as a sort of telepathic magnifier, increasing their ability to control the once-catatonic humanoids.

Something hit him in the back, and he turned just in time to see a rock aiming for his head before everything went black.

When his eyes fluttered open, he saw the female humanoid behind Dirk and called out to her.

"My love," he said, hoping to further instill a feeling of trust in her. The sand-beings had told him they needed him on the inside. He couldn't quit now.

Dirk knew this part all too well, and rushed past Korsakov's memory of his beating and binding.

***

Dirk watched his own experience of the white stone room, this time through Korsakov's eyes.

When Korsakov was asked why he was doing this, he mentioned the formation of an army. *Was that right?* he thought. *They spoke of an army. Surely that's what we're doing here.* Out of the corner of his eye, he caught a glance pass between the two humanoids. Korsakov knew he didn't know much of their plans.

The memory rushed by again as they escorted Dirk into the white stone room and went about the ritual. It slowed down again after leaving Dirk alone.

"We will take you to your quarters now, Human of Mish-rak," the female humanoid said.

"What about Dirk?" Korsakov asked, kneeling down on one knee and pretending to be interested in a small blue rock on the ground. He tried not to sound too anxious, but he knew a trace of uncertainty shone through his feigned nonchalance

"He is no longer your concern. He speaks to Mishrak, now."

Without another word, Korsakov was led back to the forest. They reached the tree village and climbed a series of wooden ramps to a medium-sized structure, roughly the size of an exploration pod.

"You will stay here."

Those were the last words he heard for nearly two days. He was left mostly to himself but was not permitted to wander far around the village. When the female finally returned, it was only to inform him that he would be traveling back to the altar, this time on his own.

"You are summoned by our commander. He speaks for Mishrak."

***

Korsakov walked up to the large, white stone to meet the Son-of-Mishrak. He saw a thin, gray cloud in the distance, the aftereffect of what looked to be an explosion, though it disappeared quickly. The sands suddenly swirled around him, forming the shape of a large bear.

The first animal he had ever studied as a young grad student had been a Red Bear from Gallenix Nine, the third moon of Castellina. The large, furry beast grew to six times the size of a man and was extremely endangered. As settlers had discovered the bountiful resources they could gather on the planet, the bear's habitat had been slowly cleared away, pushing the animals to the edge of the woods and the edge of extinction. Any bears that had stood against the settlers had met the deadly end of a ray gun.

Even in the face of adversity, one of the creatures had fought harder than the rest and survived to enact several attacks. Korsakov had volunteered to track the great beast and spent three months living alone in the forests, carefully following the bear and documenting its actions. It wasn't until the short winter set in that he'd realized the bear was a mother with a cub stashed away in her den. Closer inspection showed the cub had been injured and couldn't walk. The mother bear had been fighting back settlers to protect her young.

Korsakov knew when the sands formed the image of a bear that he was being told to stay strong and fight for his kind, even if it seemed hopeless.

***

Dirk finally released his friend from the mental connection, and as they blinked in the bright sunlight, Korsakov looked at Dirk and watched tears roll down the man's cheeks. After taking a few deep breaths, Dirk straightened his shoulders and looked into Korsakov's eyes. They knew they were on the same side, and they knew they had to stop Mishrak.

Chapter 26

E steemed colleague and friend, Dr. Declan Hathaway, always had a saying. "No matter how nature appears on the surface, be it serene and placid or tumultuous and chaotic, nature is a never-ending battle for survival and domination. Always remember that, Jenny."

Jenny opened her eyes and found herself in the Marcus Hoffman Auditorium seated center stage, three rows back.

If she concentrated, she could just sense that the other students, some listening as intently as she and others not quite so, were all just hollow images. Memories. She tried to hold onto them, but like a desert wanderer attempting to obtain the last dregs of a glass of water, they remained just out of her grasp.

Shortly, the only two left in the massive theater were herself and the speaker, Dirk Forrett. He was dressed in very modest brown slacks and a red cardigan beneath his worn blazer—just as he'd been the first time she ever saw him. He looked down from the podium and smiled.

"This isn't real, is it?" she asked him. She noticed then that she wasn't wearing any shoes.

He smiled and took a small breath. "I suppose that depends."

She stood up from her seat and made her way to the end of the aisle, never taking her eyes off him. "On what?"

"You, mostly." Dirk stepped away from the podium and sat down on the edge of the stage. He seemed quite different. "On your…" He paused and took a breath, emphasizing his next word. "…perspective."

Jenny stopped at the end of the aisle before deciding to take a few more steps toward him. Another figure stood stage-left behind the curtain. She only looked away briefly before looking back at the figure sitting before her. "You're not Dirk, are you?

He chuckled. "Again, I guess that depends on your perspective."

Jenny walked up to him and noticed a grating of cold, wrought metal where short, rough carpeting should be. It didn't seem safe, but she barely paid that any mind as she looked into Dirk's face. He smiled back with more confidence than usual— with much more resolution. This wasn't the Dirk she was accustomed to, but something existed behind his eyes, impossible to miss. Without question, she realized with whom she was speaking.

"No, it *is* you."

Dirk just smiled quietly.

"You've changed."

He turned toward the figure standing backstage before shifting back to Jenny. "You don't know the half of it." He reached a hand out to offer her a boost onto the stage, but she only folded

218

her arms.

"Dirk, what's going on?"

He held his hand out a moment longer before pulling back. "You're a scientist. If you had to wager a guess, what do *you* think is going on?"

Jenny stepped back and looked around at the lecture hall. The students, once seemingly real and tangible, had all disappeared and, while she couldn't be sure, there were definitely inconsistencies. She was sure she had arrived with shoes on, but now they were gone. She couldn't remember what shoes she had brought.

"I suppose this could be a dream, but that doesn't seem quite right. If it is, it's the most vivid dream I've ever had." Looking back to Dirk gave no satisfaction as to whether or not she had pegged the correct line of thinking. He seemed to just be interested in what she would say next.

"Go on."

She sighed, mildly irritated, and continued. "Well, I suppose all these images could be coming from my subconscious. It's the first place I..." She looked to Dirk, who just smiled knowingly. She quickly changed the direction of the sentence. "...realized what I wanted to do with my life."

Dirk continued to be infuriatingly quiet.

"I assume that's the case, considering it's a place that's..." She paused again as she slowly put the pieces together. "It's a place that's personal to me."

Dirk's eyes remained trained on her.

"So, I suppose the question there is: Is it by design or is it just a byproduct?" She bit her lip and paced as more ideas came to her.

Dirk hopped back up to the stage and slowly paced along-side her. "Keep going."

An excitement she hadn't felt since the early days of work-ing with Dirk welled up inside her. "If it's just a byproduct, I sup-pose the effects will eventually wear off. Hopefully, I'm not in any immediate danger in the meantime."

"One would hope," Dirk cut in.

"Quiet," she snapped but continued. "If it's not just some haphazard reaction and it truly is by design…"

"Then?"

"Then I need to find a way to get the hell out of here as soon as possible."

She gasped and stepped back as Dirk stopped pacing along with her and hopped down off the stage. "Good to know we're on the same page, then." He turned toward the backstage figure. "I think she's about ready. You can come on out."

Jenny gaped at the familiar figure stepping out from the shadows; it was Korsakov. "Hello, Jenny. You're doing well, all things considered."

"What's he doing here?" Jenny demanded as she turned back to Dirk.

As Korsakov hopped down from the stage, Dirk raised a hand to his shoulder to bring him in closer. "He's a key figure in what we need to accomplish, but you'll figure that out later. Right now, I need you to break through all of this." Dirk waved his hands dismissively at the hall around them.

"I don't know how, though," Jenny pleaded, suddenly feel-ing anxious.

"You've already done the hard part," Korsakov offered. "You know this is all set dressing. Now, all you need to do is snap to."

Jenny panicked. Sure, the people around her began to fade as soon as she realized they were just figments, but the hall remained resolute. The chairs, the stage, the gradual sloping of the floor. *The floor!* she thought as she looked down at her bare feet.

She stepped between the two men and over to the metal grating she had noticed before. It looked familiar. It was similar to…no, it was exactly the grating that made up the majority of the hallways within the *Ark*. Jenny walked about the lecture hall, looking for any other inconsistencies. Slowly, they made themselves more apparent to her.

A rotating beacon of light affixed to the wall would normally be found along the entrances in the corridors.

A large glass panel separating the various departments in the lab had been incorrectly located near the back of the auditorium.

Larges piles of sand…sand? Jenny stopped to run some of the grains of sand between her fingers. The cut was much rougher than any sand familiar to her, and she couldn't place the composition without any tools at her disposal. Then it dawned on her, and she spun back around to the others.

"I'm outside the *Ark*, aren't I?"

The lights blinded her as the auditorium melted away, and Jenny collapsed onto the ground, suddenly unable to stand beneath her own weight. A pair of arms managed to wrap around her and kept her from slamming directly into the ground.

"Dirk?" She looked up to see the man she dreamed would hold her close, but instead looked into the face of Korsakov.

The man looked surprisingly sullen. "Afraid not. Our boy's not doing so well."

Jenny strained to look over his should and saw Dirk, totally naked save for a small bit of fabric improvised into an awkward loincloth. He strained to hold himself up with a makeshift walking

221

stick. His skin, cracked and peeling, was a pale gray with a bright, iridescent blue shining beneath. He struggled to speak. "Hey, there."

This was not the paragon of strength and confidence she saw in her dream. Despite his protest, Jenny managed to struggle out of Korsakov's grasp and hobble her way over to Dirk. She let her tears flow freely.

"What's happened to you?" she sobbed.

Dirk smiled weakly and stumbled as he made his way closer. He just shrugged and said, "Change sucks."

Jenny became aware of all her muscles working against her. They ached with spasms as she struggled to hold her balance. She had to stop where she was but kept her eyes trained on Dirk.

Korsakov motioned to Dirk. "The worms."

Despite the excruciating pain he experienced, Dirk moved directly toward her. Korsakov stood to help, but Dirk just held a hand up in protest. He quickened his pace until just barely reaching Jenny before casting aside his walking stick and embracing her. They propped each other up, two helpless individuals stronger together.

"Quite a predicament, huh?" Dirk joked and gasped for breath.

Jenny smiled and placed her hand on the back of his neck as their foreheads pressed together. "If it had to end this way…"

Dirk cut her short. "Oh, it's not over for us. Not by a long shot." He softly cupped her face with his hands. "There's still a lot of work to be done."

She furrowed her brow in confusion. "What do you mean?"

He shifted his weight as Korsakov came up to support them. Dirk kept eye contact with her. "This world's done something to me. I'm being rewritten, and so much is becoming clear to me I can't quite put into words you would understand yet. They're primarily emotions and instincts stemming from this planet and its purpose."

"What do you mean, 'its purpose'?"

"There are so many wonders out there, Jenny," Dirk continued. "This planet is connected to all of them, but set apart. The Sons of Life and the Sons-of-Mishrak—"

"The Sons-of-Mishrak?" Jenny cut in, confused.

Dirk chuckled. "A bit of a misnomer, really. They don't have gender or a sex so much as we understand it anymore. The name is just an interpretation of a concept conveyed to us, really."

"I don't understand," she pleaded again.

"It's not important. What is important is that, despite our desire to explore and see what's out there..." A certain weight hung on his next words. "We should have never come to this planet."

Jenny stammered, "What? I don't—"

Korsakov chimed in and added, "Go ahead and tell her the grim reality, Dirk."

"The best way to explain it would be," Dirk started, then took a breath, "that this planet is under quarantine."

The full meaning behind those words hit her immediately. "So, you mean...we can't get help?"

"I mean we can never leave this planet, period."

Jenny slumped onto the ground, defeated. She could feel the worms coursing through her much more vigorously, and she couldn't quite muster the desire to be bothered.

Dirk knelt next to her and gently put his hand on the back of her neck to direct her attention. "Jenny, listen to me. This is just the reality of the situation. I can't have you quitting on me, now. Not now that you know you can break free of Mishrak's influence."

Barely able to say the words, Jenny managed to squeak out her next sentence. "But what's the point if we can't leave?"

"Life," Dirk responded. "All life. That's always been the point. It's why we do what we do." He smiled at her, as though hoping that would at least be a small comfort. Coming from anyone else, there would have been no chance of that being the case, but from him, it worked.

"I can barely move, Dirk."

Dirk pulled her closer. "I can help with that."

Ignoring the cracking of his bones and the tearing of his skin, Dirk helped Jenny to her feet. "I'm sorry about this, but this is really going to sting."

Jenny barely managed, "Wha—" before Dirk put his mouth on hers and breathed new life into her body. She felt an intense sensation coursing through her, burning out the worms invading her system. The pain was intense, but instead of collapsing on the spot, Jenny found new strength in their bond before Dirk stumbled back and broke their connection.

"The hell just happened?" Jenny stammered.

"Yeah, it was a shock to me, too. When you find me, we can talk more about it." Jenny shot Korsakov a surprised look before he added, "You seemed to take to it okay, though."

Just then, Dirk stepped away from the two of them and clawed at his temples. "That hurts!"

Jenny was just about to ask what was wrong but could instinctually tell that whatever energy he had just given her was without question weakening him. She could only respond with a muted, "No."

He turned back toward her and attempted a weak smile. "Just the way this plays out. You always think you'll make it to the end, but…" He cut his sentence short as streams of the iridescent light erupted from his body. "Listen, both of you! We absolutely cannot allow anything to get off this rock. The *Ark* is down and I've got Franklin on a job, but chances are someone will find a way to get a message back home. We cannot let that happen! Our friends will give into fear, but you need to stand resolute. I know you can feel it already."

Jenny and Korsakov nodded to each other in understanding.

Dirk cried out again as bits of his flesh chipped away. Jenny rushed to his side. "No, you can fight this!" She knew it was a lie as the words passed her lips.

"Some things you just can't fight. You need to find your place in the web of things and take solace in the balance." Dirk, again, smiled in a weak attempt at comfort. "I'm going to have to say goodbye, now." He kissed her once more before adding, "Take care of Kuhn for me."

Jenny tried to find the words to tell Dirk how she felt about him, about how she always felt about him. Dirk put a finger to her lips, moved it to her head, then back to his. He knew.

"That's how we beat them, Jenny."

She let the tears come freely. Dirk's body convulsed and he shot up out of her arms and dashed a few meters away, calling out behind him, "Remember that, Jenny! That's how we beat them! Everything we are is connected!"

Jenny stood and wanted to run after him but knew she shouldn't. "I don't want you to die!"

Dirk stopped and turned around; the light burst out of him quicker now. He smiled one last time and called out, "Die? I'll always…"

His sentence abruptly ended as his body burst into a ball of light and energy before disappearing into the ether.

***

Jenny gasped for air and shot up. It took her a few seconds to orient herself, to realize the blinking of blue lights around her belonged to the various instruments within the *Ark*'s sickbay and not to…

"Dirk," she whispered.

Chapter 27

F ive miles above the surface of Santelli Minor, Rolf Vermann was not a happy man. His splendid isolation was being disrupted by recent events, and if things continued like this, he would be forced to intervene. That meant he'd have to deal with others, to interact. And that prospect did not thrill him in the least.

He clicked his antique Parker pen—a gift from his mother, not that the sentiment meant anything to him—in irritation. Click-click-click, click-click-click. Always two sets of three clicks. Never three of three—that would require another set to even the balance. And never more or less than three in a set. No, that would wreck the balance, spoil the equilibrium.

And if anything was central to Vermann's peace of mind, it was equilibrium.

Equilibrium achieved through a complex collection of gyroscopes and electromagnets was what kept him in crypto-orbit around the planet. And an equally delicate balance kept him in his splendid isolation from his own kind, free of the obligation to interact with the kind of imbeciles who had plagued the first—tortured—twenty years of his life back on earth. When he was finally recognized for his unique skill-set and appointed as the Company's chief puppet master, he felt at peace.

The arrangement suited him just fine. His towering intellect, the very thing that made him a freak among 'normal' society, was acknowledged. All need for human contact was eliminated; so too was the vampiric leaching on his energy which mixing with people represented for someone like him. He'd been there for eight Earth years now and saw no reason why he would ever feel the need to go back 'home'.

Most days, the gentle whirr of numbers scrolling on the screens that surrounded him in a semi-circle wall assured him that all was as it should be. Clean, absolute, unblemished. Pure data did not lie, or mock, or demand attention or social niceties. Or emotions.

But today was different. A blip in a field of numbers had alerted him to an eddy in the flow of events down on the planet's surface.

Vermann frowned. Blips were not welcome in his world. They represented something that could send the carefully prepared plans askew. That wasn't how it was supposed to pan out. He'd have some serious re-coding to do if he couldn't halt the blip's replications. If worse came to worst, maybe even a reboot.

He glanced over at the giant-sized screen on the far wall. Not only was it much larger than its counterparts, floating in mid-air around his specially designed, custom-made ergonomic seat, it also displayed very different data. Less ordered. More random…unpredictable and chaotic even.

It was the central mainframe monitoring all the subconscious thoughts, hopes, fears, and dreams of everyone who had passed through the main space gate from Earth to join missions on Santelli Minor and the fifteen other planets in its solar system. Scientists, cooks, cleaners, mechanics, security staff, miners, technicians, medics, engineers—they had all been scanned and chipped coming out of the standard checks—though little did they know it.

How else could the Company be sure to keep everything under control?

Vermann regarded the giant screen with distaste. It was far too human for his liking, though he had to admit it was, by far, the most effective tool he had at his disposal to manipulate events. And, more importantly, to make it look like the result of human frailty and free will.

In its synapses flashed childhood memories, haunting nightmares, relived traumas, fondly remembered faces and voices—everything representing the unique chinks in the emotional armor of each individual. Plenty of ammunition for the battle for the hearts and minds of the second great wave of Earth's space colonists. It was a battle which Vermann was winning, easily, on the Company's behalf.

But now he felt something slip in his unseen iron grasp on events. Some small flutter of something beyond his reach, beyond his control. He could see it there on the blip on the screen, but he couldn't touch it.

He leaned forward and looked closer at the irritating anomaly in the gentle sea of code. The numbers were all wrong. Where once there had been a regular algorithm going with the flow of unsurprising numbers, Dirk Forrett's digits were now off the chart, creating unacceptable spikes and troughs and sending out cyber ripples that threatened to disrupt everything around them.

Fearful of a catastrophic butterfly effect which would ruin everything—not least the equilibrium on which he based his very existence—Vermann dug down into the code to see what was afoot.

Strange. Whatever virus or parasite had invaded Forrett's code also morphed the indicators for his already impressive mental capabilities. If the old chestnut about the average human using only thirty percent of their brainpower was true, Forrett on a normal day used somewhere around seventy percent, through a combination of natural talent, inclination, and training. But now? Now it peaked at a hundred twenty percent, if that was even possible.

It seemed there was a price to pay, though. His physical vital signs were decaying rapidly, in direct reverse proportion to his mental progression. Forrett must be living in the body of a centuries' old man, and not a healthy one at that. If the trend continued, Vermann thought, he'd be flat-lining any time.

With that, Forrett's code simply blinked out of existence. Disappeared, leaving no trace that the scientist had ever been entered into the system. He was quite simply gone—or passed into another dimension beyond the reach of Vermann's equipment.

"Scheisse!" he roared in his adopted German, a language he only used when at the height of his intellectual irritation. In an almost unprecedented fit of temper, he flung the antique pen at the screen and raged like a two-year-old, tipping chairs over and stamping his feet.

As he rampaged through the lab, he failed to notice the subtle changes on the wall screen. He didn't see the miniscule gaps appearing in corners of the grid, reflecting the disappearing act Forrett's code had performed.

Twenty minutes later, his rage spent, Vermann sat panting

on the floor. Quiet now, he stared down at the tiles as he tried to formulate a way to reverse the damage done by the Forrett bug and prevent any further consequences.

"It can be contained," he muttered under his breath. "It must."

He collected his pen from under the desk, gave it a couple of meditative click-click-clicks, and got to his feet. Putting his chair back in place, he glanced at the wall screen...and froze.

What he saw made his blood run cold and his heart leap throbbing into his throat. The small hole left by Forrett's code blinking out of existence was no longer an annoying anomaly in the field of figures covering the wall. Instead, the screen resembled some intricate lace doily—one crocheted by a madman. Gaps in the code appeared everywhere, at random, eating their way into the integrity of the system.

Vermann reached for the reboot button. There was nothing else to be done. Sure, it would mean losing all the data collected over the past twelve hours, but at least it would restore the mainframe to its state before the virus wormed its way into Dirk Forrett's little piece of the picture. At least it would prevent the rot from spreading further.

He lifted the protective cover from the master switch—it was as carefully guarded as any red button to launch a nuclear strike back in the bad old days on Earth—then entered his password and hit it with all his might.

Nothing happened.

No general shut-down and re-start. No wiping the screen clean of the damage wrought by the virus. The holes in the fabric of code just kept opening up and eating further into the data like the chomping heads in a vintage Pacman game.

For the first time in thirty years, Vermann wished for the

company of another human.

***

Below, on the surface of the planet, Jenny gave a shuddering gasp of pain and triumph and sat bolt upright in her sickbay bed. Her eyes remained closed, but her heart raced with labored breathing—classic signs of panic. The trainee nursing technician, assigned to her by virtue of being neighbors in the single female accommodation block, rushed to her bed.

"Jenny? It's me, Sami," she said, putting a reassuring hand on her friend's cheek. "You're okay. You're in the sickbay, and you've had some kind of shock, but you're fine. Everything's going to be all right."

Jenny half-opened her eyes and took in everything about her stark, clinical surroundings—the sterile flash of the life support machine lights; the womb-like curve of the cryogenic suspended animation pods in the corner; efficient personnel calmly tending to their patients; Sami's ID badge on her over-augmented chest; the hump of other supine bodies on the beds around her.

She looked within, searching her short-term memory for what had happened immediately before she lost consciousness. To understand the why, as much as the what and how. A wave of sadness washed over her as she remembered Dirk's last words to her before he…before he what? Died?

Somehow, she didn't think so. It didn't feel like a death. More like a transition to another state. Perhaps even a promotion to a higher plane—one didn't need something as tawdry and vulnerable as physical form. Maybe a state she too would achieve sometime soon.

She glanced at Sami's candy-striped uniform, then raised her piercing, laser-blue gaze to look at the young girl—and gave her a cyan-tinged smile.

232

"Yes, Sami. Everything *is* going to be all right," she whispered.

Chapter 28

B lankly staring at the chart before her, Zoe mindlessly fiddled with the pen in her hands. The entire world seemed to be passing at light speed, yet she was stuck in slow motion. It was a twisted sensation, watching reality continue whether she was ready or not, and it made her heart wrench. No matter how much every cell within her screamed to catch up with the rest of the world, she still hopelessly lagged behind, begging and pleading for someone to wait for her. She despised this feeling, for she was very capable of taking care of herself and keeping up with men and women alike, both physically and intellectually. It was a feeling she had only experienced once before in her entire life.

Just thinking about that moment sent waves of anxiety crashing through her body. Many years had passed and she'd managed to keep a tight lid on her inner turmoil. She had to; the sake of her current self, Medical Team Head Doctor Zoe Rowens, depended on it.

She had worked too hard for it all to slip through the cracks.

"Doc."

Snapped out her thoughts, Zoe turned to look at the restrained man. With his brown hair falling haphazardly around his face and his large brown eyes illuminated with the slightest spark of thrill for being restrained, Ron appeared more like a young boy than a member of the security team.

Instantly struck with another surge of guilt-laced-anxiety, she lowered her eyes from his so they rested on the ties chaining his hands. Many times over the past few days, she had thought herself too young to be dealing with such impending doom, yet Ron was even younger.

And Ron, though unknowingly, had killed someone.

Zoe's heart ached as she took a breath. She *knew* what it was like to watch someone crumble under the self-reproach of an accidental death; she *knew* how much it could warp a person and the person's friends.

Ron didn't deserve the shame that would accompany the knowledge of his deed, for that shame did more than punish a person; it destroyed them.

"Yes?"

"You okay? You look constipated." Attention immediately darting to Ron's face, Zoe glared. She felt bad, but not enough to halt her serious consideration of slapping him.

"I assure you, my bodily functions are all normal, thank you," she said through clenched teeth.

Ron's eyes widened before he spoke again. "Oh, I didn't mean to offend you, doc! I was just trying to say that you look like something's plaguing your mind."

Unsure what to say in response, Zoe hummed and busied herself with clicking her pen. He was rather talkative for someone who had only woken up a few hours ago and was restrained at the wrists and ankles, but then again, she'd never really interacted with anyone in the security team in her efforts to avoid their captain. In fact, even as she'd stitched up Ron's forehead, she'd done so in silence—partially because his voice was still recovering.

"Has Franklin stopped by?"

Zoe paused. Franklin had come by once since the first time Ron woke up and she had forced him out of the room. At first, she had been confused as to why she wanted to separate the two of them—it wasn't like Franklin would hurt the guy—but the more she spent in silence, lost in her thoughts, the clearer it became.

The similarities between Ron's current situation and Franklin's high school football trauma were undeniable, and she had witnessed firsthand the aftermath of such an effect. From the self-loathing, to pushing people away, to protecting oneself in harsh words and sneers, nothing good would come of Ron learning what he'd done. Zoe liked to think Franklin would never tell him, but she couldn't be sure, so she would keep them both separated to monitor the truth and to prevent Franklin from having a relapse.

The football incident had devastated him. It had hardened his heart, and she could only listen to hers break when he'd starting cutting everyone out of his life. He had transformed from her protective hero, her best friend and confidante, to her heart's greatest fear, her biggest vice and poison. Yet despite the change in their relationship, despite the way she hurt every time she dared to open her sealed memories, she would always protect him, just as he had protected her.

So maybe it was her hero complex slowly surfacing once more, but she couldn't see Franklin go through that again. She, herself, couldn't go through that again.

"He's been busy," she said.

"Oh."

Silence.

"Hey Doc?"

"Yes?"

"Is Franklin okay?"

"Why do you ask that?" she responded, puzzled by the question. She'd given no indication to Franklin's condition.

Ron's fingers twitched and his arm pulled at the restraint, as if he were trying to scratch his head before he remembered his current position. "It's just that normally he makes a point to see you."

That caught her attention. "What do you mean?"

"Like during combat training, he would let me get a few swings at his face—just enough to scratch him up—so he could go have you look at it," Ron explained. "Well, at least, that's what I thought. He'd never say, 'I'm going to have this checked,' but rather, 'I'm going to see Rowens.'"

Zoe's grip on the pen had turned her knuckles white. She'd always assumed he saw her just to hurt her in their stupid game of insults, so she would feel bad seeing his marred face. His heart had darkened a lot over time, and she hadn't even considered the fact that he may have done it just to see her. The things he'd said to her back then, the way he'd walked all over her feelings—she would not have been surprised if his visits were just fragments of sadistic tendencies.

"Did I say something wrong?" Ron asked.

Had he? She had been seeing new—or rather, old—sides of Franklin lately, and each time he'd looked out for her or called her name with concern rather than disgust, she found herself defying her old determination never to look at their past. Every look and every touch pushed her closer and closer to forbidden memories.

"No, you just got me thinking," she admitted.

He perked up. "About what?"

"Franklin and I used to date."

The words were out of her mouth before she could even think; the dam had been broken, her memories fully unleashed. In the back of her mind, she knew she should not tell Ron a thing—if his mind were to be controlled again, her past could only be a weapon against both her and Franklin, but there was a unique desperation to the present. If they were all damned to be stuck on this planet in the end, then what difference did it make? Doctor Zoe Rowens was a reasonable woman, but the past few days had proven that her human reason was inferior and rather useless in Santelli Minor's reality.

Plus, if she were not dragged down by her past, maybe she could be in sync with time's present flow.

Glancing at her ever-moving watch, she calculated that she had ten minutes before Franklin returned with the remains of his crew to talk to Ron.

Taking a deep breath, she started. "He and I were neighbors growing up. He was the cool kid, the one who screamed 'bad idea', and I was the popular bitch." Ignoring Ron's gaping facial expression, she continued. "We started dating in the very beginning of high school. He was just as crude as he is now. I liked to think of us as Beauty and the Beast. But, unlike that story, I wasn't the one who changed him." Her lips pulled up into a smile.

"It wasn't easy so to say, but I cared a lot about the opinions of others. I wanted them to envy me yet I couldn't have hated myself more. It was Franklin who taught me to value myself for who I was. I found my best qualities in him. He was my hero, my strength, my shield. He was my everything for three years before tragedy struck," she whispered. "He began to resent himself, doing everything he told me not to do. It was like a switch flipped—one day he was planning our future, and the next, he had decided to write me out of it."

Frowning, she forced her eyes open to prevent the formed tears from falling. "My entire life had been pulled out from under my feet. I was lost and I was heartbroken." Time had rushed ahead of her while she tediously and tenderly picked up the shattered pieces of her heart.

"How'd you end up a doctor?" Ron asked.

Zoe could only mentally grimace at that question. She'd decided to pursue medicine to prove that even though he didn't need her, others did. It was a selfish motive—one she eventually grew out of—but it was the truth. Though, as she had learned, there were thousands of other doctors just as talented as she.

A few years after she graduated medical school, she'd been working in a hospital when Franklin sauntered in, his arm bleeding profusely. She'd been on call and assigned to his case, but when she confidently approached him, white coat proudly resting on her shoulders, he asked the nurse for a different doctor.

He had thrown it in her face that he would never need her as much as she had needed him. Even when his arm had gashes and bruises, even when his blood loss had required a transfusion, he didn't need her.

He had broken her heart a second time that day.

"I just got my act together, I guess," she said quietly.

After that day, she made it her duty to move forward and stop wasting her ambitions on him. She became a doctor for herself, she applied to be on the *Ark*'s crew, and she pursued medical re-search beyond her wildest dreams. She learned to live for herself.

It was only when she arrived for her first round of inter-views with Dirk that she encountered Franklin again, and to her own surprise—and slight resentment—he seemed normal. Much crueler, yes, but he was the same large, loud Franklin who had at one point loved her.

And despite the fact that he threw verbal insults her way for the first time in her life—which she assumed were jokes, as he'd always been sarcastic—she found herself talking to him. At a moment in the conversation, she thought they could make these new versions of themselves work out together. Years of building up walls crashed down when his eyes had softened and he grabbed her hand.

If he'd asked her out at that moment, she would have said yes. But he must have realized what he was doing, because he dropped her hand and she was called into the interview.

Their breakup wasn't typical in the sense that she was still madly in love with him because he was the best thing to ever hap-pen in her life. They didn't separate because one of them fell out of love with the other; he had killed someone, and that had de-stroyed him. She had spent the first few years of their breakup try-ing to help him love himself again, but he didn't even give her the time of day. There had been no closure, just the unspoken pleas that she would leave him in isolation and that he would return back to her.

"What the fuck is with the atmosphere in this room?"

Jumping at the voice, Zoe whipped her head around to glare at Franklin. "Are you incapable of forming sentences without cussing?"

"I see that stick is still up your ass."

"Can I talk to you for a moment, please?" she asked. "Alone." Not waiting for his answer, she made her way out of Ron's room. Once they had walked a safe distance away, she turned to face him. "Don't tell Ron about Alby," she said

"He's awake?" Franklin asked.

She realized she hadn't given Franklin time to see for himself the last time he came around, and she hadn't offered the information. She chose not to go into it. "Yes." Carefully gauging his face, she was surprised when his expression remained the same. He didn't look upset, didn't argue against her point, nor was he insulted by her assuming his action. He simply looked at her. "Franklin?"

"I won't," he said, running a hand through his hair. She fought to keep her eyes trained on his face rather than admiring his arm muscles. "Honestly, I planned on keeping it from him."

"Oh," she muttered. "Sorry."

They stood in silence, her staring at his face and him looking above her head. She hated moments like this, when they struggled for things to say. Their relationship, both platonically and romantically, had always been without dull, awkward moments. They never hesitated to share anything with each other, for his joys were her joys and her sadness was his sadness, but this—this was a just a painful reminder of how broken they were.

"I'm glad you asked me not to," he said, moving his head to stare into her eyes. "I'm glad you care about Ron."

Unsure if that was a compliment or not, she replied, "And why does that make you glad?"

A small smile tugged at his lips and, just for a moment, Zoe was looking back into the eyes of her football star boyfriend—of her best friend who would sneak into her room just because he felt happier around her, of her best friend who would rob outer space of a star if it made her smile, of the one person she missed more than anyone. "Because it means you still haven't given up on people." Before she could respond, he made his way back to Ron.

Staring at his retreating figure, Zoe sighed. They could never go back to being Beauty and the Beast, and maybe that was a good thing. She was more accomplished than her teenage self could have ever imagined, and despite his own tragedy, so was Franklin.

Maybe they could steady themselves someplace in the middle.

Zoe headed back to the medical bay, leaving Franklin to chat with Ron whilst she focussed on Dr. Robinson. After Dirk had spoken to them through her, the anthropologist had fallen back into a comatose state. As she walked, Zoe reassured herself by reading back over the more-than-fatal vital signs; the last thing she needed to worry about was someone else disappearing. She scrolled through the data pad one last time, before hearing commotion from behind her.

Zoe headed back towards Ron's room, just in time to see one of the crew lunge for Johnson, who fell to the floor holding his cheek, blood gushing from his nose. Across from him, Franklin restrained the loose cannon, whose name Zoe couldn't remember. He glared viciously at the rest of the team, who appeared conflicted.

"Dude, calm down!" Ron yelled, still strapped down.

The man spat, "Calm down? They've been planning to destroy the fucking *Ark*!"

Chapter 29

C lenching and unclenching her fist one final time for good measure, Jenny sighed. After she'd smiled at Sami, the expression on the young trainee nursing technician's face had frozen. The poor girl had looked afraid to breathe—Jenny could have sworn she even gasped and held her breath. When she'd called the younger girl's name, Sami had jumped. It wasn't until she had explicitly asked the girl what was wrong that she looked at her reflection

The first thing she'd noticed was how limp her hair was. Usually sporting some natural curl, her hair was nothing more than a stringy mess of a dirt-like hue. Carefully starting to run her fingers through it, she quickly gave up after encountering knot after knot. Attention moving to her skin, Jenny almost looked away at the sight of her ghost-white reflection. She was not the tannest of girls, but she prided herself in a natural glow; she was so pale that surely she would glow in the dark. She was not a vain girl, so to say, but the thought of Dirk having seen her like this upset her slightly. Of course, he too had looked as though he'd gone to Hell and back, and not once had he brought attention to her state.

That had made her feel slightly better.

Closing her eyes, Jenny had taken a deep breath. Her own childish insecurities aside—not to keep reasoning with herself, but Dirk was also not one to judge based on physical appearances— she'd been unable to understand why Sami had reacted that way. She was not so hideous as to provoke such a reaction. Anyways, how else did the girl expect anyone to look after waking up from being in a comatose state?

Exhaling, Jenny had opened her eyes only to let out a short scream.

Her eyes were *blue*.

Her eyes were *glowing* blue.

Having moved as close as she could to the mirror, she'd all but shoved her face against the glass. How had she not noticed it before? Screw her physical appearance, her eyes were emitting blue!

She'd spent a good few minutes just staring at her own reflection until she began to think back to her conversation with Dirk and Korsakov. Dirk had given her new energy and, at the time, she had thought nothing of it. But now, with glowing eyes and glowing teeth, she was confronted with evidence to the reality that she could end up like her favorite scientist, in a plane where she wouldn't be tied to a body. It had been nothing more than a passing thought when she'd first woken up, but now, with piercing eyes looking back at herself, she had to consider what future changes her body would undergo.

And that led her to where she was now, still in the sickbay, staring at her hands. After her discovery, she'd expected to feel some sort of difference within herself. Yet besides feeling alive—despite how dead she appeared—her capabilities had not changed. She didn't have super strength, she couldn't move objects with her mind, and she couldn't speak telepathically to the other sleeping crew members. She couldn't help but be slightly disappointed, for even though being able to do none of those things kept her closer to humankind, it kept her farther away from Dirk.

He would always be five steps ahead.

Shaking her head, Jenny swiftly patted her cheeks a few times. Now was not the time to be thinking about stuff like that, not when there was a bigger picture.

Not when she had information she needed to tell the others.

Looking around the room, she was met with the silent bodies of the sleeping members. Sami had stepped out when she screamed, but where had she gone?

Who was left?

Moving towards the door with new determination, Jenny carefully maneuvered around her crewmates. Dirk had said that Franklin was in charge of destroying the *Ark*, so he had to be here at least, and if Franklin was here, then surely Dr. Rowens was as well. Allowing herself a small smile, her heart felt lighter when she thought of the bumbling crass giant and the delicate witty intellectual. She wasn't sure if others saw it, but she had spent enough time with Franklin to know how much the Olympian-like male adored the doctor. Even though he knew she had slept with Korsakov, he loved her. Maybe if they ever got out of this mess, they could go on a double—

Jenny mentally slapped herself. She couldn't afford to think of things like that; she had to focus on finding someone.

Carefully opening the door of the sickbay, she slowly stepped outside. Pausing, she waited for any type of sign from the others, the clicking of one of Dr. Rowens' pens, a random expletive sounding from Franklin, the sound of crashing or anything that signaled impending doom—but nothing. The *Ark* remained eerily silent.

Forcing herself to move beyond the door's threshold, she randomly turned left. Of course, she knew the *Ark*'s layout like the back of her hand, but being unaware of recent events veered her on the side of chance. Acting like she had some clue as to where to go when she knew nothing of what had transpired recently wouldn't do her any good—it was the people in horror films who acted like know-it-alls who died first.

And that was what this had become: a horror film.

Plus, she could not deny the voice in the back of her mind, telling her she would have better luck finding others if she aimlessly wandered than if she checked specific places.

Her soft footsteps echoed relentlessly throughout the hallway. If something were lurking and waiting to attack her, she was doing a horrible job at being subtle and incognito. She practically stomped through the empty halls like a giant, and while the fact that her steps were the only noise put her on edge, it was better than no noise at all.

Before she could decide which direction to turn next, a loud crashing sound broke her out of her thoughts.

Unable to even process what the sound might have been, Jenny took off running towards it. If it were something dangerous, she would just have to reason with herself that others would eventually show up.

Hopefully.

She must have been running faster than normal, because

suddenly, she stood in front of an open room she was sure was on the other side of the *Ark*. Panting, she took in the sight before her. Doctor Rowens crouched next to the pilot—Arthur, that was his name—who clutched his cheek. Standing across from them was Franklin, who held back another member of the security team as the others looked on. None of them seemed to have noticed her arrival.

"Oh, hey, Jenny!"

Ignoring the sudden increase of attention on her, Jenny moved to find Ron's small figure hidden behind Franklin's massive one. Restrained at the wrists and ankles, he shot her a friendly smile.

Now she remembered why Dirk liked him so much.

"Jenny?" Doctor Rowens questioned, standing up and making her way towards the other girl. Warm hands on her shoulders, Jenny was startled by the look of genuine relief decorating the doctor's features. "When did you wake up?"

"Just now. What's going on in here?"

"We've had to make a choice—"

"Ha!" barked the man being held by Franklin. "Like she doesn't know! If you say you got your orders from Dirk, then of course *Jenny* knows! She's the captain's—"

"Jacob, shut it!" yelled Franklin, tightening his hold.

Jenny had a pretty good idea what she was witnessing; Dirk had told her that Franklin was in charge of destroying the *Ark* and that the rest of the crew might not react so well. She, too, could not deny feeling upset when he'd told her. She had dedicated a great portion of her life to this project, and to know that the tangible remains would be nothing more than shards of scrap metal hurt. She felt a pang of empathy course through her as the man grunted in pain.

"Doctor Rowens—"

"Zoe."

Caught off guard, she stared at the doctor for a moment. She had always addressed the woman by her title, not only because it was a sign of respect, but also because she always had a hardened glint in her eyes. But this was not the same woman who had initially been assigned head medical team leader. This woman was softer. It was in the way her eyes had lit up upon seeing Jenny and the way she consistently seemed to have part of her attention on Franklin that forced Jenny to realize *this* was Zoe Rowens.

"Zoe, what's going on?" she asked. A tentative look crossed the woman's face. Of course she would be nervous telling her—she knew how important the *Ark* was to Jenny. Silence continued to reign until Jenny decided to break it herself. "You have to destroy the *Ark*."

Zoe's eyes widened. Nodding slowly, she asked, "How did you know?"

"I had a conversation with Dirk. Well, not really a conversation, because it was in my head—but not, like, he was a voice in my head, because I saw him! Or, well, I saw him in my mind with Korsakov and—"

"This planet is fucking weird," Franklin said. "Listen, it doesn't really matter how the hell you spoke to Dirk. I'd believe you if you said he appeared to you in a fucking tutu with goddamn wings, but what else did he say?"

"He said to find him and Korsakov."

"Korsakov?"

"Yeah, he's on our side." She and Franklin held each other's gazes for a moment before he nodded. "Okay, we'll find Korsakov," he agreed.

That set Jacob off. "You guys are all insane! First destroying the *Ark* and now believing that Korsakov's the good guy? And what about Ron over here who shot—"

Jenny let out a quick scream as Zoe punched Jacob in the face. Hands over her mouth, she watched as Franklin howled in laughter and Johnson cracked a small smile from his spot on the floor. But just as quick as the brief relief came, it went. Before Jacob could say anything else, Franklin changed his hold on him to wrap his arm around the other's neck.

"You listen the fuck here, kid, got it? In case you haven't figured it out, this place is a goddamn shit show. Anything can fucking happen. If Dirk says Korsakov is good, he's pretty fucking good," he said. Jenny could only watch in amazement, for despite the fact that his words were cruel, his tone was calm and reasonable. "I get it, you love the *Ark*, but you're pretty fucking delusional if you think you loved it more than Dork-face himself. This ship was his *life*—the guy is a thirty-seven-year-old nerd who studies *zoology*—and he ordered me to fucking blow it up."

Jenny held her breath, and Jacob, shaking slightly, stared at Franklin. Whether he was shaking out of anger or fear, she had no clue. It was only when his gaze dropped to the floor—shortly followed by his body, as Franklin let go of the guy—that she released her breath.

Turning to look at Johnson, Jenny began, "So how should we start—"

"Wait, he said I shot something," Ron stated, his eyes swimming with confusion. "What did I shoot?"

"Nothing," Zoe said. "Don't worry about it."

Looking at his accuser, he asked, "Jake, what did I do?"

Jenny waited as Jacob finished his staring contest with Franklin. What was going on?

"Franklin. You shot Franklin's arm by accident," Jacob said quickly.

Before Ron could ask any more questions, Jenny asked again, "Where do we start?"

"Well if we're looking for Korsakov, then logically the first place to check would be the altar," Zoe muttered, more to herself than anyone else.

"I'll go," Jenny volunteered.

"And I'll go with her!" Ron announced. Seeing Zoe and Franklin turn to him, he continued. "You know, so that you two don't have to argue over why neither of you should go because you love each other and whatnot and you want each other to return safe and sound."

Silence gripped them momentarily before Zoe quickly tended to Johnson, though Jenny could see the blush on her face, and Franklin faced Ron.

"You fucking twat."

Chapter 30

*A*rks selenium roof panels flickered—BLINK-BLAH-BLINK-BLINK.

Jeremy Bericote was working the long nightshift. It was called the long night because Santelli had a twenty-six-hour day, and while the *Ark* maintained its own daylight routine, this was broadly synchronized with the local solar system. So the two extra hours were pushed into the night, giving eight hours of sleep rather than the solar standard of six. *Ark* staff rotated through a timetable of five days on and two days off, circling between a ten-hour day-shift, an eight-hour evening shift, and an eight-hour nightshift. There was normally a reduced skeletal staff working at night, but the biological mission of the *Ark* never stopped with the science staff, always analyzing, classifying, and cataloguing new specimens. In addition, the support services were in a constant program of preventative maintenance and repair. Jeremy frowned, rubbing his eyes and stifling a slight yawn.

BLINK-BLAH-BLINK-BLINK

Yes, the constant maintenance, he thought to himself. An image flitted across his mind— biocleansing the *Ark*'s hull. It required two staff at all times whenever they were on a new planet. He was glad to be on the science team.

The last week had been a complete whirlwind. He'd been desperate to join Korsakov's party on the initial science mission but had been required to stay behind and form part of the relief team to carry on the scientific work.

When the science team had returned, he'd been asleep and completely unaware of the new humanoid specimens and subsequent infection of the crew. Their catatonic state was a significant shock for the well-knit team, making it really hard to leave them quarantined and helpless until we found out what had caused it. When Franklin returned, without Dirk, a depressive mood dominated everyone. The only good news was finding out a worm bite was the cause of the catatonic state, so with the quarantine lifted, Jeremy had been working tirelessly, under the leadership of Dr. Rowens, to search for a cure.

His shift routine consisted of randomly screening three catatonic crew members; a laser injector was used to withdraw five milliliters of blood, which was then tested for zebra worm larvae in order to monitor the concentration of the infection. All crewmembers were also screened twice daily and charted against the individual's personal biology, all known diseases, and all unknown constituents. Any deviation from their predicted biorhythm meant they would be suspended from duty and sent for a full-body scan.

Dr. Rowens' team had noticed both the increasing density

and size of the larvae in infected individuals. They fed off nutrients in the blood stream, increasing the buildup of CO_2, which led to the slow emaciation of the victim; this increased the strain on the heart and lungs with the need for greater amounts of oxygen.

BLINK-BLAH-BLINK-BLINK

Jeremy was nearing the end of his shift, feeling weary as he'd been studying the development of larvae across a range of individuals. He rubbed his eyes again. They were dry, aching; he needed sleep. He closed his eyes, pressing his thumb and middle finger against the sides of his head next to his eyes, holding the lids shut. It offered him a moment of relief. With his eyes closed, he visualized the specimen he'd been looking at, then imagined flicking between a number of samples.

BLINK-BLAH-BLINK-BLINK. What was that? His eyes were closed…

***

Ron cast an amused smile back at Franklin. The tension in the room was broken as Zoe crouched on the floor, applying a clotting agent to the lacerations on Johnson's cheek. Jacob sat in the same position in which he'd been dumped. Jenny stood across the room, taking in the scene before her. Ron's eyes flicked back to Franklin.

Wait a minute, he thought. He looked back at Jenny—her eyes were blue…*blue*! "What the…"

Ron slumped back onto the bed; the effort of the last few hours had taken its toll and he felt weariness wash over his body. The selenium roof panels felt scorchingly bright to his now sensitive eyes. The light seared through his head, and he tried to reach up to press his forehead to ease the pain. He couldn't move and remembered he was still restrained at the wrists and ankles.

"Ugh."

"Easy, boy. You okay?" Franklin asked. The hubbub in the room continued, but Franklin could see Ron's pain.

Ron paused to breathe deeply—then it hit him. He was ravenous, like nothing he'd felt before. His stomach wasn't just empty, growling for food. It churned, convulsing with an insatiable need for nourishment. His breathing fell short and he felt clammy as he took shallow breaths.

"Franklin...I can't...breathe..."

"Zoe, quickly. It's Ron." Franklin turned, directing his request straight at Dr. Rowens.

Dr. Rowens' shoes squeaked on the floor as she jumped quickly to her feet. She appeared in Ron's line of vision and he tried to smile. She barked at the intercom, "Sami, get to Ron's room, now."

Almost as soon as the intercom had clicked off, Sami appeared in the doorway, out of breath. "I was just looking for you, Dr. Rowens. Jenny's awa—" Her sentence stopped abruptly as she saw Jenny standing in the room.

Dr. Rowens inspected Ron's stomach, feeling the convulsions and checking for abnormalities. "Sami, we need an intravenous. He needs high-carb fluids, and now."

There was a scurry of feet as the team launched the gurney to which they'd strapped Ron, aiming for the sickbay. He felt hands on his arms as they started to prep him. Then he heard Sami's voice.

"What the hell is this? Dr. Rowens, look at these nodules on his arms. These are in an advanced state compared to the others I've been monitoring in sickbay."

"Just get the damn Nutriform in him as soon as we arrive. He'll die without it."

Jenny ran ahead and pulled out the supplies she needed,

256

placing them next to the emergency bed. Franklin and Zoe transferred Ron over in one swift move, totally in sync and focused on the patient.

"Are you sure?" Sami hesitated as she attached the Nutriform to Ron's IV drip. "Is this safe, Dr. Rowens?"

"Yes, do it, then we'll switch on the biocontainment field and monitor him. *Now!*"

Sami connected the last valve—Ron gasped in ecstasy. The sensation of the fluids was dreamlike while affording heightened awareness. He felt a cold tide flow into his arm, zipping round his body, revitalizing and refreshing him. For a body so drained and depleted, the dense dose of carbohydrates provided an extreme buzz, almost lifting him off the stretcher. The sense of energy and pleasure heightened to a dangerous extent. The fluids contained a barbiturate to depress the nervous system, allowing him to relax while being replenished.

Having been bitten by the zebra worm, Ron had become host to the rapidly multiplying larvae infesting his cardiovascular system, now approaching maturity. They had literally lived off of him, utilizing nutrients in the blood stream. These anaerobic lifeforms naturally increased the amount of carbon dioxide, thriving in parts of the body low in oxygen.

When small, they flowed to the arms and started to form nodules under the skin, increasing in size as they grew. However, the pulmonary artery had the greatest concentration of larvae. The artery was large, accommodating the biggest individuals, allowing them to grow to excessive sizes. It was also hugely deoxygenated, being positioned immediately below the lungs, transporting the blood before it was infused with oxygen. What set the larvae apart from most other infestations was the rapid growth and extreme mandibles that developed. These were not only large, affording great leverage, but razor-sharp—at the final stage of development, their protective exoskeleton was shed.

Ron felt a surge of energy, but his breath grew shallower. His vision swam. He could see he was inside the biocontainment field, faces peering in—Sami, Rowens, Franklin, Johnson, Jacob, and Jenny. He smiled weakly.

Then he felt searing pain in his heart—the infestation was complete. At maturity, the larvae had now transformed into fully grown zebra worm adults. The teeth sliced pieces of tissue away from his artery. He felt the pain rip through his chest—worms cutting, dicing. His heart exploded as his artery was punctured and blood poured into his lungs. Ron felt them filling. He coughed, vomiting blood, gurgling as he tried to suck in the precious air to keep him conscious, keep him alive. His mouth frothed vibrant red. The worms feasted on his alveoli, the fine nodules of his lungs forming the perfect meal. Worms and blood mingled as they filled his lungs. The worms shed cysts, infecting the blood further.

Ron then felt his arms popping as the infested nodules erupted and smaller worms burst out. With one last, large fit, his chest convulsed, heaving into the air, and he vomited blood across the biochamber, where it spattered on the far wall.

On the outside of the chamber, the onlookers watched in horror as Ron went limp, the alien infestation feeding off the remaining carcass. Worms dripped down the transparent walls, squirming. Ron lost consciousness before he lost his life.

***

Jeremy's eyes flashed open. He was instantly awake, his mind racing as he wondered about the meaning, the implications. What *was* it he was seeing? He felt completely wired as he looked back at the matrix display in the laboratory. Using finger taps, he isolated the samples he was interested in, then zoomed in further.

He saw the larvae, but… He zoomed in again, down to the molecular level, and there it was.

BLINK-BLAH-BLINK-BLINK

The molecules oscillated in unison to the same rhythmic pattern—the same pattern as the lights. Jeremy sat back on his chair, focusing beyond the screen to relax his eyes and allow himself to think.

What was it? The thought niggled and needled at his tired brain.

Jeremy went back to the screen and accessed the ship's maintenance logs, where he isolated the monitoring of the lighting system for the previous twenty-four hours. There it was—a rhythmic variation to the voltage feeding the system. He had a hunch, a big hunch. If it was correct, the ramifications were…

BLINK-BLAH-BLINK-BLINK

Jeremy jumped the log back to Earth-dock just after the *Ark* came out of biocleansing before its last mission. He scanned through a seventy-two-hour block, but the voltage stayed monotonic, static, unvarying.

"So when?" he muttered to himself.

He jumped forward to the day they landed on Santelli—still nothing. He knew something, *something*, must have happened since they'd landed. He skipped through twenty-four hours at a time, monitoring a one-hour window. Day 1, Day 2, Day 3.

"Bingo!" he shouted.

There it was—BLINK-BLAH-BLINK-BLINK.

"What happened on day three?"

He paused for a moment to think. The humanoids! Yes, Franklin had come back from the first excursion and unloaded them from the pod. Dirk had gone berserk when he'd returned to the *Ark* to find them. Jeremy scanned the log again—there it was at 16:24 Santelli time.

"But what triggered the change?"

One answer simply threw up another question. He knew what he was looking at, but why? What changed at 16:24 to cause the variation in the lighting system voltage—that same variation now matching the rhythmic pulsing of the larvae in the infected crewmembers, inducing their catatonic state?

"Causality. Action and reaction." He liked talking to himself as he worked and often ended up using quotes from old "movies" to fit the moment.

Jeremy ran a memory dump across all the *Ark*'s systems at 16:24, with a three-minute window on either side. He filtered for an "exception", an event classed as unusual. He saw the exterior antimatter shield go down at 16:23, followed by a bioscan of all living forms at 16:24. The humanoids were a new species, so their molecular signature triggered a full-body bioscan to index their DNA and isolate any known viruses. This was cleared at 16:25 and the interior shield raised to allow them in to the cargo hold.

But, there it was… Jeremy flicked back to the lighting log at 16:25. The rhythmic pattern initiated at 16:24 during the bioscan. Jeremy inspected the bioscan log more carefully. Yes, there was sample xt701, the humanoids, but also a new lifeform. xt702—a striped worm, a zebra worm. Jeremy cross-correlated the zebra worm bioscan with the lighting log. Once the bioscan was complete, the lighting rhythmically pulsed—as if it was…infected.

Besides the lighting system, was there any evidence the *Ark* really was infected? Jeremy knew it would take a while to complete, but he started a ship-wide system scan anyways, looking for exceptions. He then paused to think for a moment, to understand. Where else?

"Replication," he whispered.

Had the virus managed to replicate? His attention immediately turned to the replicators on board the *Ark*, used for the production of synthetic products, including foods. He isolated the system and scanned for replications considered foodstuffs. He skimmed through the list—high-protein breakfasts, carbohydrate boosters. He found what he expected to see. The logs also contained encrypted entries; these must have been replicated by senior staff and, given his reputation, likely Johnson. Jeremy had clearance for all systems, so he completed a retinal scan to have the full logs decrypted. There was synthetic whiskey, which he also expected, but additionally GHB, ketamine, and Dirk's Compound. He pondered for a moment on individual crew members and their past. You never escaped it, no matter where you were.

Jeremy shook his head; he'd digressed. He didn't want *known* foodstuffs, he wanted living tissue that wasn't a standard replication. He inverted the search function—nothing. He stopped again.

"Where else...where else can you replicate?"

There was only one other system—the holodeck. He ran the same scan and there, flashing on screen before him, was xt702. The zebra worm. Jeremy replayed the holorecording, saw Johnson enter the holodeck, select an opponent, and begin his kung fu workout. There it was at the end—a red, glowing light. A striped zebra worm.

Jeremey was momentarily stunned. Thoughts raced through his head, but he kept coming back to two key facts. The crew were infected with a biological virus that formed replicating larvae in the bloodstream. The ship was infected with a virus that could self-replicate biological forms. This was the first known instance of a bioinformation virus. The enormity of the discovery caused him to pause.

Jeremy barked at the intercom, "Rowens, this is Bericote. I've made a major breakthrough with the virus."

The intercom clicked and then Jeremy heard screaming. "Bericote, get to the sickbay. *Now*. We've got an alpha medical emergency."

Jeremy spun round on his stool and ran out of the laboratory. The room was quiet, the activity of the moment a past memory in the system records. The ship-wide scan completed, the cursor blinking as the results were compiled. Only one sub-system showed an exception, indicating interference—infection. The exterior long-range scanners kept working on their own—the virus was scanning the planet, searching.

***

Heartly felt consciousness return to her. The fogginess of sleep gradually gave way to her senses, her thoughts. The combined memory of the crash from the dropship and the nauseous smell of liquid Molybdenum caused by the high temperature and pressure melting of the hull rocked her awake. She lay in a small depression formed by the surrounding dunes, with Grewder sitting across from her next to the humanoid. They spoke quietly, and she could only pick up the rising and falling cadence of their voices. Grewder looked weary, tattered, the scarring to his face seemingly blending in with his disheveled state. But his eyes—they were different. That detached, lonely, hardened character was gone. She saw a glistening, the quiet confidence of knowing, of having known. He had changed.

Grewder looked across at her and, seeing her awake, walked over. "Evening, Major. You've been asleep for the whole day. That really took it outta ya. Here..." Grewder grabbed both Heartly's hands and pulled her to her feet. "Have you looked in the mirror?" he asked.

She paused, open-mouthed. What an odd question. Looking on the ground next to her, she saw the open black case and crushed vials. Sifting through the remains, she grabbed her compact mirror and flipped it open. The same eyes stared back at her, except now there was a freshness to her gaze, her skin, her complexion. The orange tint to her skin had gone.

Her remaining memories returned in a rush—the crash, escape through the plasma window, following and finding the humanoid, then watching Grewder approach her, ready to restrain her. He had stopped, motionless—not catatonic but as if he'd lived the moment in a dream. Heartly had collapsed, moving in and out of consciousness, and the conversation with Grewder had just been her cure. With her memories flooding back, she had a renewed sense of conviction.

"Okay, Grewder. How do we find this goddamn ship if she's forgotten where it is?"

"It's a bioship. Biological. We need to scan the subsurface."

Chapter 31

The black, six-inch stilettos struck the pristine, white marble corridor with such force her ID badge swung wildly from the breast pocket of the grey, woolen, pinstriped suit. Sweeping her long silver fringe from her face, she tucked it back into the bun at the nape of her neck and adjusted the starched white collar of her shirt. Rounding the corner, Alexandra Powers took a deep breath while nodding to the two guards, who quickly opened the frosted glass doors to the boardroom. There, a table of eight of the Company's key investors awaited her arrival.

"Good evening, everyone. I am sorry to have called you all here on such short notice, but we have experienced some 'bumps in the road,' shall we say. Nothing we cannot iron out to accomplish our end objective. However, we need to make a decision right now on how you would like to proceed."

Alexandra took her seat at the head of the table and motioned for everyone to put on their virtual display glasses while she pressed her right hand to the glass tablet for five seconds as it scanned her biometric code. A few seconds passed before Rolf Vermann's gaunt face appeared before them.

"Mr. Vermann, I just want to let you know I have the investors here on the call with me."

Rolf stopped clicking his pen and quickly put it down in front of him, then cleared his throat and re-adjusted his glasses.

Alexandra continued. "Upon receiving your latest communication, I can confirm that we do in fact have a backup copy of the data you lost after quote, 'Dirk Forrett has disappeared from the system.' Unquote. We will upload a copy and transmit it via the subspace relay after this meeting. I expect a report back in four hours explaining what happened."

Rolf nodded and tried to stutter out an explanation. Alexandra cut him off quickly, not wanting the investors to know the true extent of the problem. Rolf picked up on the tone of her voice and nervously wiped the sweat from his brow. He had worked so long on this project and was so close to his payday. Unfortunately, little human contact over the years had weakened his skills of perception.

"You may or may not be aware that we have lost communication with Major Heartly's Dropship One."

Rolf sat up a little straighter, unsure of what was to come next.

"It has been decided, due to your contractual obligations with the Company and your close proximity, that you are required to enter into Santelli Minor's atmosphere and find the ship. We will send you the trajectory from the last known coordinates of the ship after receiving its distress call some twenty-four hours ago.

We have had prior confirmation that the 'cargo' was secure and onboard. Find the dropship and you will find Major Heartly. Extract her and her team, including the cargo, and return to orbit where you will be intercepted."

"Intercepted by whom?" Rolf stammered.

"Classified information, Mr. Vermann."

Beads of sweat finally broke free from the confines of Rolf's matted brown hair, dripping onto his glass lenses, the enormity of the task hitting him sharply in the chest. "Ms. Powers, I'm flattered that you install such trust in me, but would it not be wiser to wait for a more—"

"Mr. Vermann, I am fully aware of your skillset. It's why we hired you. The Company feels you have been playing with your pawns too long, and the timeframe has been extended one too many times. The Company wants this wrapped up before the next Universal Election here on Earth, so you have three days. Are we clear?"

Rolf nodded and thanked them all for their time before the line went dead.

Alexandra removed her glasses and looked around the table. "I motion to take our best warship off its current course. At present, it is only a two-day journey from Santelli Minor to rendezvous with Mr. Vermann. I will be honest. I do not think he's up to the task. However, even if he locates Major Heartly's ship and the cargo, it will make for a swift extraction from the planet once the warship arrives. I have full faith in Major Heartly and Master Sargent Grewder. They won't let the Company down. I'd like to take a vote in favor of this action." She scanned the table. "It's unanimous, then. I will keep you all updated on the progress."

***

"Holy Mother of fuck-balls!" yelled Rolf at the top of his

lungs as he rocked back in his chair. "What the actual—" He slumped head-first down onto the console. *This cannot be happening, this cannot be freaking happening,* he repeated over and over in his head, somehow feeling that, if he said it enough times, it would come true and he would wake up.

Sighing loudly, he sat back up and removed his glasses, wiping his face with the arm of his jacket. As he looked out through his viewport, Santelli Minor seemed so peaceful from up here. But Rolf knew of the mayhem and pain this planet had suffered. The fact that it had been dormant for so long, only now to have flared up to its current level, was not part of the plan. He couldn't help but feel some guilt; he was the reason Dirk Forrett and his team were even there in the first place.

"Right, let's get this ship ready. Time is of the essence," he muttered.

His computer system immediately rebooted, and there on the screen was his precious data. All thoughts of his mission were temporarily cast aside.

***

"Ron!" screamed Zoe, tears pouring down her cheeks. Clutching the plastic wall of the chamber, she slowly fell to her knees. The stress and shock of what she'd just seen rattled every nerve in her body, and she had been completely unable to stop it. *Are we ever going to win against this?* She buried her face in her hands.

Franklin picked her up from the floor and hugged her tightly, wiping her tears with his thumb and smoothing her hair back from her face. Ron had been the first one of their exploration team to have been bitten, and the harsh reality of the rest of the crew's fate hung heavily in the air.

Zoe pushed herself away from Franklin and regained her

composure, keeping herself busy by checking on the others. *Get yourself together Zoe,* she thought. *The crew needs you!*

"Bericote, Johnson, Zoe, and Jenny, I want to see you all on the bridge in fifteen minutes. Sami, lock and seal off this room with biohazard status. Everybody else, out now. You all have work to get back to, especially you, Jacob. I'll deal with you later." Franklin waited for everyone to exit the room before taking one last look of what was left of Ron's body. Bowing his head, he recited a small prayer for the man and automatically made the sign of the cross. "You did good, kid. Your parents would be proud," he whispered, then turned and walked out the door.

***

Franklin stared out through the *Ark*'s main viewport on the bridge. He watched in wonder as the moon Mearon slowly rose into the night sky. It shimmered so brightly, as though covered in millions of diamonds. In truth, it was due to the huge gold deposits spanning across the entire surface and heated by surrounding volcanoes. This, in turn, produced a gas littered with melted gold fragments.

Franklin thought back to the night Dirk explained that to him. *Maybe I'm finally understanding Dirk's genuine love for this planet.* Hearing the others come onto the bridge, he brought himself back to reality. Turning slowly, he took in the four faces looking at him, pale and blotchy from lack of sleep, malnourished from little food—and Jenny, with her crazy blue eyes. Franklin saw the pain in each of their faces, and he began.

"Look, everyone, before we decide on our next plan of action, I just want to say, in case I don't get a chance to later, that I can't thank you enough for everything you've done to support me, each other, and the rest of the crew. I know Dirk would be proud of us all for what we've been through. I can't promise you that we'll make it off this planet, but whatever happens, know that I will try to do everything I can." As the words rolled off his tongue, the undertaking of the next few days weighed heavily on Franklin's shoulders. He looked at the floor for a moment before snapping his head back into the game, asking Johnson for an update on the pod.

"Good to go, boss. Any time you're ready, just let me know." Johnson swallowed hard, obviously trying his best to sound upbeat.

Franklin nodded. "After everything you've told us, Jenny, I do believe we'll find Korsakov near the altar. But first, we need you to give blood to Jeremy, see if there's any way we can somehow replicate this 'Star Stone'. It may be the only way to save the other crew, unless Korsakov knows something we don't."

"I might have something as well," Jeremy piped up.

"Spit it out!" Franklin barked.

"It happened just before the Alpha Emergency. You wouldn't believe it." Jeremy summarized his findings with a glint of excitement in his wide eyes. "I have a theory, but I just need a little more time. I do have to ask you, Johnson, when you were running the holodeck program that day, who were you fighting? I couldn't quite make it out on my screen."

Johnson gulped and looked at Franklin, whose eyes bore down into him "It was a humanoid."

"Really? The computer randomly selected a humanoid for you to fight. Interesting. Then afterwards, there was the worm, right? What happened to it?"

Johnson's discomfort oozed off the man. Franklin wondered just how many rules the pilot had broken. "I took it back down to Matt Babbage to quarantine it," Johnson confessed. "I thought I was doing the right thing. Later, I picked it up, and it felt like it seared my hand. When I dropped it, it slinked back to the humanoid's cage. That injured one, right? But my hand was fine, and I...I don't remember much after that."

Franklin's eyes shrank back down to size as he moved his gaze from Johnson to Jeremy. "Jeremy, I want you to keep working on this. We need to know what we are truly up against, and what this has to do with the *Ark*. We may still have to destroy it, as Dirk said, but I want answers first. Zoe, I think we need to prepare for the worst with Korsakov. Fingers crossed he can give us the answers we need. It's still possible for us to get back home. I think its best if I go myself with Zoe and Jenny. We need the extra seat to bring back Korsakov."

Johnson looked at the floor in disappointment.

"Johnson," Franklin continued, "we'll leave at dawn. I'm leaving you in charge of the ship. If we don't make it back, you know what to do with the iTransmit."

The pilot raised his head, pride restored once again, and put a fist to his chest. "Of course."

***

Left alone on the bridge after the others went about their work, Jacob slowly pushed back the lighting panel in the ceiling above which he'd been perched. He'd followed them, not wanting in any way to be left out of the next decision. There was no way he would just sit around and let them destroy the ship that was both his current home and his only way to get off this damned planet. Whatever insanity had consumed them, he hadn't subscribed to it. He'd heard them perfectly, and he also knew exactly what an iTransmit was. Now all he had to do was find it.

***

"Come on, Major. Just over the rise. I can see the wing."

Grewder led the party back towards their crashed dropship.

271

To find the humanoid's ship, they needed long-range sub scanners. The dropship's scanners had been completely destroyed in the crash, but they knew where they could find one. The *Ark* was still on the planet, after all.

First things first, they needed supplies and the compass readings for the *Ark*'s location. Grewder knew most of their hi-tech equipment would have been damaged in the crash, but he was fine with going old-school. He almost felt like he was back in the Academy. Night was falling as they approached the hole in the plasma screen.

Grewder turned to the group before entering. "I think it would be safer if I go in alone. I know exactly what we need and where it is, hopefully. Major, rest here with Amber. I won't take long."

Major Heartly watched him re-enter the ship, unsure of how she felt about this shift in roles. She was still his commanding officer, but something had changed within her. Was it the residual effects of Dirk's Compound wearing off, or was any sort of emotion just now foreign to her after having suppressed them for so long?

Collapsing down into the nearest sand dune, she hung her head between her legs. She was still skeptical of this creature and its strange powers. Yes, she was grateful that it had cured her, but what did it ultimately want, exactly? From her? From Grewder? From this planet?

Chapter 32

Korsakov stood over the unconscious co-leader of the Sons-of-Mishrak. The humanoid slowly stirred, but he was still incoherent. While the doctor waited for him to awaken fully, he replayed the past few minutes over in his mind, trying to comprehend what had just happened.

"We have to destroy the *Ark*," Dirk had said with determination. "This is bigger than ourselves. This is deeper than I imagined. I can feel it in the planet. In the wind." Dirk had then proceeded to shut his eyes and mutter to himself. "Jenny," he whispered.

Korsakov watched as Dirk's entire body glowed a translucent, electric blue. It was a soothing color, despite the fact that, as he glowed, his skin had slowly peeled away from the intense illumination beneath. It wasn't long before Jenny had seemed to materialize before the two men, and Korsakov realized Dirk had connected the three of their minds. He wasn't sure if Jenny's mind had been brought to theirs or if their minds had traveled to hers; all he knew for sure was that the three of them were together again, if only for a moment. He also knew that, with Dirk in his weakened state, they had to share what information they could before this crucial opportunity slipped through their fingers. Dirk's skin flaked off and drifted down to the sands with every move he made, and what little skin still hung to his captivating blue body was grayed and brittle.

Dirk immediately filled Jenny in on as much as he could, but her appearance flickered slightly—like a candle when a breeze tickles the flames—and Korsakov knew they were running out of time.

Jenny had looked weak. Dirk cupped her face in his hands, and a blue haze had escaped his mouth as he breathed into her. The change was visible instantly. Her skin had regained color, her back straightened with restored energy, her cheeks flushed, and her eyes filled with the same electric blue as Dirk's. Korsakov had recognized the emotions and feelings displayed across her features; he called out to her to tell her it was okay, that he knew how she felt. And he did—the worms had been burned out of him as well, albeit through the lizard venom rather than Dirk's newfound power.

"We can talk about it more when you find me," Korsakov had called out. Hopefully, Jenny could remember they were at the altar. Dirk had finished filling Jenny in on what little more he could manage to say, but it wasn't much. Korsakov barely heard the last bit of their conversation; he was too distraught watching Dirk fall apart. Dirk's skin flashed blue, and bursts of energy escaped the cracks in his peeling flesh. Knowing his time was up, Dirk ran off into the distance, keeping his friends safe from the final energy blast.

"I'll always—"

Those had been the last words Korsakov had heard from Dirk before his captain had exploded into a bright blue light then faded into the wind. The connection had been broken; Dirk and Jenny were nowhere to be seen.

Korsakov didn't know what had happened, not really, but he had the feeling that Dirk wasn't truly gone.

***

The humanoid laying before Korsakov now groaned groggily, pushing himself up off the ground and bringing himself to his knees. He raised a scaled hand to his head, then looked up at Korsakov, his eyebrows drawn down in confusion.

"Wh—what happened? Where is the other human? The male?"

"He disappeared," Korsakov said. It wasn't exactly a lie. "He entered my mind, and I was afraid. But all I can remember is waking up here a moment ago. He was already gone." That *was* a lie.

The creature let out a low-pitched growl, slamming his fists into the ground and stirring up a flurry of white sand, which nestled into his fur, before jumping to his feet.

"You stay here," he snarled at Korsakov, who immediately tossed his hands up and backed away from the angered humanoid. "I must return to the village and inform the others of the traitor. Watch for your people. Destroy them if they come too close. And find a way onto your ship! Mishrak has demanded it!"

With that, the humanoid turned to the altar and a green light erupted between the pillars. He shivered, shaking the sand loose from his fur, then tossed one final glare toward Korsakov before striding through the sheet of light and disappearing, the green glow blinking out behind him.

Korsakov was left on his own and was glad for it. He'd told Jenny to find him, and hopefully she had seen he was at the altar. All he had to do now was wait for her to get there. He looked around, somewhat impatient. What if the Sons-of-Mishrak returned first?

About an hour had passed, and Korsakov was still alone at the altar, resting his back against a large white rock and absentmindedly watching a lizard sunbathing on a flat stone by his feet. He felt safe near the lizard, knowing it as the same species of lizard whose venom had saved his life.

A muted hum filled the air, and he watched the altar, certain someone was about to come through. The humming grew louder, and the ground began to shake. The lizard scurried off his stone and into a small hole in the ground beneath another nearby rock. The sound quickly escalated into a dull roar, and Korsakov spun around, searching for the source of the strengthening noise.

Coming down from the sky behind him was a small ship. He recognized the conical nose and wide quad-boosters in the rear as those of a much older model, one he had been certain was discontinued years ago. The roar of the engines soon drowned out even Korsakov's thoughts, and he ducked down behind the large, white rock against which he'd just rested, never tearing his eyes away from the fast-approaching ship.

The side thrusters flipped around, facing downward and operating at full capacity, slowing the ship's descent as it neared the surface of the planet. It hovered in place for a few minutes, as if the pilot were unsure whether or not to land. The heat from the thrusters melted the sand beneath them, forming liquid pools of glistening, orange glass. Finally, four angled legs unfolded from beneath the ship, straightening out from between the boosters and extending down at a forty-five-degree angle to the ground. The ship wobbled the remaining few yards to the sand, landing loudly and ungracefully. A flurry of sand pushed outwards from the ship, sending a rough spray across Korsakov's face and causing him to rub his eyes profusely.

As he blinked back the sand, he heard the ship's hatch door open up as the atmospheric pressure equalized with that of the ship and the air-tight seal was broken. A figure stepped down and paused at the foot of the short, fold-out stepladder extending downward from the doorway.

When his eyes finally stopped itching and he could see clearly, Korsakov realized the figure was a man. The stranger cleaned a pair of wire-framed glasses with the bottom of his button-up shirt, then brought them to his face and straightened them against the bridge of his nose. The man took a deep breath, cleared his throat, and stepped forward.

Korsakov wasn't afraid of this man, who looked more like an office employee than a space-traveler. He stood up from behind his rock and walked up to greet the stranger, extending a hand out in front of him to introduce himself. The man stopped short and reached into his pocket, which Korsakov only just then realized had an odd-shaped bulge and the end of a handle protruding from it. The man revealed a gun and confidently brought it straight up in front of him, aiming directly at Korsakov's head.

Korsakov halted just a few yards from the man, and at this distance, he could see this new stranger sweating profusely. The scientist stood there awkwardly, his hand still extended, his mind suddenly blank. The newcomer used the back of his other hand to wipe the beads of sweat off his forehead, then pushed his glasses further up his nose with his index finger.

"That'll be close enough, Rodney Korsakov."

Korsakov made no move, still staring incredulously down the barrel of the gun. The only sign he gave of having heard the man was the raising of his eyebrows, which climbed so high on his forehead they nearly blended into his hairline.

"My name is Rolf. Vermann. I'm in a bit of a pickle, but I think we can work everything out, if you cooperate. Right, Rodney?"

Korsakov simply closed his mouth, which he realized had opened on its own, and nodded slowly.

"Now." The man cleared his throat again, and wiped the line of new sweat from his brow. "Your friends should be here shortly. My data tells me they've already left the *Ark*. What I want shouldn't be too far from here, but I'm going to need the *Ark* as well. To achieve any of that, first I need you."

"Why?" Korsakov finally managed to spit out. "I'm a scientist. I'm just here to—"

"I know why you're here. Three days ago, I watched your ship pull into the atmosphere. Unfortunately, something got messed up…strings got tangled…and if I have to be here to straighten them back out again, that's what happens. But we're going to do this right, and we're going to do it quickly. The sooner I get off this planet and back into orbit, the better."

Korsakov's eyebrows trailed steadily downward as Rolf spoke. His features drew together in confusion. "Three days ago? Look, I don't know what you want, but you've got your days mixed up. We came here over a week ago."

"The twenty-six-hour day you experience here in Santelli's gravitational field is just under four Earth hours. You may believe yourself to have been here for much longer, but I can assure you, it's only been three days back home. It's all relative, Dr. Korsakov. I have three days—just about three Santelli weeks—to fix this problem. And you…you are going to help me."

A high-pitched whistling shot through the air, and the two men looked to their left, just past the altar, to see an exploration pod in the distance heading their way. Korsakov looked back at Rolf, studying the man's features. He didn't look like an inherently dangerous man, and the amount of sweat he produced far exceeded the heat of the planet. No, this man was nervous and out of his element. Korsakov feared him for that aspect alone; a nervous man was an unpredictable man.

"When my crewmates get here, they aren't just going to suddenly help you when you have a gun to my head."

"No, but they will help me when they realize who I am and the power I possess. You alone have the trust of every faction on this planet—the humans, the Sons-of-Mishrak, the Sons of Life. It's the only reason I came to you first—the only logical decision. And you will inform them that they can, in turn, trust me."

"I don't even know you," Korsakov countered. The pod moved closer by the second; he could make out detailed features on it now. It slowed upon its approach.

"Sure you do, Rodney. I'm Mishrak."

Chapter 33

The cool morning air snaked over the sand dunes to the crashed dropship. Major Heartly awoke shivering, her head feeling heavy in the sand. Tugging the collar of her ripped jacket up around her neck, she licked her parched lips. Pulling at her memory cords, she tried to work out how long she'd been asleep this time.

Looking up at the sky, she started to pull fragments from the dream she'd just had; the pieces all scattered in her mind. Drawing them together, her father's face flickered again in front of her eyes before disappearing into the glow of morning sky above her. Major Heartly's eyes welled with tears; she knew her father would be proud of her choice to finally return to the right path in life. She wondered why she had desperately avoided it for so long.

Turning her head to the side, she saw the humanoid looking up at the twin suns rising in the sky, slowly stroking the fur on its chest. Heartly wondered if the humanoid had been responsible for the dream. Wiping her eyes with the back of her hand, she kept her gaze on it. She couldn't help but wonder if the humanoid wanted to go home as desperately as she did at that moment. A clatter of metal from inside the ship jolted her upright.

Grewder appeared from the opening of the wreckage, and Heartly felt a wave of relief that he wasn't hurt. Hours had passed since he'd entered the crashed ship; Heartly didn't know what she would have done had he not appeared now before her. When she stood up, the sky spun, and she fell back down into the sand.

"Easy there, Major. You're severely dehydrated." Grewder dropped the box of supplies he carried and cracked the seal of an electrolyte hydration pack, putting it to Heartly's lips. Placing her hand over his to take the pack, he smiled down at her before gradually letting go.

Then he knelt in front of her and organized what he'd salvaged into two packs. Weapons, food ration packs, flares, and medical supplies. "Good news, Major," he said. "I found one of the satellite tracking units we used in the operation. It's still intact and it has the *Ark*'s last known coordinates. The ship's stationed around twelve miles due west of here. If we leave soon, we should be at the *Ark* in four hours—provided the creature can keep up."

They turned to look at the humanoid, who seemed blissfully unaware of them both. Still staring at the sky, it looked lost deep in its own emotional thoughts. Heartly couldn't shake the feeling that it knew more of what lay ahead than it was willing to let on.

***

Not wanting to startle the creature, Grewder hesitated momentarily before approaching it slowly. Dropping to his knees, he tugged some padding and a bandage from his pocket. The humanoid turned and looked at him, but did not pull away in fear. Grewder applied the padding to the bottom of its stumped leg and wound the bandage around to secure it. As his fingers moved over the creature's fur, his vision momentarily clouded over and an image of Amber shimmered in front of him.

Grewder stopped wrapping, lost in the dreamlike state. Amber put her hands over his. "Look up at the sky," she whispered. Grewder tilted his head back and looked at the layers of pinks and purples blooming above him. "My planet—our true planet—is up there, not this wasteland on which a fraction of our people thought they could make a new home. The others you encounter, they are Sons-of-Mishrak, a blight on our race who have been trying to get off this planet for hundreds of years. They will lie, deceive, and stop at nothing to get what they want. Remember that." Grewder looked back at the creature. "We need to hurry before your people disappear forever," said Amber.

The cool morning breeze hit Grewder's cheeks, bringing him back into the present. Tying off the bandage, he looked at the creature and smiled.

"Major, let's get moving. The sooner we find this ship, the quicker we can get home."

* * *

Korsakov felt the sand stirring at his feet. It slowly whipped his ankles before pulsing further up his bare legs. The pod approached rapidly to land beside Vermann's ship. However, he was unable to move, his legs paralyzed by what he'd just heard. Korsakov's mind scrambled to process the last ten seconds. His own laughter surprised him. *This* was 'Mishrak,' who claimed to be the so-called puppet master of Santelli Minor.

***

Rolf widened his stance, tilting his head to the side, unsure what to make of the man dressed in rags whose face contorted even more by the second. Vermann could only imagine this was what may have been the beginnings of a madman now unleashed inside the doctor. Maybe Korsakov was not the man he should have approached first. Korsakov's laughter erupted even further as the air whipped the sand faster around them. Vermann's glasses slipped down his nose. He lifted his hand to push them up. Korsakov took that moment to lunge at him, tackling Rolf to the ground. The force knocked the wind out of Rolf's lungs and the gun from his hand. Crawling on their hands and knees, they both scrambled to find the gun in the now-churning sand.

Franklin focused on the scene before him, the vein in his forehead pulsing in rhythm with the pounding of his heart. Whatever was happening on the ground, Korsakov needed his help like he himself needed air. He maneuvered the pod to stop beside the unknown aircraft. The pod punched the ground, causing them all to jerk forward in their seats. Franklin grabbed his space gun from its holder before Zoe even had the chance to look back up.

Franklin slammed his fist against the ramp control button, the vacuum seal disengaged, and the short ramp lowered to the sand. Before it could hit the ground, Franklin slid down the ramp and propelled himself forward, hitting the sand with such force that he rolled a few times before coming to a stop.

Switching the mode on his weapon to 'kill', Franklin aimed at Korsakov and the stranger. The sand still swirled around them, causing havoc with everyone's sight, while the pod's engines shut down. Franklin rested the weapon's barrel on his left forearm, looked down the infrared scope, and fired.

As the sand finally settled back into its usual patterns, Franklin shook his head from side to side and glanced back down the scope. Both men lay motionless on the ground.

Zoe stepped down the short ramp, nervously aiming her weapon ahead of her. Jenny followed hesitantly behind. Franklin noticed her blue eyes radiating even more from her gaunt face; a blue tinge had seemingly swept over her entire body. He wondered briefly if it had anything to do with their close proximity to the altar now.

Zoe and Jenny joined Franklin at the bottom of the ramp, and together they moved cautiously towards the bodies.

The stranger regained consciousness, coughed, then inhaled sharply and pushed himself up onto his elbows. Frantically groping around in the sand, his fingers brushed against the half-buried hilt of the gun.

Franklin pushed his boot into the man's back, causing the stranger's torso to slam down onto Korsakov's chest. "I wouldn't do that if I were you," Franklin snarled. "Turn around so we can see who you are…slowly…that's it." The man turned to face him. "Zoe, grab the gun. Jenny stay behind me," he barked. Zoe pulled the gun from the stranger's fingers and tossed it to Franklin.

The man turned to face Franklin, sitting down hard on the sand. He blinked against the sun. "Even without my glasses," he said in a whining voice, "I'd know anywhere the man who casts that colossal shadow. It's nice to meet you, Franklin."

Zoe tightened the grip on her gun. "How the hell do you know that?"

The stranger smirked. "I know everything, Dr. Rowens."

Franklin felt Jenny tap him on the shoulder. "Look at his chest," she said.

The foreigner looked down at his own chest to see the red smudge there. Ripping open his shirt, his anxious breathing matched his frenzied hands as they moved over his body. Franklin distinctly noticed the lack of any blood on the man's bare torso.

Zoe pushed past the man and knelt beside Korsakov, pulling his head into her lap. Her hands nervously pulled back his shirt. "Jenny, get my medical kit, now. Korsakov's been hit." She applied pressure to the wound.

Franklin met Zoe's gaze as she glanced at him for help. Passing the stranger on the way toward her, Franklin punched the man in the chin. The stranger's head spun to the right and he fell back onto the sand.

A familiar hum permeated the air around them, followed by a green glow forming between the pillars of the altar.

"Well, this should be interesting," the stranger slurred, then slumped back onto the ground, unconscious.

Chapter 34

Rolf Vermann started life as a nobody. His own parents forgot about him half the time. He was one of seven children after all, and the youngest at that. By the time he came into this world, pink and screaming, they had checked out. They didn't have time to fawn after him—or really parent him much at all. Rolf was left to his own devices. His six older siblings had taken their parents' looks, each of them gorgeous in their own way. There wasn't anything left for Rolf except brains and a deeply rooted desire to make himself known.

It was at the age of six that Rolf found himself to be an incredibly skilled chess player. He beat everyone he was up against, his mind calculating moves ahead, predicting what the other person would do. He was never wrong. Not even once. After four years of undefeated chess, Rolf grew bored. He needed a new challenge; figures moving across a board could only keep so many people occupied. He was sure he had already discovered every combination of moves, and now he wanted something with a hint of unpredictability.

One day in his eleventh year, his oldest sister Bethany had misplaced her diamond necklace. It was a gift from her boyfriend—she just *had* to find it. Bethany wailed for days about the jewelry, frantically searching everywhere and begging everyone to help her find it. Rolf found the necklace tangled in her sweater on the bathroom floor. He hesitated in the room, holding the jewelry in his hand. He could easily give it back to her—end her hunt. Or…he could place it in one of his siblings' rooms. Bethany would be furious if she thought someone had stolen it, especially someone in their family.

With a taunting smile playing on his lips, Rolf headed to his sister Amanda's room and hung the necklace in plain sight on her dresser. He couldn't wait to see how this would play out—just the exact unpredictability he had been craving. Maybe Bethany wouldn't get angry at all. Maybe she would forgive their sister.

He bounded out of the room and down the stairs to where Bethany lamented her lost jewelry on the couch. Rolf pretended he didn't want to tattle, that she was dragging it out of him. When she ran up the stairs to see if it was in fact her necklace, he ran and hid outside, where Amanda was reading a book.

Not even two minutes later Bethany, stormed outside. She yelled and screamed while Amanda denied ever taking it. She didn't know how it got there. The girls bantered back and forth as sisters often do, and soon Amanda was in hysterics, swearing up and down that she hadn't ever touched her sister's necklace. Someone must have placed it in her room to get her in trouble.

Rolf watched their every movement, followed their body language and cues, and committed it all to his brain. This would come in very handy, he thought.

After that day, people became his new pawns. The more intimately he knew the person, the better he could predict their behaviors. People were creatures of habit; they ordered the same food at the same restaurants, ate with the same people, and hardly ever deviated from their patterns. The saying was true—people don't change.

College was harder for Rolf. After practicing his new skills on people he'd known for years, he had to start from scratch with the strangers in his classes. He tried making friends within different groups, but everyone rebuffed him. He was a nobody, after all. It was then that he decided to try his hand at reconnaissance work. Three weeks he spent following a boy in his mathematics class, learning the kid's schedule and habits so well Rolf wasn't quite sure he hadn't picked up a few of them himself.

After that first boy, Rolf followed other students, then he moved on to strangers. He filled notebook upon notebook with everything he could learn about them—what they did when they were alone and thought no one else would be watching. Those private, intimate moments anyone would want to keep secret from others. Rolf found his way in and used it to collect his own data, turning every person into a living chess piece he could manipulate at will when needed.

In Rolf's senior year of college, a man dressed in all black approached him midday next to the water fountain in the middle of the campus. He sat down next to Rolf, his back turned slightly away from him as if he were admiring some view across the lawn. His suit was tailored expertly, not a stitch out of place. Beneath raven-colored hair, the man's sunglasses hid his eyes from the bright sun. He stuck out like a sore thumb amidst all the coeds in sweatpants and the previous night's outfits.

"How would you like a job?" he asked Rolf.

Rolf did not recognize the stranger's heavy accent; that didn't happen very often. "What's the job?" he asked. "I'm assuming it's not a normal nine-to-five gig, seeing as you've chosen quite the public time and place to approach me."

The man smiled slightly and adjusted his sunglasses. "That it is not. But it *is* of the utmost importance. It could change everything we know."

Rolf's interest peaked. "What do I have to do?" he asked.

The stranger stood, nodded, and walked away, leaving Rolf a bit bewildered. He picked up the business card the gentlemen had left behind; it was colored black with the slightest tinge of electric blue. As he flipped it over in his hands, he felt a soft voice calling to him, saying that this was his destiny. That he was needed. That he wasn't a nobody.

Rolf shook the voice from his head and focused again on the words on the card—"THE COMPANY" written in bold letters, and beneath it was inscribed a date, time, and location. Somehow, Rolf knew he was going to dive in with both feet. This would be his life-changer.

He arrived at the specified location two hours early, taking a seat at an outdoor coffee shop. He sat back, watching the restaurant across the street, waiting. He wasn't there fifteen minutes before someone slipped into the seat across from him.

"My employers had a feeling you would be scouting," said the same man who had approached him on campus.

"What is this job?" Rolf asked, pushing his glasses off his nose. The man pushed an envelope across the table, and Rolf opened it to find photographs of various individuals with basic biographical information printed on the back of each. He glanced over each and every subject photo. "I don't understand." Rolf shook his head.

"My employers would very much like you to find these people and ensure they end up in the same place at the same time. This needs to be as controlled and contained as possible. My employers want to guarantee there will be absolutely no surprises."

"What if I say no?"

"You won't." The stranger smiled. "Not only will they pay you handsomely, you'll get your very own chess pieces on a board over which you will have complete control."

"Variables?" Rolf asked.

"Classified." The stranger tapped a few fingers on the envelope.

Rolf shuffled the pictures back into the envelope. He stood and offered the man his hand. "I'm all yours," he replied. They shook, and the suited man handed him a flash drive, saying he'd be in touch.

Rolf plugged the drive into his computer, and not only did it pull up the dossiers of each person in the file, it also included manuals on how to pilot different aircrafts, the weather patterns and conditions of a planet called Santelli Minor, and a date fifteen years in the future.

Taking a deep breath, Rolf took off his glasses. He rubbed his eyes and groaned. This was deep. Did he really want to get this involved? Fifteen years? He would be middle-aged before the mission even really started. His new employers remained awfully cryptic, and he had a feeling this was not entirely a vision of legality. Then again, all the time he spent "watching" people hadn't been, either.

Before he could rationalize himself out of it completely, Rolf Vermann opened his closet, pulled out his only ratted suitcase, and threw what little personal belongings he had into the bag. He doubted anyone would even notice he'd left. Zipping up the bag, he pulled out his passport and the envelope, printed what was on the flash drive, and headed out of his dorm room. He knew he'd never return—not if he could help it. Rolf wasn't going to be a nobody any longer. He was finally going to be a somebody, and that all started with finding Dirk Forret.

Chapter 35

Dirk's consciousness bounced back and forth, seemingly through the fabric of reality itself. It bounced just as his thoughts did. Dirk went from moments of immense clarity of his current predicament to moments of intense confusion. He wasn't sure what had become of him, if there was any way to go back, if he was any place right now. And whenever confusion began to overcome his thoughts, they would drift out, replaced by thoughts of peacefulness. A feeling of being one with his surroundings. Like waves on the beach they flowed in and out, washing over Dirk's being.

The waves began to break from their monotonous motion and change their approach. Instead of a wave coming from one direction at Dirk, it seemed to flow around him. He felt it whip around him like a breeze, then he felt something that was hard for him to understand. The wave felt like wind whooshing past him, but he no longer had a physical body. He felt it push up against him. He felt the resistance. He wasn't bouncing back and forth anymore; he was grounded.

The confusion subsided and he concentrated with every part of his essence on being a physical being again. He felt himself rise up as the wind swirled around him. He felt a form for the first time in what seemed like an eternity. He felt eyes form and instantly opened them. Sand.

All he saw was sand. He saw it when he looked forward. He saw it when he looked back. He saw it when he looked down at his current form.

Sand. Just like the sand-beings they'd encountered on this planet. He focused on his form and felt it bend to his whim. The appearance and texture of his body changed until it resembled his old body. The form he'd had all his life. He felt his own power. His mind and consciousness still felt unchained, as if it had outgrown the use for a body. But the form he existed in now calmed him. Even if he didn't need a body, it gave him comfort. Whatever problems he had left to overcome on this planet, he wasn't going to face them as a blue spirit of energy or whatever the inhabitants of this planet had left him to be. He was going to face them as Dirk.

The first steps were a task. The form of his body was a familiar one, but its functionality was not. Dirk was determined to figure it out, to save his friends, and end the destructive conflict on this planet.

He took a deep breath and focused his mind. He could feel different landmarks on the planet. He felt where he was needed at this time. He felt the Altar to his left. He started walking to his right.

***

Franklin dragged the unconscious stranger to the altar. The green glow pulsated all around them in a state of excitement, apparently due to the man's proximity.

"Every damn time we've been to this altar, it's been blue. Hell, half this goddamn planet glows blue. What makes you so special, huh? How come you get green?" Franklin said over his bested opponent. Franklin turned the man over to face him and slapped him in the face. "Wake up and answer me!"

"Franklin, that's enough," Jenny said.

Franklin turned to look at Jenny. Her eyes shot through his thoughts. He could see her aura of blue shift slightly, moving ever so slightly closer to the green hue of the altar. That wasn't what stopped Franklin in his tracks. What stopped him was past Jenny's aura, in her actual eyes—the spark of red darting out towards him as she stared him down.

"Whatever you say, Jenny. Just...help me, then. I need some answers. I can't keep track of all of this and this guy just rolls in here out of nowhere. If he doesn't know what's going on with this planet, with us, then who does? He's got to, and I'll be damned if we don't find out from him. I'm not letting any slimy alien touch this man until I know what's going on." Franklin tried to hide his newfound fear of Jenny with his normal bravado.

"Let me have a turn." Jenny left Korsakov with Zoe and walked toward the stranger. She held him down with one hand on his chest and put her other hand on his forehead. "Wake up."

Her words seemed to have made a difference, as the man's eyes opened. He struggled for a second to move, then relaxed.

"Who are you?" Jenny asked.

"Somebody," he said.

"I'm serious. Tell us now," Jenny pushed.

"Does it matter?" the man asked. "How will learning my

name impact any decision any of you make from here on out?"

"I've always found it at least slightly more difficult to kill someone when I know their name," Franklin said.

"You won't kill me. I have information most valuable to you, and you will keep me alive as long as you're able because of the misguided perception that I will share it with you for any reason. Personally, I love the dilemma. I'm too valuable to kill and yet I'm of no use to you." The man grinned.

Franklin pulled his gun out and pointed it at the man's head. As he pulled the trigger, Jenny pushed the gun away, causing the bullet to hit only the ground beside the infuriating stranger.

"Predictable," the man said.

"Just tell us what you know about what's going on, and I won't have to push away another shot," Jenny said.

"Nothing that hasn't been planned and predicted. You all had parts to play, and you played them with gusto. Every last moment for the last fifteen years of your lives has been perfectly planned to lead up to this moment. Everything down to this conversation has been accounted for." The man sighed, and it somehow made his smile even larger. The reactions on Jenny and Franklin's faces were more than enough to make up for the intense work to which the man had dedicated his life.

"So why tell us this now?" Jenny asked. "All this work to predict all of this just to tell us about it before you get what you want?"

"Because there isn't anything you can do at this point to alter the outcome. We know what you are going to do from now on. And allow me to commend you. Every one of your decisions is wrong. Even if you made the right choices, we would get what we want, but you make our job easier. The Company always gets what it wants," the man said.

A cough came from Korsakov's direction, whose chest wound just barely did not include any major organs. "Mishrak," he said.

"What? Mishrak?" Zoe asked.

"He's Mishrak," Korsakov added.

"He's right. You know some of the beings on this planet worship me as a deity. You know something else? They might not be wrong." A small explosion on the altar released smoke so thick and painful to the eyes that even Jenny couldn't help but close her eyes as she tried to clear the air in front of her.

She concentrated and opened her eyes again. An energy released from her body and sent all the smoke in the area away from the altar in an instant. Then she quickly eyed their surroundings. Franklin stood beside her, wiping his eyes. Zoe lay with her head face-down in the sand. She was unhurt but had had to resort to extreme measures to avoid the smoke.

Korsakov and the stranger were gone.

***

Heartly, Grewder, and the humanoid continued their pace across the desert, approximately two miles away from their destination.

"Grewder, stay back with me for a second?" Heartly asked.

The Master Sergeant instantly obliged, leaving the humanoid a few feet in front of them. "What is it?" he asked.

"How can we truly trust that thing? I know it's helped us—me—in an incredibly generous way, but I can't shake the feeling that this is all wrong," Heartly said.

"You're usually more of a 'by the numbers' thinker, Major. Going with your gut isn't usually your thing," Grewder said gruffly.

"I know," Heartly said, "but something still stinks about

297

this. You said the creature appeared to you as Amber, more than once, to communicate with you and explain whatever she explained."

"So?" Grewder shook his head even though Heartly hadn't even finished her thought yet.

"My point is that if there's a communication gap between species, I could see why using the appearance of a human would make sense. But using a specific person with such emotional attachment to someone—why would *you* do that? It reeks of control. Getting someone to do something they don't want to do by coating in the memory of their love. If a random person told you to kill someone for them, you wouldn't. If someone you loved said it, it might be a different story."

"What are you trying to say?" Grewder asked, eyeing her. "That the being who completely cured you of your addiction to Dirk's Compound and rid you of the need to take it in the first place is using us to do something against our directive? Just because they're different doesn't mean they're bad. If you want to judge creatures based on actions alone, I'd say this creature has made its intentions clear." He tried to turn back towards the humanoid, but Heartly pulled him back.

"That *is* my issue. Using good deeds and love, not to show intention but to create attachment. I'm not worried that this thing is trying to make us do something right. I'm worried it will prevent us from asking whether it *is* right," Heartly said.

"Is everything all right?"

Grewder and Heartly both turned to see the humanoid in Amber's form. This time, the creature had projected that image of itself to both of them. She walked alongside them clear as day, Amber's smile bright and warm.

"Everything's fine," Heartly said quickly. "I just needed to discuss something with my subordinate here. It doesn't concern you."

The trio climbed over the ridge of a dune to see a great, open horizon line. Just over a few hills sat the *Ark*. It looked quiet, peaceful.

"I'm not sure that should be our next stop," Amber said. "We should keep going."

"We came halfway across the galaxy because of this planet and that ship. We're going there, and we aren't stopping until we get what we need," Heartly said.

She led the way down the hill towards the *Ark* when a low rumbling caused her to stop. She ushered Grewder and Amber to stop right behind her. Amber took a few steps away from Heartly, and the Major had to physically stop Amber from continuing.

Eight figures emerged seemingly from nowhere, surrounding the trio in a perfect circle. Heartly instantly palmed her weapon. It was just a steel mace, but she wasn't going down without a fight.

"We are the Sons-of-Mishrak, and you will go no further," one of the figures said. The way the voice travelled made it impossible to tell which figure had made the sound.

Heartly took the mace in her hands and held it in a strong grip up to her shoulders. The figures all took one step inward towards the trio, and that was all the provocation required. Heartly lunged forward and swung her mace.

"No, stop," Amber said.

Heartly swung through toward one of the figures, but her weapon seemed to go right through the Son-of-Mishrak. She swung over and over again, but her weapon never seemed to make contact.

"Heartly, get back," Grewder said. He reached forward and grabbed her, receiving a stiff hit in the face from her weapon in the process. He fell to the ground. Both Heartly and Amber kneeled down to assess his injury. Heartly peeled her gaze away to see the Sons-of-Mishrak stepping even closer.

Then the wind began to blow.

It encircled the trio, creating a seven-foot shield around them. As the Sons-of-Mishrak attempted to reach through the sand, they all recoiled in pain. The circle of sand expanded, pushing the Sons further away. Then it exploded in a gust of wind and energy, sending whatever Sons had survived the pain rocketing away from Heartly, Grewder, and Amber.

The sand circled around them for a moment longer before gathering in a single spot in front of them. Then it grew and warped, piling upon itself until it rose in the form of Dirk Forret.

"Major Heartly, Dirk Forett," he said, extending his hand.

Heartly found herself reaching out to shake the thing's hand, still trying to take in what she'd just seen—to understand how the hand she gripped felt like a hand at all. "Dirk. I, uh—"

"No need," he interrupted. "We don't have much time to catch up at the moment. We have a lot of work to do if we're to save this planet and the *Ark*'s crew. And it starts with dealing with that." Dirk pointed behind Major Heartly.

Chapter 36

Dirk had been the easiest target to find. The renowned scientist had only been twenty-two at the time, but even then, his brilliance was nothing to scoff at.

Rolf would give him that much, at least.

Already having completed his undergraduate degree in engineering, the guy had been in the middle stages of finishing his doctorate, according to his file. When he'd first read that, Rolf had wanted to knock that man from the Company who'd found him right off his chessboard. He himself lacked social skills, unable to tolerate the mindless blabber of the peasants and laymen who used up the majority of the earth's oxygen, and the pawn he was supposed to maneuver was too cramped up in his own dissertation to be bothered or interrupted.

If he were to interrupt Dirk's current lifestyle to complete his job, there could only be two outcomes. One, he would be brushed off and forgotten about, or two, he would be remembered as that guy who would not leave the other alone. He had memorized all of the information given to him—nowhere did it say remain incognito—but something in Rolf's gut told him to remain the player of the game and keep an eye out from above.

Lines would get blurred if he were both player and piece, and there were no guarantees that there existed a common goal between the two.

So he would let Dirk go about his life, double-checking numbers and making sure everything was just so; he could still move the other pieces. He just had to find common ground among them.

Eyes jumping from screen to screen, Rolf watched in boredom as his system ran background checks on the other targets. He did not expect to find anything that the Company had not already told him, but he would not be taken for a fool. In fact, he had done some research of his employers, and the fact that nothing came up was much more telling than if miscellaneous chunks of information were to present themselves. Of course, he could care less about the reputation or the credibility of the organization, for they had managed to entertain him, but it was an undeniable fact that information was power, and right now, they had more than he did.

Hell, they had managed to find *him*.

He had never dealt with an enigmatic entity such as the Company in person; the only observations he had as a foundation were those found in science fiction novels. But any institution, no matter what title was assigned to it, was nothing more than a gargantuan collection of humans; the Company, in essence, was human, too.

And any human had patterns.

And patterns were why Rolf Vermann was the master of the board.

He was thorough, cunning, and curious by nature, a deadly combination. The Company may have appeared out of the blue, but they did not change the grand scheme of his game—all they did was give him a larger board and assign new meaning to some pieces. He would do their dirty work and let them think this fifteen-year chase was enough to keep him interested. He would find these people and move them around and watch them fumble and think their lives were their own. He would work for this invisible company that thought they had lured some stereotypical, socially inept brainiac into their grip to do with as they pleased by playing to his desires. In the end, they were only fooling themselves by thinking they had any influence over him. They had promised him a chessboard and they would be his king. After all, the king was nothing more than a nuisance to the game, barely capable of moving on its own.

Hiding.

Waiting.

Yes, the Company could be king to the moons of the most distant planets and back, for nothing would change the fact that he was the player, and the king could only remain safe for as long as he allowed it to be.

The Company was under his thumb.

The mystery of the names on his files—Dirk, Franklin, Rodney, Zoe, Jenny—and the importance of Santelli Minor were intriguing, yes, but they paled in comparison to the Company itself.

And fifteen years seemed like sufficient time to learn the patterns of the unsuspecting Company.

***

Rolf had spent the first two weeks doing nothing but going

over files and cross-referencing histories inside his hotel room. Only leaving to force food into his body, Rolf dictated very clearly with words and money that he did not want anyone cleaning or stepping foot into his room. He would know if anything was out of place; he had set up cameras. The cost of the equipment littering the room was not his concern—they could take that for all he cared. It was owned by the Company and set to wipe itself if removed improperly. Rolf's caution stemmed from a much more selfish reason than that.

This was *his* game, and he refused to share it.

Not that any random plebeians could even understand it.

In the short period of time that had passed, his new pawns had proven they would surely make the next five thousand, four hundred, and seventy-five days interesting. All their paths had crossed at one point, though Rolf doubted each of them remembered meeting all the others, and it would only be a matter of time before he started bumping them into one another by accident.

After all, he had found the common ground.

Two days earlier, Dirk had set up a brief presentation for the public regarding his dissertation. According to him, his thoughts could change the world, so the world should be invited to hear. Rolf had watched the presentation through the live stream while manipulating one of the auditorium's security cameras. The man spoke of creating a spaceship, going so far as to show the schematics and everything. He was smart and imaginative, but if it had not been for two things, Rolf would have yawned.

First, Dirk Forret had mentioned an ultimate goal of traveling to Santelli Minor, and second, by moving the security camera, Rolf had been able to find a familiar face sitting in the crowd.

Rodney Korsakov.

The man, who was only a few years younger than Dirk at

the time, had nodded along, absorbing every word the future scientist said.

It seemed as though his pawns were moving together of their own accord, beginning their orbit around Dirk.

And he had just the ship to bring them together.

***

His favorite subject had to have been Franklin. The man's patterns of behavior, though different from the vast majority of others having been struck by tragedy in high school, was still a pattern and, henceforth, still predictable. After the accident, Rolf noted Franklin's recovery phase was pretty typical—shutting down, getting angsty, acting like everything was okay—and he only acted out when he was stressed.

And he was only stressed when a certain Zoe Rowens was involved.

Even years after the incident, Rolf was certain that Franklin was not okay. The giant was interesting to watch flounder around pretending, but if he wanted all of them to be accepted into Dirk's *Ark* program—which had been announced to start accepting applications in two years—Rolf needed to ensure that all of his pawns were in good condition and would make it onto the official crew. Korsakov had done a lot of the work for Rolf, connecting with Dirk and showing interest, and he already had plans for Jenny. But Franklin and Zoe were their own train wrecks.

In order for any progress to be made, Franklin needed to understand he was not okay.

Zoe, on the other hand, needed to be kicked out of her safety net as a doctor. She had gotten too comfortable, and even worse than the fact that in her current state she was unlikely to apply for the *Ark*, she was beginning to bore Rolf. Her moves were beyond predictable—they were practically scripted. He would fix that.

He could kill two birds with one stone, hijacking a traffic light close to Zoe's hospital to get Franklin in a car accident. Rolf watched in pure amusement through the hospital's cameras as Franklin had sauntered into the hospital, caught sight of Zoe, and refused her aid outright. He had continued to watch as Zoe later ripped off her nametag and chucked it across the room as Franklin held his head in agony, crying out in one of the hospital beds.

They were both on track.

***

Halfway into his job was the moment everything picked up the pace. Jenny, who had been a student at the university where Dirk taught, was required to attend the lecture of a professor at the university for one of her research classes. Students were required to sign up ahead of time, and Rolf watched in apathetic interest as the girl tried again and again to sign up for the Astronomy lecture only for the system to say the lecture was full. Rolf had, of course, changed the programming so she could only access Dirk's class.

Jenny went, and the rest was history.

Things at the Company, on the other hand, had taken a much more convoluted turn. For the first time in eight years, he was contacted by the Company and asked to come into the central office. It was an opportunity he both anticipated and dreaded. His own observations of the internal operations and actions of the Company had been very limited, as one had to be invited to the main office, so this was his chance. But at the same time, he despised social situations; that much would never change.

When he arrived, a woman—Alexandra Powers was her name—told him they were pleased with his work and wanted to reward him. He must have been sweating, having been surrounded by unfamiliar walls and security guards, because they brought him a glass of water. After he took a large gulp, she told him of a chance to exist above them all: in the sky. He would have his favorite pawns at his fingertips—the planets would basically be at his disposal. He would be away from all the useless lifeforms on Earth. It was all that Rolf could have ever dreamed.

Yet some part of him wanted to say "no." Being up there meant he was going to be in a machine made and owned by the Company; there would be no way to observe the institution itself if they had him on a chain. But before he could even think it through, before he could reexamine the chessboard, a ring sounded through his head and he found himself saying yes.

***

His head ached.

His mind felt as though it had just been ripped open and put back together. What had happened? He had landed on Santelli Minor, made his way to where he knew the *Ark* crew was, and had even spoken to Korsakov—or, he thought he did—right? Clearing his mind, he tried to remember the events, only for more blurs to present themselves. The more he thought, the less clear the picture became.

Rolf Vermann had a perfect memory.

Something was wrong with this planet.

No matter how much he concentrated, he could only grasp random fragments of memory. The more he considered his conversation with Korsakov, the less he could recall all of it. The last clear memory he could recall was crossing the planet's surface with intent to find Korsakov.

Did they actually speak?

He was losing his mind.

Groaning, Rolf forced his mind to stop banging and focus on the now. Slowly opening one eye, he found himself staring at the glowing green altar, only it wasn't the same altar next to which he'd landed his ship. He was vaguely aware of Korsakov sitting a few feet away from him, but he could not bring himself to look away.

"Ah, he's awake."

Startled by the voice, he looked up. Sitting on top of the new altar was a translucent figure. He looked mostly human, though humanoid features were predominant on his face. Adorned in beads and jewels, a wicked grin decorated the figure's face.

Who was he?

"Pitiful human, you've already forgotten me. I am Mishrak, and you," his eyes danced with fire, "helped bring me here."

Chapter 37

The whirlwind of the last week on Santelli Minor still filled Jeremy's mind—foremost in it was the elation of identifying the bioinformation worm which had infected both the crew and ship, but this had been tempered by Ron's horrific death. It was the following day, and he was now back at the console after a fitful night of broken sleep. Franklin and the insertion team had already departed. He was focused—had to be focused—on investigating the infection of the *Ark* and, more importantly, how to undertake decontamination.

Once he was seated in position, a retinal scan authorized access to the *Ark*'s onboard systems. He sat back, reviewing where he'd gotten and what he should do next. The system initialized the holographic displays and restored all the status information as he had left it yesterday. Activating the history slider, Jeremy was able to review the analyses he'd run, then time-slice between different data views. At exactly the same moment as he saw it, he remembered he'd left a system-wide scan running, searching, for infection, for systems that had been initiated by the worm. There it was: 'Sub-surface scan…'

Shit, he thought. *What's it searching for?*

He accessed the *Ark*'s higher-level runtime architecture, enabling him to define a search parameter across the programmatic cascade. If he could isolate the codebase running the sub-surface scan, he could identify the top-level worm interface and so directly access other systems that had been initiated.

The retinal scan authorized his access but the screen remained blank; he ran a console command and saw there were locks against his access to the *Ark*'s top-level systems. The worm appeared to be locking him out. This was much more serious than he thought—if the worm had locked him out of this system, what else could it take control of?

"Okay, you clever little bastard…if I can't list the systems, can I guess which one's you've taken?" he cursed.

"Oxygen—Check.

"Anti-gravity—Check."

"Replicators—Check.

"Security—Check.

"Shields—Check.

"System records—locked. Why?" Bericote was puzzled.

"Navigation—No..." His voice trailed off. What were the navigation systems needed for?

"Weapons? No." The *Ark* had no weapons; it was a science vessel.

"But…mineral exploration. No. Shit. *Shit*..."

The *Ark* had a direct-induction laser-based mining system

intended for sub-surface drilling. There were locks against that system, and he couldn't access it.

"Johnson, Bericote here," he commanded into the intercom.

"Yeah, B, what's going on?" came the reply.

"I've got a lock-out against system records, navigation system, and the mining laser. Can you access them manually? What are they doing?"

"Just looking…" responded Johnson. "I can do a syslog dump from the system records for you to investigate. The navigation system has a course plotted on Santelli itself—two locations. The first point is at the search pod—no, just east of that, at the altar. The second is eight clicks due south. Looks like an open depression, bare, barren." Johnson was focused, concentrating, reading out information from the manual control system.

"The coordinates are being fed—holy shit—they're being fed to the mining laser! The ship has to physically move to reach that target. If the laser hits the altar, it'll vaporize everything in a twenty-meter radius, including the pod."

"Bericote, the system's locked out. I can't access it. The *Ark*'s stabilizers are engaging while the laser capacitor charges. We've got about thirty minutes of initialization before the system is live. We've gotta get a message to them."

Jeremy froze—he was locked out, and Johnson had no manual control of the *Ark*. The worm had control of all principal systems—it was clearly malevolent and they were increasingly under its control. It was imperative they evacuated the ship.

"Johnson, we have to leave, have to abandon ship. We can't stay here if the ship's systems are out of our control. Order an evacuation."

He heard the intercom click on, but no voice—just the sound of hoarse breathing. He imagined Johnson sitting up in the cramped bridge—in what was normally his domain—knowing that the decision was inevitable but not wanting to make it. There was an intake of breath, then…

"Sure thing. Can you start the evac procedure? All personnel to the lifepods, jettison the specimens. I've got to…" There was a long pause. "I've got to do what Franklin said…destroy the *Ark*. I'm heading to engineering. I'll meet you at the lifepods in ten minutes."

"Roger that, Johnson. Bericote, out."

With that, Bericote accessed the command and control safety module and started the ship's automatic evacuation. The lighting panels became brighter and brighter to the point that they were painful to look at—at the same time, a rhythmic white-noise waxed and waned. This was part of the multi-sensory program which alerted staff to the well-drilled procedure. They were required to make their way to the upper deck of the ship where fully equipped lifepods for ten crew members each were positioned. These had life support for thirty days and were ejected upwards and outwards. On Santelli Minor, they would use atmospheric boosters to hover away from the *Ark* to a biosafety perimeter. The safety systems were synchronized with live telemetry from the main computers—as soon as the self-destruct sequence was initiated, the lifepods would then move twenty kilometers away before landing and embedding themselves into the surface.

The crew made their way calmly along the corridors, climbing through the decks toward the lifepods. Bericote loaded the specimen ejection protocol—or SEP, as it was known—on his console. The SEP opened the cargo bay, and then, for the larger specimens in cages, lifted them on a maglev conveyor belt to the ship's main ramps. They were ejected before an air-filled cushion system was used to parachute them to a safe landing—the dead-bolts on the cages were then fired, releasing the specimens. All of the smaller specimens were in a centralized climate-controlled storage area and were ejected as one pod in a similar manner. This area lay at the rear of the *Ark*, immediately in front of the medical center. Once evacuation commenced, the medical center retained all injured personnel and a skeletal staff and was the first system area to be separated from the *Ark*.

Bericote initiated the SEP, locked out his console, then glanced around the lab. He paused, remembering the times he'd spent here—colleagues, friends, discoveries, their hopes and dreams. With a sigh and a shrug, he left for the lifepods.

***

Back on the bridge, Johnson sat back in the pilot's chair—he paused, taking in the scene. He knew he didn't have the time but wanted to savor the feeling of being the pilot just once more. With a wistful smile, he slowly pulled himself up and left, his footsteps echoing as he disappeared down the corridor.

Outside the bridge door, there was just the faint hum of the ship when, with a judder, the roof panel slid sideways. Jacob slowly lowered himself down and lightly dropped to the floor. He'd overheard the entire conversation. "Over my dead body," he muttered. And with that, he entered the bridge.

Jacob had a hunch. *Where would a pilot hide his most valued possession?* he thought. *As close as possible!*

He went straight to the pilot's chair—pulling a knife from his boot, he slashed the back of the chair, ripping the padding out. Nothing. He tore the seat cushion from its base. Still nothing. Putting the knife away, he dropped to his knees, sliding his hands underneath, feeling the material much like a security guard frisks his target. He felt a small bulge in the chair lining and, tearing away the edge of the fabric, found the secret compartment. He pulled out a metal safebox, opening it. Inside lay the iTransmit.

Flicking the safety catch off, he hit the 'Transmit' button before attaching the device to the control panel. The beacon immediately sprang to life, sending an alpha-one coded emergency signal, transmitting it via the interstellar sub-space relay. Then the iTransmit showed the successful transmission—upon reaching Earth's communications gateway, the high-priority message was intercepted by the Company's communications center and from there re-routed to Alexandra Powers.

***

Johnson hurried down to engineering. The corridors were strangely quiet with the crew now evacuating the *Ark*. His eyes hurt with the bright light, his ears with the white noise, and now his head with the prospect of destroying the *Ark*. As a space veteran, he knew his course, the path he had to plot then take. With calm rationalism, he entered the engineering department; the area was cramped. The *Ark* was really one large rocket with large laboratories and storage facilities bolted to the front. Engineering was then squeezed in and around the rocket with a range of computer consoles, giving control of the propulsion system along with direct physical access to the rockets themselves for maintenance and repair. The command and control system for the rockets was located on the port-side toward the rear. This was where the warp injectors were located—these were used to vaporize the fuel rods before ignition. The self-destruct mechanism overheated the injectors, building up large quantities of fuel in the exhaust chambers before igniting them, so destroying the ship.

Johnson carried on down the narrow, winding corridor, ducking below an emergency pressure release valve before arriving at his destination. He reached within his shirt and pulled out his ID tag; this held his bioimprint, medical records, and system access rights. For the self-destruct sequence, he not only needed to complete bioauthentication but also have the hardware key to perform the final authorization. The computer performed the retinal scan, and he then pressed his tag against the console. This automatically flashed up the top-level control functions. He tapped 'Self-Destruct' and set the countdown to fifteen minutes, maximizing the time for crew to safely evacuate before the mining laser completed initialization. He turned swiftly on his heel and made his way back up to the lifepods.

***

Bericote reached the lifepod level—he had to wait for Johnson and ensure everyone evacuated safely.

The syslog, he thought.

In the frenetic activity, he'd forgotten about the third system which had been locked out—system records. He activated a temporary terminal and, after the retinal scan, initiated the holographic display; the syslog dump showed all activity across system records. He set up a filter, removing all scheduled activity, leaving only exceptions. He was expecting this to be fairly randomly distributed across different systems, mostly initiated by environmental sensors.

"Crew records?" he mumbled. That surprised him. "Actually..." He drilled deeper into the data records. "Biomedical... DNA!"

He pulled off the first record. Jenny Adonna. In fact, it wasn't her full DNA profile, just a DNA variation...a marker

"A difference? A marker?"

He copied the marker and ran it across the other crew records. "It matches! We've all got the same DNA trait. But for what?"

He heard steps behind him and an out-of-breath Johnson

appeared. "Get in the lifepod, Bericote. We've not got long," he uttered breathlessly.

"Johnson—the worm has been…profiling us."

"What? What do you mean?" Johnson was confused, impatience showing clearly on his face.

"We've all got the same DNA variation—a marker or tag. We're…connected."

"We haven't got time for this. The ship is about to self-destruct, man! Let's go." With that, Johnson grabbed Bericote by the arm and dragged him to the last remaining lifepod. The hydraulic delta wing doors of the capsule closed and they strapped themselves in. Johnson took his position at the front, where he could assume manual control in case of an emergency.

The front display flashed up a five second count—5—4—3—2—1. The lifepod rapidly accelerated, thrusting them back into their seats as it soared over the planet's surface away from the *Ark*. The thrusters fired them further and further away before the compressed gas canisters ejected the retaining pins, deploying the large parachutes. They slowly floated through the sky.

The terminal at which Bericote had stood completed the DNA match and flashed the results on to the screen—there were two DNA markers. The crew were split into two groups. Two *different* groups, each with unique markers. By design? Jenny and the rest of the science team were in one, the remaining crew in the other.

***

"Perfectly timed." Alexandra Powers smiled as the iTransmit message flashed up on her display. Pursing her lips, she concentrated, scanning the intel that the device provided on the *Ark*'s operational status. Lifepods all evacuated, crew on board, and specimens and medical center ejected. "Excellent," she muttered.

She composed a direct message to send to the Company investors—*Self-destruct sequence has been initiated on the* Ark *as anticipated. Proceeding to final phase in preparation for delivery.*

Powers switched her display to the iTransmit command console, then initiated a series of programmed commands transmitted back to the *Ark.* Finally, she called up the voice message system for transmission via the sub-space relay.

"Mishrak, this is Powers. We have now entered the final phase. You may utilize Vermann."

***

LEDs on the top of the iTransmit blinked, indicating data reception. Through the console interface on the bridge of the *Ark,* the device was able to relay a series of commands to the main computer, effectively controlling the ship remotely. The self-destruct sequence was halted, enabling the stabilizers to fully come online while the capacitors charged on the laser. Five minutes remained before the ship would be able to move to its initial target—the altar site. Finally, a series of commands were relayed to the lifepods.

***

Bericote and Johnson were both looking for the first indication of the ship's destruction. They waited... As the lifepod closed in on the surface, the air-cushions deployed and they came down with a barely perceptible bump. Still, nothing happened. The other members of the lifepod strained their necks, looking at what was happening, bracing themselves.

The relayed commands came from the *Ark,* releasing a colorless, odorless gas into the cabin. Bericote felt his mind numbing, his eyes closing, before he dropped unconscious. The bulkhead at the back of the lifepod opened, and the striped worms wriggled and writhed their way into the cabin.

Chapter 38

"You're who?"

The man's face twisted into the shell of a pleased leer. Though outlined with a mocking taunt, his lips held more than just amusement. Having been a socially inept observer his entire life, Rolf had seen a lot of unpleasant looks directed at him and others, but all of those glares and sneers and mirthless smiles could not even compare to the look of barbaric enjoyment contorting the figure's face; it was the most inhumane sight he'd ever witnessed. For the first time since he'd joined the Company, he felt utter terror.

Unable to suppress the shudder passing through his body, Rolf struggled to keep eye contact with the figure standing above him. His body protested with all its might against any sort of exertion—including the strain of forcing his eyelids open against the wind, sand, and altar glowing fiercely in the background. Plus, despite being partially translucent, the apparition before him radiated an aura that could only be described as oppressive. From the moment he had opened his eyes only seconds before, he'd felt the shift in the atmosphere around him. The soil and the plants and the air had gone from being simply things existing in the physical plane to somehow emitting a threatening vibe. They were like dormant weapons, waiting to be wielded by their master.

And Rolf Vermann had no trouble guessing just who that master was.

"I am Mishrak," was the reply, spoken in a tone as unpleasant as his expression.

Heart pounding from being pinned beneath a ruthless gaze, Rolf used all of his strength to stay as still as possible. He was in no state to run, yet it was the one action his body urged him to take. Everything about this situation radiated negativity, but attempting to leave would only make it worse.

"I must thank you for being such an obliging vessel, Rolf Vermann, for you have made this possible."

I must thank you for being such an obliging vessel.
Such an obliging vessel.
Obliging vessel.
Vessel.

Vaguely aware of the gears spinning rapidly in his mind, Rolf froze in horror as the words sunk in, his world breaking apart at the seams. This man—this *creature*—was giving him credit for hosting him, for making him stronger.

His mentality was different than that of most people, brutally crafted from the hardships of being an outcast his entire life. He did not sympathize with shallow heartbreaks or flesh wounds, and he couldn't care less about politics or theology, but even he had a moral compass. Though his was much more liberal than most, the appearance of *Mishrak* and the concept that he had been the one to breathe a new degree of life into him, was positively *wrong*.

It was wrong because at the time since Mishrak had appeared, things which should have been natural became unnatural. Everything felt tainted; Rolf had never felt filthier.

It was wrong because he would never willingly aid and abet something like this, confusing, unimaginable. Not even Rolf could foresee this; he had lost control somehow without even realizing it.

It was wrong because by losing control, he had relinquished his title as the player of the game instead unknowingly becoming a piece on the chessboard. He was brilliant and cunning and any being that could force him to play his own game was dangerous.

"Vessel?" he mumbled, still staring at the humanoid creature.

A chilling laugh sounded from his lips. "Yes. From the moment your little metal container began orbiting Santelli Minor seven years ago, you became mine. The Company, as you call it, gave you to me. It took many patient years developing the company on earth, to orchestrate special humans being set here. You do realize how special you are?"

Upon seeing Rolf's expression of confusion, a satisfied smile marred his features. "You may have been in the sky, but it does not change the fact that you are nothing more than a slave to this planet, at the mercy of gravity's whip. You have no right to the celestial beings."

With those words, any control Rolf had been holding onto for dear life was torn out of his hands. World shattering before him, he could not hold back the tears wracking his aching body, only adding to the pain searing through him. Just when he'd thought he had found somewhere he belonged, free of human contact, he was shoved right back to the ground. Even with no one to compare himself to, he did not belong. He was nothing more than a grown man trying to play pretend among the stars. He'd been so wrapped up in his game—so foolish—that he had forgotten the fact that he was under the orders of the Company. They were always present in the back of his mind, but his fascination with his new position had blinded him, and now he truly had nothing.

The realization stung.

Calming down from his sobs, Rolf caught his breath. Slowly turning his head to the presences he'd felt when he'd first woken up, he found himself staring at Korsakov. The man stared right back, confusion distorting his features. But Rolf had spent his entire life observing people and reading them, and he could see that beyond the man's disoriented eyes burned determination. He was still fighting to save himself and his colleagues, pushing back the rationale that was forcing bile up into Rolf's throat as the realization of how serious this was hit home.

Rolf no longer had a goal; his life had been torn to shreds and stomped into the ground before his very eyes.

He was exhausted, in the purest, most literal meaning of the word.

He just wanted to close his eyes.

But before he could give into his desires, he had to know one thing. He did not care about the motives or anything remotely human; he wanted to know how he had lost control of his own game.

"How?"

"Just because you are earth-bound does not mean I am," was the reply. "I am not chained anywhere. My reach can extend into the skies of this planet and my body does not need a form. It was simple to infiltrate your mind through your computer systems. You were so transfixed by the bleeping lights that you did not even realize I had taken over."

He had been hacked. His computer programs, his body, his mind—everything! As he was processing the words, another voice cut him off.

"Mishrak, this is Powers. We have now entered the final phase. You may utilize Vermann."

A wicked grin danced across the humanoid's lips. "At least this time, you'll realize it."

Mishrak lunged for Rolf.

***

The handicapped humanoid stared back at him. In his current state, Dirk could see the humanoid for what it was, yet also faint traces of the veneer it wore. It was fascinating, and under any other circumstances, Dirk would have loved to research the phenomenon further, but the face the humanoid wore was not what mattered.

"You're different," he stated, ignoring the exchange of glances between the two figures next to the humanoid. When he had regained his consciousness, something drew him away from the altar. His first priority should have been Korsakov and the others he sensed in the area, but something hung in the air that pulled him in the opposite direction. He could feel the goodness of the planet clearly in the air, and he could also feel the darkness. Yet there existed something in between the two—something which upset the already tilting balance, and it radiated from the humanoid.

"You are Dirk. The wind whispers your name."

"And you are?" he prompted again. There was not much time.

"Different, as you say, but you may refer to me as Amber."

"You know you're different—"

"What do you mean different?" the woman beside Amber interjected. "What's going on?"

Ignoring the woman's interruption, the humanoid gave Dirk a meaningful look. "You can feel it, right?" He nodded. "Then I will explain, if you agree to help me save my home and protect the rest of this galaxy from unimaginable destruction."

Though lacking a true physical body, Dirk could feel the adrenaline rush through him. They could do this. Even without the explanation, he could see the will shining in her eyes and that was enough to make him agree. He could tell they shared a common goal, for if the wind had not told him, the look she gave him did. It mirrored what he was sure his own reflected, filled with grief and spirit.

"I agree."

"Then I will tell you," the humanoid said. "Unlike your race, which has painted the world in shades of grey, Santelli Minor is black and white. There is good and there is evil, and nothing exists in between. It has been so since the beginning of time. The existence of a variance would shake the grounds and lead to disruption in the balance. Only complete control will allow Mishrak to reach his potential. We can't let that happen"

It clicked—the way he felt the equilibrium tipping, the tug he felt.

Quickly, Dirk said, "You're grey."

"I am the only, and Mishrak wants me dead," she stated. "While I can do nothing, I represent a change in the stability of Santelli Minor—a change that has been building for years. Good wants evil gone, and evil wants good gone, yet I recognize that both must exist, though not equally."

"Why would evil need to exist?" the man grunted.

"Because to eradicate one completely would destroy this planet. The Sons of Life and Mishrak are not just idols, they are the names given to good and evil personified—they are, in essence, lightness and darkness. They are the powerful forces that hold Santelli Minor together, and at this point, to erase one is to tear apart the planet. Ideally, at one point, Mishrak would be banished, but for now, Dirk Forret, I am asking you to help me weaken him."

He ran over her words in his mind. Somehow they made sense. If he had heard them before this trip, he never would have understood them. It would not have made sense to the past Dirk that evil should be eliminated in increments rather than all at once; it seemed fundamentally wrong. But he had seen the Sons of Life speak to him and he could feel the balance upon which Santelli Minor's fate hinged.

"How do we do that?" he finally asked.

"He has taken a human host. To kill the host is to weaken the parasite. He has engineered your very need to be here, he can manipulate humans easily, but he underestimated my strength as a grey, and the allies I have gathered. I have managed to intervene enough that we have a chance to stop him this time. Now, I'm simply asking for your help in finishing what we started."

*　*　*

Jenny ran faster than she ever had in her entire life. She had never been an athletically inclined person, but she felt as though she were flying at her speed.

After all the dust and sand had cleared, Jenny used her heightend senses to try and locate Korsakov and Vermann. They hadn't gone too far, using the altar to move to another gateway. She had pinpointed them, but just before she could take off running in that direction, she picked up on the faintest pulse of distress in

325

the opposite direction. It had not even taken her a minute to tell Zoe and Franklin the direction of the *Ark*'s second in command before she bolted away to assist the crew.

Minutes swiftly passed before she found herself standing in front of the lifepods. Confused, she peered inside. Johnson sat unnaturally still with his eyes closed, but what alarmed her was the sight of zebra worms crawling up his body. Without a second thought, she backed away, and with strength unbeknown to her, she smashed the glass.

***

Watching in horror as Vermann's body went limp, Korsakov held his breath. Before he was able to release it, the man's head snapped up and turned his way. No longer was his face warped with misery. Instead, he looked demonic, his grin wide and eyes wild. This was not the same man who had cried moments earlier; this was the creature who caused those tears.

This was Mishrak.

"It seems you're no longer under my influence, but I doubt you did that on your own," the man mused. "It seems the Sons of Life helped you out."

He said nothing. Nothing he could say would make this situation any better. His best bet was to run.

Wait.

Pausing, Korsakov listened again and sure enough the word was repeated.

Wait.

He knew that voice.

Dirk.

He had to buy time.

"You said the Company gave Vermann to you. What do you mean?"

"You humans are always so foolish, searching for all the wrong things. I was finally contacted by the Company through this earthling, after years of focussing my energy on one human that I managed to pair with. Aliens are not so dissimilar, there is always some connection between us all, and when I figured out how to utilize my telepathic energy, I finally connected with a host, on a near by spacecraft. All I had to do was get the right people out here, that carried a tiny mutation in their DNA that makes communication with humans possible. That's why you are all here. You will help me, and I will spare your planet the destruction I have planned once I transcend, finally able to leave this place."

"You are saying I have a rare mutation in my DNA?" Korsakov prompted. He was not even truly listening to what was being said. Instead, he focused on stalling. Counting heartbeat after heartbeat, he deafly waited.

"And you think that's a coincidence? You're part of a game you don't even understand," Mishrak taunted. "Since you've landed on this planet, nothing has gone your way. You've added to the unrest fueling the Sons-of-Mishrak. Fueling me."

"Okay, so you've won. Santelli bows to you. Why are you still in Vermann's body?"

"You humans are all so stupid. My reign does not end here, for I intend to spread it to every planet inhabiting this universe. Vermann, here, knows the coordinates of a bioship to help me accomplish just that."

***

Hands pressed against Johnson's forehead and chest, Jenny watched as the worms on his body died one by one. Not sparing a second, she moved to Bericote and repeated her actions, each pulse of her powers making her feel farther and farther from her body. She attended to each member in the lifepods before she heard a

327

groan.

"Something…wrong…" Johnson mumbled.

"What's wrong?"

"iTransmit."

She did not know what was wrong with the iTransmit, but that only propelled her quicker towards the *Ark*. If there was one thing she knew about the engineering of the *Ark*, it was that the iTransmit ran on a countdown timer. She hadn't heard anything blow up yet, which meant the timer was still running.

She had to be quicker.

***

Losing his physical sand form, Dirk was able to travel fifty times faster. It was only a matter of moments before he found himself materializing next to Franklin and Zoe. Both of them sprinted towards where he knew Mishrak was.

"Franklin, how's your aim?"

The man's eyes grew wide as both he and the doctor came to a halt. Dirk was sure this was terrifying for them, for he had just come out of nowhere, but there was no time for lengthy explanations.

"How is your aim?" he repeated.

The hulking man blinked a few times before steeling his eyes. "Fine."

"Mishrak has taken a human host, and the only way to destroy him is to shoot him while he's in a physical form." He twisted the truth a bit, for the shot would not kill Mishrak, but there was no time to explain everything the humanoid had told him. At this moment, Grewder, Heartly—as he'd heard them call each other—and Amber were heading towards the bioship. He had been able to sense it and sent them in that direction, but he needed to go to the *Ark*.

"Do you understand what I'm saying?"

"Dirk—" Zoe started, but Franklin beat her to it.

"Yes, Captain."

***

She found Jacob sitting in the captain's chair. From his slouch, to the fact he sat in Dirk's chair, to his hand running through his hair—everything about him infuriated her at the moment. Taking long strides over to him, she almost screamed when she saw the iTransmit in his hand. His eyes shot to her and widened.

"What did you do?" she seethed, but her question only ignited the argument.

"What did I do? What were you thinking, destroying the *Ark*?" he shouted.

"It's to keep everyone safe!"

"Bullshit! I gave up everything for the *Ark*! It was my one chance to make enough money to pay for my sister's medical bills, and you want to take that away!" he yelled, tears falling down his cheeks. "How is that keeping *her* safe?"

A beat of silence consumed them. She watched in grief as he cried, though malice still hardened his eyes, and for a moment she felt horrible. Everything was happening in such a rush, such a flurry of insanity, that second by second they all were becoming less sensitive to the things which made them human. She had never heard about Jacob's family—or about any of the *Ark*'s members' families—and despite the fact that she was going to rip the iTransmit from his hand, she sympathized with him. The destruction of the *Ark* was a lot more than just destroying a spacecraft. For Dirk, it was destroying his dream—for some, it was their jobs and for others, their families. But no matter what, someone was losing something. But they had to do it, Dirk's message was clear, there was no scenario that would allow the ship to return to earth, the outcome wold be unimaginable.

Just as Jenny prepared to make a move towards the iTransmit, a beeping noise sounded. Spinning around to the control panel, her heart stopped.

"Why is it pointing there?" she asked, breaking the quiet.

"What is what pointing where?"

"Why are the *Arks* lasers pointing at the altar? I thought you just turned off the self-destruct sequence!"

"I did!" he yelled, "well I think I did, it seemed too easy… but…I didn't access the onboard weapons system at all. In the silence that followed, he stared at the screen in confusion just as the *Arks* pre flight door seals initiated, and the engines fired up.

Both Jenny and Jacob jolted, staring at the timer as it counted down the last five minutes, Jenny's mind raced. Why was the *Ark* set to take off? What were the implications? Her head pounded as the red numbers blinked.

Placing her fingers on the keyboard, she took a deep breath, but before she could press anything, she felt a presence next to her. Though she could not clearly see him, the outline of the man she loved was traced in the air.

"The system's been hacked," he said.

"Why would anyone want to destroy the altar?"

"Amber said it's because it's what ties Mishrak to this planet. By destroying the altar, he's free to move around as he pleases."

"Amber?" she questioned, but quickly caught herself. "How do we fix it?"

Dirk and Jenny stared at each other. In all of the times she'd ever daydreamed of seeing Dirk Forret speechless, never had this scenario been one. Years ago, she figured it would be if she ever confessed to him, but this—this was never in the plan book.

"I overheard Jeremy mention something about a worm hacking the system," Jacob offered, staring at the floor. "I'm not sure if that means anything.

Dirk used his life power to remove the iTransmit from Jeremy's hand, causing it to hurl across the room, smashing against the far wall.

"Jeremy, this ship is infested, it has to be destroyed now. Do you understand what I'm asking you?" Finally the puzzle pieces came together, Jeremy didn't have a moments pause to understand how his actions had led to his own impossible predicament.

"I can stop the Ark from taking off, and ensure the self destruct command completes on site. If you don't complete your mission Sir, I sure as hell will do mine."

Four minutes flashed on the countdown and Dirk nodded. In that one motion, Jenny understood his plan. If the worms could hack the system, so could he, and if they could destroy worms with their powers, they could do it in the computer as well. He was free of the constraints of a physical body, free to travel through any medium. He could stop the countdown from the inside out after the infestation is removed. She could kill the worms. She would try to attack from the outside. Sharing one last glance, she allowed herself one moment of insanity—a smile in the midst of impending doom.

It was crazy, but life was always an adventure with him.

***

His lungs burned, but he paid them no attention. They were so close, he could feel it. The bushes grew thinner, and he slowed his pace. Behind him, Zoe panted heavily.

They were getting too old for this.

Motioning for Zoe to stay still, Franklin heard voices from

beyond the foliage.

"—ck…you…"

"Shut up."

Peering through the bushes, Franklin's breath hitched as he saw Vermann—no, Mishrak—holding Korsakov by the throat, strangling him. The *Ark's* second in command kicked his feet uselessly, resulting in nothing more than the bandages on his sides coming undone. His face was turning blue. Franklin's grip on his gun tightened.

"And what do you know, it seems as if your friends have arrived. Shall we greet them?" Mishrak said, turning to face where Franklin and Zoe hid. "Come out, come out."

Exchanging looks with Zoe, Franklin nodded and walked out first. Without turning around, he could hear her lithe footsteps following his, standing slightly behind him. She was not the type to play damsel in distress, and they both knew she was capable of taking care of herself, but this was not the time for a bantering match. In the back of his mind, he truly appreciated it; when they'd dated, one of the most difficult things for either of them to do was admit they needed help or protection, and the fact that she allowed him to do this for her meant a lot.

If they made it out alive, he'd tell her.

Raising the gun, he aimed it at Vermann's head. He had not killed anyone since that night in high school, and the idea scared him, to be honest. He had to tell himself over and over that this was different—that by doing this, he was saving people, including the man who was Rolf Vermann—that he was making the right choice. That if he did this, he would not be the monster he was in high school.

The longer he waited, the more his hand began to shake.

"It seems all you humans like to play pretend," Mishrak

said, tightening his grip on Korsakov. Franklin watched as his hands moved to snap the man's neck. Just as Korsakov raised his hands, just as Mishrak started to reposition Korsakov in front of his own head, just as Korsakov closed his eyes, Franklin pulled the trigger.

In the silence that followed, Zoe held her breath. She heard a two bodies fall to the ground. One of them dead, one of them living.

Franklin never missed.

For what felt like the first time in eons, Rodney Korsakov took a painful, gasping breath.

***

"Major Heartly and Master Sergeant Grewder escaped on a separate bioship while we got the *Ark* travel-ready. The ship now sits in quarantine. We still hope that one day it will be relocated to a site as a dedicated space museum.

"The *grey* humanoid remains on Santelli Minor to this day, bringing about peace to a world with a history of nothing but unrest.

"Once Mishrak was without a host, his influence lost its grip on Alexandra Powers. The freedom from unknown control left her so confused, she was inevitably committed. I'm not sure she truly understands how close she came to unleashing true evil on our universe.

"The planet of Santelli Minor is currently going through a period of great change. Unlike here, where we elect political leaders who pass laws, the humanoids of Santelli Minor are ruled by lightness and darkness. In the past fifteen Earth years, there has been a shift in the balance favoring lightness. The idol of insanity, Mishrak, is being repressed, though there is never any guarantee that it'll remain so—yeah, Hannah. Question?"

"What happened to Doctor Dirk Forret? He led the expedition fifteen years ago, right? Is it true he and Jenny Adonna ended up staying on the planet? And what about the DNA marker? What did that mean?"

A fond smile graced the man's face. "Well, Hannah, you see—"

"Professor! Professor!" Standing in the doorway of his lecture hall was the dean's office secretary—he could not remember the kid's name for the life of him. Holding in the few cuss words on the verge of leaking out—the whole political-correctness-don't-swear-in-front-of-young-impressionable-minds bullshit was really getting on his nerves—he raised an eyebrow, waiting for the guy to continue. "Sorry to interrupt, sir, but your wife and son are here. Apparently it's urgent."

"Did Zoe say—"

"Dad!" Pushing past the messenger, a mop of auburn hair made its way towards him. Giving a fake salute, he ruffled the boy's hair.

"Alby! Don't just rush into your father's classroom!" a voice called. Chasing after the young teen came the professor's wife.

"Oh, the irony," he drawled as she, too, ran right into his classroom. The beautiful woman flashed him a dangerous glare before smirking. Digging into her purse, she pulled out a slightly wrinkled white envelope. Holding it up, a huge smile broke out across her face. The address was written in familiar handwriting he hadn't seen in fifteen years. It was narrow, loopy, slightly slanted, and undeniably belonged to only one person.

"Franklin," his wife said, "he wrote."

THE END

Human Against All Odds
By Cayce Berryman

Villains are not determined by their actions but by their potential to do bad things. I wasn't always a villain, just like I wasn't always human. No one wants a deformed creature living amongst them, and when that creature is young, humans find exile easier.

"Get rid of the abomination before it destroys us all!"

That's what they said and what they tried to do. The only problem is that they failed, and their actions created the enmity needed to make me what they feared I'd become.

The wet grime providing life for the sickly green shoots in the warm season forms a ghastly white to my gray skin. The sun warms the land, and my body swells until the return of the cold season.

The ground isn't good for much. It makes my hands brittle because it gives way to my claws easily, like wet soil to the burrowing Silkien fish in my own world and the beach clams which claim sand in this world.

Oh, how I remember my world, its turf expanding for turns longer than the Earth's curved surface could dream of stretching. Though I had only lived there a year, a Silayan never forgets. I've never forgotten the day my world fell to the death of the black hole consuming its surface, pulling it bit by bit into nothingness forever. I've never forgotten the screams echoing through the last portal I selfishly buried in the ground for my own use. I've never forgotten the pain I experienced upon my arrival to a new plane, so much closer to the sun that my skin wished to melt off my back. I've never forgotten, and for a young Silayan offspring who left their colony to die, the memory alone is enough torment.

I circle my claw in the dirt above, licking my lips as water drips off the hovering roots, warning me of the new rain welcoming the warm season again. Humans celebrate this time, and even after years of my heart slowing and succumbing to a constant chill, I cannot bring myself to do the same. I despise what the sun will do to my skin, darkening it to mirror porous, human flesh. The sun has powers of change not unknown to those of my world but still unfamiliar to us.

I do not know the humans' lifespan, so I make sure to hide beneath the soil until I feel the hatred dissipate. After one hundred years, I watch humans from a distance, scrambling for food and shelter before the cold season. They rejoice when the sun returns with food.

Every warm season, I call upon the stars to take the life of a child, and they curse the villain they know still lives. They think me an evil being, so I comply. Every cry resounding from a young life reminds me of the one I couldn't live…the one I was denied because of a human's incapable mind. No amount of life satisfies my thirst.

I have to stop after a century passes, and I wait for another century to return. Death doesn't please me, and I will never feel satisfied seeking vengeance from a helpless tribe. My heart is slowing even more, now; I know I need to walk into the village this time. Silayans cannot survive more than half a millennium without a colony, else we do not adapt to the changing climate. I can feel the Earth change, but I'm not changing with it. As Silayans live off the flowing blood within the colony, mine has slowed in the last century. Now, even the sun's warmth does not alleviate the chill of a slowing heart.

A weakening body does not help me walk into the human colony, but without their acceptance, my heart will stop before the cold season returns. I've waited too long to accept the fate of joining such a primitive species. Because my skin mimics their own, my towering above them only provides them one oddity to glance at, disturbed, before norms of society remind them not to stare.

Walking down rows of small houses and thatched roofs, I glance at small children chasing each other across the soft ground. Each child sends sharpened staffs, large fires, and screams into my mind, and the memory of reddened human faces quickens my pace.

The blue linea of interitus stretch from the sky, ready to strike down anything I wish, as they did centuries before. The power of stars never leaves a Silayan, but I swore never to use it, else I will give into the frenzy and will kill another race.

Uplifted voices tug an irritated thread in my chest, but I swallow it, knowing I have to learn to like those who would hate me if they knew me.

Another child races by, and I turn around, feeling the slivers of interitus plead for further direction and a target. I could give them one—every child in this generation. Their small faces bring the gray face of my youth into the forefront of my mind, fear shading the once selfish innocence of my being.

"Sir?" a miniscule voice whispers.

I turn to face a child whose eyes look the same color as my skin once had. I recognize "sir" as a gender affiliation; however, I never understood the purpose of gender, aside from procreation.

I nod and the child flashes its teeth at me before grasping one claw with the other. "Do you have any food?"

The words make me face him completely. I know of young children who ask for food or shelter. They are denied the same as I. I have always made sure not to strike them, but to instead strike the children who are entitled to such things. I never need food, but while I've sought a colony to sustain my life, humans seem to thrive by devouring other life.

I shake my head, regretting immediately that I have not taken time to learn the words of humans. I hadn't thought of it, nor did I feel the need. Communication works equally well through the body, but humans seem to need multiple languages. Watching them allows me to understand their words, but I never considered trying to speak them. I don't even know if I can.

"Well," it persists, brushing back the fur atop its head and holding it at its shoulders. "Do you have…"

I shake my head before it continues; I have nothing to offer. Still, I hurt for the child. I came to Earth expecting help, though I received only hate for my oddities. This child threatens no one, yet it still is denied the right to life.

A sparkle leaves its eyes and it remains as defenseless as it was when approaching me. Without any hope for sustenance, the child turns and asks the next passerby, who turns away before it finishes asking. I dig my nails into my palms, holding back the urge to change my target and strike the elders who deny helpless lives their needs. The humans are worse than I thought.

I growl at myself for having nothing for the child, feeling as useless as the humans. The language of movement allowed me to see much, and this child only wants what anyone could have provided. Before digging another hole into the cool soil, a soft thump draws me to a hollow trunk. Small, brown creatures with long ears cower after a glance at the face recognized as human, and I smile. I grab the two thick pairs of ears and turn back toward the colony.

The child looks up, startled, when I kneel on the ground beside it. A glint of hope shimmers in its eyes, and it pulls long locks of hair away from its soft, gentle face. After risking a quick glance at the creatures in my hand, it smiles softly. I hand it the dead carcasses, and it throws me another pair of wide eyes.

"For me?"

I nod, this time giving it a smile of my own. I close my mouth when I remember the odd sharpness of my teeth, but the child doesn't cower and, instead, throws its body into mine, covering me with tears. Immediately, the heat of the sun bares on me harshly. My eyes dart around at the forming circle of elderly humans. Tears form on a few faces and they turn away, returning with round, brown lumps and colorful fruit. Before long, other rejected children meet the one beside me, sharing their tears and thanks.

It doesn't make sense, but I don't care. I continue ensuring the lives of those children prosper, and the act encourages the colony to come together as mine once had. My blood flows strongly, and my winter-gray skin barely surprises them when it appears.

They once declared me to be an evil creature for my appearance, but this time they don't. This time, I am an angel. This time, I'm the guardian.

Wytch Born
Chapter 1

The saloon was filled with its usual nightly ruckus—the laughter of men plied by drink, a slightly out-of-tune piano keeping a lively melody, sultry murmurs of the prostitutes looking to lure a patron upstairs, and the occasional outburst of men in dispute. Once again, above all the other commotion in the Frontier House of Vice, Sal heard the same voices.

"Hit me again, Charlie," called the disheveled coalminer at the bar. The man had been making a spectacle of himself since Sal had dealt the first hand of the evening. No less than six times this night had he caused a deafening scene of drunken buffoonery. The coalminer was a local by the name of Dan Pearly, and this was a usual occurrence. The reason Charlie, the barkeep, put up with Dan's inhuman volume was the fact that every bit of coin Dan earned at the coalmine went right into Charlie's pocket.

"That man clearly doesn't mind making a scene in public," Sal muttered.

"Dan don't mean nothing by it. Now deal them cards and let me win a hand," said the railway worker beside Sal.

"Now there's the spirit. That is the kind of poker player I like to see at my table." Sal bared his perfect, white teeth in a joyous grin. He shuffled and cut the deck, but before he could deal the next hand, an enchanting voice took him aback.

"Gentlemen, is this seat taken?"

Sal turned to address the owner of such an alluring voice. He stood as he laid his eyes on her, her elegance and beauty more overcoming than he had ever seen. Her bright orange petticoat matched that of the prostitutes of the saloon, but Sal had to believe this woman was more than a simple lust trader. Her thick, raven hair flowed softly around bright green eyes and fell against her skin, its soft tan like a perfect clay in the dim saloon. Apart from faint lining around her lips and eyes, she wore no makeup; she did not require any. Sal squinted at the ink of tattoos partially obscured by her mesh sleeves, but he could not tell if the tattoos were tribal or oriental in origin. Sal would have sworn that this woman carried Gypsy blood.

"Ma'am, a creature as lovely as yourself is free to sit where she pleases. It would be our privilege if you would join our table," Sal said as he stood and placed his grey hat over his heart.

"Oh, sir, you are too kind, indeed," the woman said with a practiced bat of her long-lashed eyes.

She raised her right hand, and Sal immediately picked up on the signal, taking her hand in his. "I wouldn't be so quick with that compliment; you don't know me yet." Sal gave her his best smile. "Please allow me to see you supplied with whatever drink you might fancy to keep those exquisite lips of yours from getting too parched by all this desert heat."

"If I said you were too kind, would you be agreeable this time?"

"Ma'am, if you keep on batting those eyes at me, you will find I am agreeable to all kinds of things."

"My, I have to say it is a pleasure to make your acquaintance, mister…"

"Folks around here call me Sal."

She threw him a breathtaking smile. "Interesting name. Is Sal short for something?"

"Why, yes it is, but only my best friends call me by my full name," Sal said, returning a playful smirk.

He wanted to maintain a bit of mystery about himself, though he could tell she was the sort who was used to having men answer her every whim without challenge.

"Oh, can't I be your friend?" The woman mocked distress, and he considered continuing their game, but the curious eyes at the table caught his attention, and he acknowledged them with a nod.

"Ma'am, just sit and play a hand, and I'll show you how friendly I can be." Sal cleared his throat. "I will confess, you do have me at a disadvantage. You are stunningly beautiful and have the voice of a lark, but I have not the pleasure of your name."

She retreated into herself for a moment, glancing hesitantly at her lap. "A lark, you call me. A lark is a beautiful bird with a beautiful song. Sir, you may continue to call me a lark."

"As you wish, Miss Lark." Sal pulled the empty chair out for her to sit. "The game is Brag, ma'am. Are you familiar?"

"Why yes, Mr. Sal, I am acquainted with Brag. I confess that game has never held my fancy. It's too…gentle for my tastes.

I prefer Pochen."

Sal raised an eyebrow. "I appreciate a woman who knows her way around a deck of cards. Pochen it is, providing you gentlemen are agreeable to Lady's Choice." Sal glanced at the surrounding men, and all the other card players nodded their heads vigorously in agreement.

They played for hours. Sal and Lark continued their shameless flirtation. To their credit, neither Sal nor Lark managed to relinquish the slightest shred of personal information. Even the ever-increasingly boisterous outbursts of the inebriated Dan Pearly were a muted hum and blur of faded colors next to Lark's divine voice and radiant beauty.

"That's the snake who cheated me!" came a shout above the roar of the saloon.

Things immediately quieted. The town sheriff, two of his deputies, and a man who Sal had relieved of his money much earlier made their way through the saloon's swinging doors and headed for Sal.

"I don't reckon I know you, stranger," said the sheriff.

"My good Sheriff, folks call me Sal. I assure you, there must be a misunderstanding."

"For yer sake, I hope so." The sheriff held back a snarl as if he were ready to spit. "We don't take to card cheats, do we, Ross?"

"No we don't," one of the deputies said. "Cheats get their hands brought down to the blacksmith's. Big John likes that."

Sal took a moment and pulled at his shirt collar, which had grown tight around his neck. "That sounds unpleasant. It is a good thing I'm not a card cheat. We all have a run of poor luck from time to time. When you have been drinking hard, the head becomes cloudy." Sal grinned lightly at the man who continued to scowl at him. "My good man, why don't you have a good night's sleep, let your luck replenish itself, then tomorrow you can find me here and win some of your money back. If it will ease your mind, I'm sure my good friend Miss Lark here would be agreeable to shuffle, cut, and deal for us." Sal turned his smile to the stunning woman. She returned the gesture with a smile of her own before casting a seductive look in the posse's direction. "For now, why don't you let me buy you another drink?"

It took a moment for Sal's fast-talk to set in, but his accuser hinted growing favor toward the proposal. Sal fought another grin as the man glanced at the radiant woman beside him. The glance from Lark had sealed the deal.

"Why not? Never pass up a drink," he said.

"Please, a bottle of whatever my friend here cares for," Sal called to Charlie at the bar.

As the saloon returned to its usual hum, the sound of Dan Pearly pierced above all once again.

"Charlie, more rye!" It looked like this time Dan had overdone it. Without warning, the man clutched his belly and doubled over, retching and howling toward the floor. The onlookers waited for the standard spew of bile, but a long trail of flames shot from the coalminer's gullet and put the room in a fearful silence. It burned hot and long for several moments, roaring with life like a dragon's breath, then faded.

No! You have just killed us both, you damned fool! Sal thought, frozen in his chair.

"Wytch!" The sheriff pulled his pistol and fired a shot into Dan's belly. The coalminer fell while blood soaked his coaldust-stained shirt. "String this monster up and burn him!"

The posse pulled the bleeding Wytch into the street amid terrified screams of onlookers. Sal's mind raced. He could already feel powerful hands tighten around his heart and the blare of the Wytch's First Tenet echo in his mind.

My name is Magic. I am your mother. You are my children, my blood, a Wytch. Should any Wytch spill the blood of our kind or stand idle while our blood is spilled, their life is forfeit. This I command above all else.

Sal pleaded, hoping he could manage to aid his fellow Wytch without calling attention. He closed his eyes and called upon her.

Mother, as your child, I ask of you, let the winds of your brilliant blue sky and the breeze across your vast meadows confuse the minds of all here with false whispers of forgetting, so that it may serve your blood and your children.

She did not answer this. Sal called upon her again.

Mother, as your child, I ask of you, let my brethren's skin be as your enduring mountain's stone and his constitution be that of your great valley's Redwoods. Let him withstand the flame of those who would harm him, so that it may serve your blood and your children.

She did not answer this. Sal grew desperate. He pressed his eyes tighter and called upon her again.

Mother, as your child, I ask of you, tear your clouds in the starlit heavens asunder and bring forth a deluge to hinder those who threaten your children, and let the your purest of waters coursing beneath the flesh of my brethren heal his wounds, so that it may serve your blood and your children.

She did not answer this. Sal could see them fix the noose around Dan Pearly's neck and light torches. Sal grit his teeth, clenched his fists, and called upon her one final time.

Magic, I call upon you by my true name. I, Salem Taker, last of the Taker Bloodline, ask of you, as the sun's morning rays

warm the endless face of your prairie, let that kiss of fire fill my
hands and boil in my veins, so that it may destroy your enemies.

This, she answered.

The doors of the saloon exploded from their frame amid a shower of splinters as a cannonball-sized orb of fire launched from inside, striking the sheriff in his chest. The man's body immediately set ablaze, and he fell to the ground screaming. Another ball of fire came through the saloon doorway, engulfing Deputy Ross.

Salem exited the saloon, holding a fireball in each hand. Flames burned in his eyes, and thick black smoke trailed from his mouth and nostrils. The last remaining Deputy went for his gun, but Salem threw a fireball and let the man burn before he could draw.

Salem sent a grand burst of sparks and fire into the sky. The supernatural display gave any lingering spectators cause to run for shelter, so Salem went to the fallen Wytch.

"You didn't let them burn me," Dan said with a sad smile etched on his face. His eyes glazed, but a burning pain remained in him, and Salem tightened in recognition of the effects of a silver bullet. Salem went to call on Magic again, but it was too late. Only a silver bullet could take a Wytch's life so quickly, and nothing could save Dan from it.

The click of a gun's hammer beside Sal's head brought him slowly to his feet. He turned to see Lark holding an ornate pistol carved out of dragon's bone—the trademark weapon of a Paladin, a Wytch hunter.

"I'm guessing Sal is short for Salem Taker," Lark said triumphantly.

"And I reckon I should call you Dame Lark," Salem replied.

The Wytch and the Paladin smiled at each other.

ABOUT CW PUBLISHING HOUSE

CWPH was founded in 2015, dedicated to publishing CWC novels. Due to numerous requests, we have opened our doors to submissions from completed collaborative novels and will work exclusively with collaborative novels written by two or more authors. CWPH has also arranged a number of Anthologies, with more to come. To learn more about our books and our authors, please visit: www.cwpublishinghouse.com